For Eileen,

The Hungry Piper

An Irish Famine Story

Sláinte!
Faye Green

Also by Faye Green

The Boy on the Wall	2012
Dicey	2013
Gertie	2014
A Daughter is Given	2017

The Hungry Piper

An Irish Famine Story

Faye Green

ISBN 978-1-62806-252-6 (paperback)
ISBN 978-1-62806-253-3 (hardback)
ISBN 978-1-62806-254-0 (ebook)
ISBN 978-1-62806-255-7 (ebook)

Library of Congress Control Number 2019914043

Published by Salt Water Media
29 Broad Street, Suite 104
Berlin, MD 21811
www.saltwatermedia.com

Cover design by Faye Green.

Dedication

This book is dedicated to
the music of Ireland
that came across the ocean
to the Appalachian and Smoky Mountains
where it was played
in the parlors and
on the summer porches
for succeeding generations
and still brings joy today.
Some of those parlors and porches were my family's.

Acknowledgement

The Portumna Workhouse was a real place, located in Portumna, County Galway, Ireland. The buildings are still standing and maintained as an Irish Workhouse Museum. It is partially restored and open to the public so the workhouse system can be understood by ensuing generations. I visited the Portumna Workhouse Museum in preparation for writing this novel. Although, much research was done on the workhouse system, reading accounts of different workhouses across Ireland, and stories of families struggling in them, the visit to Portumna gave me inspiration—so strong that I used it as the setting for The Hungry Piper. I walked through Portumna's large entry door, the reception hall, dormitories, open yard, laundry, punishment cells and hospital.

I want to acknowledge the help and assistance I received when I was at Portumna. The museum staff welcomed my interest and endless questions. We were invited to cake and tea—true Irish warmth and hospitality.

Writing historical fiction is always a remarkable journey through time and place. This trip in Ireland, with the Doyle family and the workhouse, was challenging and rewarding. Maybe it will inspire you to visit Ireland; if so, go to Portumna Workhouse Museum. The spirit of Patrick Doyle, the Hungry Piper is there.

The Hungry Piper is a work of fiction. All the characters and events are fictitious but, after researching many overcrowded Irish workhouses during the famine years, they are probable.

Writing a book is a solitary job but when it is time to get

it ready for readers, the author must open her work and mind to editors, proofers and readers. I'm not alone in my work any longer. My editor, Judy Reveal, did an amazing job and taught me so much, even on my 5th novel. It is an ever-learning experience. This novel is better constructed, clearer presented and more worthy of a reader with my partnership with Judy Reveal. I am delighted to have her on my team.

Ann Messina has done the fine-tooth combing with her expert proofing eye. She is an invaluable member of my team along with Penny Reuss who always ready to read with the red ink pen in hand. I could not get a book within a cover without Judy, Ann and Penny.

Prologue

Ireland 1848 - the Famine

The potato—black, odorous, mushy, decaying, blighted like a plague—marched over hills and glens, leapt walls, changed lives, brought starvation and death, left no one untouched. Absolutely nothing would be the same.

There was a time at the Doyle table when a potato was tossed to the children to play. Patrick, Fiona, Sean were well taught—keep it safely on the table.

Twelve-year-old Fiona was quick. She caught the missile. "One potato, two potato three," off to Sean.

"Here it come from me to ye," off to Patrick.

"Make it fast before it be," back to Fiona. And then again.

"Cooked in the pot. Tra-lee. Tra-lee."

Patrick was oldest, almost fourteen. He liked to test his younger brother, Sean.

"Stuck with the spud."

"Stuck in the mud."

"Sean, stuck in the mud."

"With the spud." Amid, laughing, the game would start all over

"One potato, two...."

It was sport today but tomorrow that potato would be first in the pot.

A year ago, rows and rows of potatoes flourished on the hill behind the house. Annie and Andrew prepared the ground each year. Patrick and Fiona worked alongside pushing the seed potatoes into the softly mounded earth. Soon lush green growth promised a good harvest before the final potatoes from last year were eaten. During the summer the whole family sat by the cottage door and watched the evening breeze stir the green ribbons of life. Patrick played lilting melodies on his fife. Andrew let the fingers of his right hand softly beat his flat drum. Fiona and Sean would dance over the rows whilst Annie nursed baby Mavis. It was idyllic and although life was hard, backs were sore, and there was little else to please the family, they were content with each other, their cottage, and the potato field.

Stories about the blight were told before its black presence made itself known down the coast from Galway Bay. One day, a day like many others, Andrew saw some black withering leaves on his potato mound. He knelt down in the dirt and pulled six mushy ebony leaves from the plant. Then in desperation he pulled the whole plant and carried it to the woods. There was no stopping the plant plague when it starts over the hill. Picking leaves or pulling infected plants will not stop it. Nothing does. One day your rows are healthy green and suddenly black blotches are everywhere. To add insult to injury, the whole garden was wrapped in a horrible odor. The odor drifted into the cottage and there was no denying—the potatoes were dying and so was hope for the survival of the Doyle family. Their future was as black as the potato leaves.

Starvation did not come quickly, but slowly and insidiously, as food rations decreased. Andrew and Annie Doyle did without to feed the children. But their self-deprivation no longer put food on the children's plates. Food was gone and so was hope. When there was no more; there was no more.

Annie had always been a strong person but there were no strong places left. She went inside and sat beside her children on the floor of the empty cottage.

Andrew Doyle stepped on the door jam and let his eyes become accustomed to the dark. In the dim light he saw his family—swollen bellies, dry red-ringed eyes—quiet, inanimate. His whole world sat huddled, hungry and waiting for nothing. He turned and walked the green hill beyond the stone wall. "If only we could eat the green grass and chew the grey stones." he spoke to the land.

All choices for Andrew Doyle were bleak. The rent for his cottage and land was not paid. Eviction was coming. He saw his neighbors thrown out of their stone cottage and the roof of wood and thatch crushed in so the family could not take shelter for one more night.

Andrew and Annie could huddle in the corner with their children until the constable and landowner came to force them out. They could seek shelter among the stone walls on the hills until starvation took their final breaths, or...they could go to the workhouse.

Chapter 1

The voices were hushed but concern and frustration drifted across the cottage to where Patrick pretended to sleep.

"'Tis a terrible place. The Feeneys won't go. Kathleen told me. They're gonna stay in their cottage...leave it t'God." Annie whispered.

Andrew shook his head slowly, side to side. "I can no' choose that." He struggled with an emotional, dry swallow. "Can no'. A long, hungry death? Leave it to God? Starvation? Watch our children die? Let them watch us?" A terrible truth ran through his mind. "Should we sit together in a corner and wait? Who goes first? You? Me? Patrick? Fiona? Sean? Little Mavis?" Andrew looked at each child as he reached across and took Annie's hand. "I canno' watch any one of them go. Nor ye, Annie. God wants us to save our children. And any day now the constable will be putting us out." He squeezed her hand, "We're goin' to the workhouse t'save the children. That's why we're a-goin'"

Annie dropped her head in final submission. The last time Andrew brought the rotten potatoes to the cottage, the smell was horrendous. Annie cut around each one trying to salvage a small part that was not black with blight. It was nearly impossible. The potato was mushy, stinking and repulsive. Tears fell to her hands as she tried to block the smell from her nostrils. She knew what giving up meant. And so, she continued to pick up rotten potatoes as Andrew brought another bucket to her. Finally, in disgust, she threw the whole black, odorous mess to the ground.

"'Tis nothing here. Nothing," she proclaimed to her husband.

If she had strength to run, Annie would run away but she had no place to go. In her younger days she was beautiful. Her hair a mix of gold with red highlights curled around a lovely face. She was a runner. Her strong legs gave her sport across the glen. Annie Doyle could outrun her husband and children. She was a natural athlete and sprinter. Now, her legs had no strength, there were no highlights in her hair, her skin was grey, and her eyes had no life. Like the potato, she was soft and mushy. There were no strong places left.

"All we need do is show up at the door." Andrew brought her back from her revelry. He tapped the document from Father Moynihan attesting to the complete Doyle family, the only requirement for entering the workhouse. "There be no choice. We go together and we eat. Do ye see another way?" He asked his wife as he had asked himself over and over. "Annie, 'tis our fate."

Patrick brought his head up, looked first at his parents, struggling to keep their issues under the dim light of the candle, and then to the faces of his brother and sisters sleeping like lambs. He moved his eyes to his mother's face and to his father's just before the light was blown away by his father's last words.

"To bed, Annie." Andrew said. "Tomorrow, to the workhouse—all together— the Doyles—one and all."

The room was cold. Patrick drew Sean close, sharing the warmth of his body. It was not the cold that kept sleep away; it was the gnawing in his stomach. The boy had long ago learned that it was not good to think about food—it kept him awake. He worked his hand around to the corner of his straw mattress where the seam had been pulled open many nights before. His fingers found a piece of straw. He chewed and chewed until the fibers were wet, crushed, and minced enough to swallow. Patrick did one more hard brown straw before turning on his bloated stomach to sleep at last.

Dawn brought bright streaks of sun into the stone cottage at the bottom of a hill that rose from the glen and the beautiful green hills north of Galway. Its beauty belied the hunger and destitution of the people inside. Andrew and Annie Doyle did not see any beauty in the morning. Hunger had not only taken beauty from the bodies of the six Doyles, it had stripped their home and land. Except for the straw mattresses and a single candle, nothing was left. Their meager possessions had been sold or bartered for food. Andrew's beautifully crafted furnishings fed them for several months. Annie's mother's table went before winter. Her heirloom linens were only a memory. They secured some salt fish two months ago. Three weeks ago, Annie let her family Bible go for some dried grain that caused the starving bodies intestinal bloating and unimaginable pain. The battle was lost. Hunger—powerful and ugly—had won.

The Doyles and their lives were down to bare bones. There was no food. None. Not a crust of bread or a potato to share. Andrew had not eaten for many days—Annie, either. After weeks of pitiful rations, the children would have another day with nothing. Nothing for breakfast. Nothing for lunch. Nothing for dinner. And worst of all—nothing tomorrow. The family did not know the word *famine.* They only knew that there was no work for Andrew, no help from starving neighbors and no potatoes in the small plot next to the cottage wall.

Patrick was a lean boy, even before hunger became part of his life. He had begun to grow tall, like his father, when hunger and stomach pain kept him bent over. Patrick had red hair from his mother and all efforts to keep his curls back failed. They were mostly on his forehead. He leapt from his bed this fateful morning. With all his energy he pushed his languid body from the cottage and over the stone wall. The straw that he had eaten gave him cramps. He got over the wall before convulsions of his bowel punished him. Blood and watery stools spewed forth and frightened him. It was not the first time eating straw had brought him over the wall early in the morning but it was the first time he saw blood. "Me dyin'" he told himself. He embraced the notion and lay down exhausted and prostrate on the sod. "Get this over with," he demanded in a weak prayer.

Suddenly, angry at his plight and himself, he pounded the sod with his fists. His childish tantrum forced him to grow up. As he lay on the ground the sun broke the line of the wall and cut into his eyes, blinding. With the light came a vision. As sure as if it were painted on a wall—he saw Fiona and Mavis walking toward him and Ma and Da walking away. *Where's Sean?* He wondered.

Patrick rose, pulled up his trousers, and embraced a new defiant attitude. Blood and hunger might scare him but could not suppress his will to survive. He did not want to die so he cried for the only help he could hope for. "God! Hunger 'tis terrible.

Let me live past being hungry!"

Bloody stools did not kill Patrick. He recovered from the cramps, blood, and doubts of the morning. He straightened up and went back into the cottage.

Two-year-old Mavis was whimpering a longing, tearless moan. Patrick knew the sound and it would make a long day.

Sean, nine, and twelve-year-old Fiona sat quietly on their bed. There was no crying from there and no reason to get up. They had stayed in their bed most of the last week—yielding to weakness and knowing the uselessness of tears.

Patrick looked at Fiona and saw her begging, pleading eyes. There was nothing he could do for his sister except hold her hand. Da's voice called him from the only tender moment of the day.

"Patrick, me boy, 'tis our last day here. Help your sisters and brother put on all the clothes we have. It be easier to wear what we have than carry them."

Patrick went to work pulling whatever fit over heads and pulling arms through sleeves. It was not a big job. The older children had no extras, but Fiona and Mavis drew on things that were handed down. Altogether, three extra shirts and two pairs of pants constituted the wardrobe. In less than twenty minutes the family was ready to go.

"Da, do we take the candle and flint?"

"No, Paddy," he used the tender nickname of softer days. "Just the things we are wearing. John Hanlon will come to get them later. He gave me three carrots."

Patrick noticed his mother was unusually quiet and left the directions to his father. He watched Annie walk to the place where her beautiful table with the lace tablecloth used to be.

Then she went to the window and stood where a small table once held her family Bible in the light. Patrick kept his eyes on her as she went to sit by the cold fireplace and pretend to warm her hands over cold ashes. It was only a few minutes, but it seemed a lifetime before Annie stood up and locked eyes with her son. Patrick stood riveted as she came and brushed his curls off his forehead. Then he resumed his tasks.

Patrick went to the bed and forced Sean to move aside while he felt for the fife he had fashioned and kept under the mattress. He took a moment to feel the richness of it—the smooth hard maple wood that he had tenderly carved. Even the inner tunnel that floated his notes was perfected. Patrick was proud of the thinness of the body, almost sharp at the end, to bring the clearest possible sound. It had a value beyond possessions; it housed the boy's soul. He would not abandon the cottage without it and the music it made.

Patrick accepted his father's announcement. Today they would leave. It really did not matter if they stayed or left. When the stomach hurts, the bowel bleeds, the head aches, the heart is denied, and tears fail, it really does not matter.

Andrew, Annie, Patrick, Fiona, Sean, and Mavis Doyle are going away from this place that had once been their paradise. A dozen years ago, Andrew cleared the land allotted to him. He built the wall and cottage—stone by stone. He patted the floor down flat, poured fat on it to make it dust-free and smooth. He wove a rug from the rushes and built the furniture, piece by piece, except for Annie's beautiful table. Annie made the curtains from flax, made a flower bed by the door, and welcomed each baby as a gift from God. They lightened the burdens of life and celebrated joys with music. Annie sang while Andrew beat a makeshift drum and Patrick played the fife. The boy's music was magical. His notes painted the Irish world and eased every burden.

Andrew loved working with raw wood until plain boards became things of beauty. And, he grew the best potatoes in the glen. The Doyles' dreams and their paradise died with the potato vine and the hard attitude of the lord of Welford Manor. No allowances would be made to the humble cottage dweller. Lord Welford would not allow his faithful gardener a rabbit or a fish from his fields and streams. He would export cheese and grain to England rather than extend charity. His eyes were blind to the plight of his sharecropper. The cottage was reclaimed for paying tenants and the Doyles had to go.

Annie and Andrew faced their own pending deaths gallantly, but they could not accept it for their children. It was a hard decision but ultimately, they had no choice. The Doyle family would move into the workhouse in Portumna and try to stay alive.

The ragtag family started the walk to Portumna. Andrew lifted Mavis onto his shoulders. Patrick took Fiona's hand. Annie took Patrick's. They would walk as a team, sharing strength. Sean, refusing a hand, reluctantly followed. Annie turned to look back once more at the cottage. The stone walls glowed a soft silver-gray against the startling green of the hills beyond. Her hand went over her pinched mouth to stifle a cry.

As they passed the cottages of their neighbors no one was seen. Behind the walls no one wanted to watch them go or see themselves in the fate of Andrew and Annie. Everyone knew there would be no reversal of fortune; they would never see the Doyles again. In the path, a small cloth was spread. Andrew bent down and picked up a generous slice of bread cut into six pieces. He stood and turned a full circle to honor the gift from an unknown donor. The Doyles' going was not watched but was felt inside the cottages, beside the walls, between the stones and in the hills of Galway.

Fiona sat beside Patrick when it was time to rest and eat a piece of carrot and bread. "Paddy, Connie Feeney said her family would die before they'd go to the workhouse. Would you rather die in our cottage?"

"I don't want to die and we've got to eat."

"Food in the workhouse. And school. Why won't the Feeneys go?"

"I don't know. I know we are not going to stay in the cottage and die. The Feeneys can do what they want." Patrick was taking an attitude. "Do ye want to live or die?"

"Live, for sure. I've thought about it but right now with this carrot and bread...I feel different."

Patrick stood up and faced her. "Good. The Doyles are gonna live. You understand, Fiona?' He was red-faced. "Live. We not be hungry forever. We be strong again." He plopped back beside her. "I'll take care of ye in the workhouse. Brothers do that, ye know." Patrick stood in his own invulnerability. "I'll take care of ye, and Sean, and Mavis, too."

"What about Ma and Da?"

Before he could answer a call came. "Up! Let's go." Da was picking up his burdens and Ma had her hands out to Patrick and Fiona.

❖ ❖ ❖

The workhouse, located in the city limits of Portumna, about 25 miles east of Galway, had five long buildings arranged in a figure H. The open space at the top of the configuration was the yard. A separate building north of the H housed the hospital. The workhouse was a squared quilt-like pattern. Two rows of high windows indicated two floors above the ground floor. In the huge building, facing the road, a large door centered the stone wall. A bell hung beside with a rope on the clapper.

The Doyles would live in Portumna Workhouse. They would be fed; they would not die of starvation. They would be put asunder and rarely, if ever, see each other. Andrew had been told this by his priest, but he did not tell Annie.

"Ring the bell, Paddy," Andrew instructed.

Patrick moved to take the rope in hand and pull it to the side—three times. Clang! Clang! Clang! The bell clamored into his clutched hand. As the years went by, and he passed into manhood and another life, he never forgot his part in bringing the family into the workhouse. He was the one who summoned the devil to let them into hell.

Chapter 2

Seamus Sweeney, doorkeeper, was a hard, hard man with a mean spirit and a face that twisted to a weak chin. His eyes were unevenly embedded in a skull barely covered with thin pale skin drawn over his hairless head. He stood tall, nearly six feet, and he used his bulk to claim his space and part of yours. Sweeney made a habit of always keeping his large, thick hands where they could be seen—generally slapped onto his chest—rather awkward but effective, much like a soldier holds his weapon. At the clamoring of the bell, those weapons grasped the latch with an attitude of annoyance. He would allow some more poor souls in the workhouse without recalling the tragic circumstances that made him keeper of the door.

Mavis, frightened by the foreboding figure, began to cry. Andrew stepped forward to present the paper prepared by Father Moynihan. Sean stood silent with his hands pressed hard in his pockets. Patrick instinctively stepped in front of his mother, Fiona, and Mavis. He spread his arms wide to make a barrier between them and Sweeney. His feet set firmly as challenge crossed his countenance and hid his trembling.

Sweeney's crooked mouth pulled to the side—almost a smile, but the look in his eye made it a sneer. A teenage boy with defiance; another lad to tame. The Doyle family brought Sweeney sport and made an otherwise boring day into a good one. The change in the doorkeeper's face was not lost on Patrick.

"With or without papers?' Sweeney demanded, spitting

saliva with both p's in papers.

Patrick waited to hear his father speak, hoping against hope that some miracle would allow them to turn from this place and all the fear this doorkeeper represented.

"Papers," Andrew announced, thrusting the document forward, as if it would make things better than horrible. Partial families could not come into the workhouse. Sweeney could not read but he glanced at Andrew's paper, attesting to the complete family, and stepped aside to let them enter—pointing in the direction of the registry. As Patrick passed, Sweeney shot his foot out and sent the boy face-first through the door and down on the stone floor. Patrick was in Portumna Workhouse.

Neither parent took note, but Patrick understood the deliberate act. He had an enemy in this place.

The paper did in fact help the family move quickly into the workhouse. Entry meant the family was officially wards of the state, and they would soon eat. The papers meant that they would not have to wait outside and deal with Sweeney.

The registrar's office was slightly more pleasant, with pew-like benches lining the walls. The exhausted Doyles, completely spent from their walk, were able to sit down and rest their legs. An air of apprehension stifled the family and kept them silent. Annie and Andrew avoided a conversation that would bring questions from the children—questions they could not answer. Fiona moved closer to Patrick, claiming his protection. The younger children anticipated something good—maybe milk.

Patrick was not focused on food. He carefully studied his surroundings—the massive walls and high windows that no one could look out or look in. The bleak looks on the faces of anyone who passed through this room. There were no bars across windows or doors. *What keeps us in?* He wondered. He was trying to assess everything he needed to know to get himself and his family out of this place. He looked at his father hoping to see determination to overcome these circumstances. His eyes demanded his father look at him. He silently screamed, *Look at me, Da.* But, Andrew could not. He did not raise his eyes to any of the children's demanding or pleading faces. Patrick blinked and softly gazed again at his father. His heart broke as he saw the thin, emaciated, weak and defeated man who was his hero, his everything.

Da's given up. he thought. *Nay, me...*Patrick straightened his back. *Whatever 'twill take—whatever—whatever,* he talked to himself. He stood and paced across the room and back, looking around. *This no place for me. Canno' be,* his brain demanded. Patrick resumed his seat in silence but with new inner resolve.

Andrew bent forward and spoke to Annie about something that had tortured him for the past two weeks, ever since he went to see Father Moynihan. "Annie," he whispered, "tell them Mavis not be two. Be sure. Nay yet, her second birthday." He turned to the children. "Patrick, Fiona, Sean. Listen carefully. Ye sister no' be two. I'm askin' ye to lie if ye have to." His face told the importance of this direction and they did not question.

Annie held tight to her baby as a tear seeped from her eye. There must be an important reason to lie, but the lie would be found out. Annie made the sign of the cross and whispered, "Holy Mother."

The registrar came through the door and addressed the family. He did this daily and it never came easy. "Doyle. Andrew Doyle."

"Aye." He rose with great effort. His weakened muscles did not want to respond.

"Your papers are in order. The whole family—wife and four children. You can sign for the family. Three of your children are of working age." He paused and looked at the children. Then his eyes passed to Mavis. "How old is the wee one?"

"Mavis be two on her next birthday," The registrar nodded. He would have to go to the parish records and verify that ever-occurring lie. Today, he would let it pass. Andrew stood and followed him into the office.

"Patrick, fourteen. Fiona twelve, Sean nine, Mavis one. Sign here for your family." Andrew could not read but Annie had managed to teach him to sign his name. It was hard to attest to the lie about Mavis' age, but the office worker made it easy by moving quickly. Andrew signed the document with the lie. "Now, Andrew Doyle, let us go tell your family how we do things in the workhouse."

The registrar spoke loud and slowly so there would be no mistake. "In the workhouse living arrangements are as follows. There are dormitories, 1, 2, 3 and 4. The north building is divided into 1 and 2—males. The south building is divided into 3 and 4—females." Andrew—dormitory 1 for adult males. Sean and Patrick—confined to dormitory 2. Males six to fifteen." He looked at Andrew, Patrick and Sean. "You'll all be working six days a week, mostly on the premises, sometimes in the fields."

Annie missed nothing. She winced at the word *confined.*

"Females six to fifteen will live in dormitory 3. Fiona, that's you." He pointed at her, cowering beside Patrick. "Mavis and Annie will be in the nursery, third floor of dormitory 3, until Mavis has her second birthday. Then she will move in with girls two to five, confined to the floor above number 3. You," he pointed to Annie, "will move to dormitory 4, for adult women when Mavis is two." He hardly paused to breathe. Annie had no breath. "At that time, you will be assigned work—six days a week—on the premises."

The registrar paused and the room went quiet. Patrick tried to understand his place assignment while trying to remember where the others would be. It was difficult. So much to take in. So weak from the trip. So scared. So hungry.

"All children will be schooled two hours each weekday. The young ones in the morning; the older children in the evening. Classes will be divided by sex and again by age."

He took a deep breath and gave his final proclamation. "There is absolutely no passage building to building. No allowance to pass from floor to floor. No admittance to a building except your own. No admittance to a dormitory except your own." He paused for emphasis. "Never." And then went on. "The path you travel from meals or work or school to your dormitory is set. No variance." He paused a moment for this bitter message to sink in. "Meals and exercise time in the center yard are arranged by dormitories—no exceptions." He paused again. "Never."

Annie let out an audible gasp. "When will I see them? Not at meals? After work or school?" Her voice raised an octave as she grasped Andrew's forearm.

"Annie Doyle, this is the workhouse." The registrar stepped in front of her. "You're all here to work and be cared for. There are rules. Simple unchangeable rules. They must be obeyed. Make sure your children understand. Life will be much harder if you don't follow the rules. Tell them." He pointed at the boys specifically.

Annie stood and demanded again. "When? Tell me, when will I see my children?" Her voice was shrill with emotion. Andrew took her arm and pulled her back to her seat. Her question went unanswered.

Annie could not breathe. She turned an angry look on Andrew and cursed God. "You...and God did this."

The registrar gave the Doyle family a weak smile. His final rehearsed line made this job possible. "You will go and be fed now."

The Doyles stood and instinctively took hands, except Sean. He would proceed as if not a member of the family. They were all so hungry. It had been hours since they shared a piece of carrot and crust of bread. Each of them wanted whatever food was beyond the next door, except Patrick. He straightened his back and embraced hunger even as he went through the door to the dining hall.

"One more thing...," the registrar stepped into Andrew Doyle's face and spoke loudly and clearly, "...you can take your family out that front door at any time, but you leave with no more than you came with. Your landlord has taken your cottage. No place to go. No work. Never forget why you brought your family here in the first place. To leave, all need be done is check out in the registrar's office. It is not a swinging door. You must officially leave to be able to come back. Think carefully about your decisions."

The registrar opened the door to the dining hall and invited them in with a wave of his hand. Sean bolted into the room. Patrick hesitated... looked back at the front door... took Fiona's hand and followed his family.

After eating the Doyles were led to the quartermaster room where they would receive their de-lousing bath and workhouse uniform—male and female separated by a curtain wall. One by one they stepped behind a curtain for the first humiliation as all clothing was stripped from them.

Patrick managed to squeeze his buttocks to hold his fife while backing behind the curtain and stepping into the bath. He did not want to get his fife wet, but instinctively knew it had to be hidden. He dipped into the water quickly and out again.

Sean set his feet, tightened his fists and refused. "Nay, not me. No bath." He screamed and held tight to his shirt. The male attendant lifted the lightweight, fighting boy and ripped his clothes off, exposing his nakedness to the whole family. Patrick, already behind the curtain, looked out to see his father crying but doing nothing to help Sean through this passage. He watched as Sean was carried past Da and, with his clenched fist, landed a solid blow, fired by his indignation and adrenalin, into his father's stomach. Andrew doubled over and slowly went to the floor. The splash of Sean's bath was heard before silence, deep and sad, circled the room and the entire family. Patrick buried his face in the rough and scratchy towel.

A young worker, looking about Patrick's age, passed out blankets and waited for the tasks to be done before speaking to Patrick. "Me name be Willie"

Willie was shorter than Patrick and more muscular. He appeared unkempt but had an air of confidence. His dark hair stood out in all directions and friendliness seemed a physical characteristic.

"Patrick." He answered but held back his nickname, not sure he wanted a friend in this place that was going to be temporary at best.

Willie was wise and understood the reserve of the new boy and busied himself packing away the Doyles' raggedy clothes that would be returned if they ever left. Then he stepped close to Patrick and whispered, "Ye kept the fife so far. Best hide it away good or it'll be taken from ye. If ye manage to keep it; 'tis a treasure worth stealing." Then he returned his attention to the family. "Mrs. Doyle, can ye manage your blanket and the wee one's too? Canno' help ye to the south building. Me can get a woman to help."

"Fiona and I will manage."

At last, Willie gave the final direction. "Males to that door." He pointed north. "Females to that door." He pointed south. "Someone'll be at each building to divide ye."

Annie ran to Andrew and invited his arms. They held on while the children came and formed a human pyramid of love; Mavis was almost crushed in the center. Patrick grabbed Sean, pulled him in and stepped outside of the circle to surround the whole group with his arms.

Fiona looked at Patrick. "Remember ye promise, Paddy." He took her gaze and nodded assurance.

Annie and Andrew started with Patrick giving farewell kisses. Sean, embarrassed and confused by his feelings, did not raise his face for his parents' kiss. They insisted and bent to him.

Patrick leaned into his father and whispered. "We be parted soon, Da." The devastated look on Da's face melted Patrick's resolve. "Da," he pleaded. He needed *something* from Da but got nothing—no acknowledgement, no assurances, no secret pact—nothing.

The Doyles drifted to the floor. Annie and Andrew ran their arms over each child, rubbing backs, arms, and legs, kissing heads and cheeks, wiping tears, finding weak smiles, whispering encouragements and making promises. In a matter of just under two hours they were stripped of their former life, dehumanized and dumped like identical rag dolls into the workhouse—scared, scarred, scorned, and scattered.

Chapter 3

The huge north building stretched down the right leg of the H-shaped complex. "Yard," Willie pointed out as they crossed the open space. The windows were high in the thick stone walls. No step holes to climb up and look out. Patrick took Sean's hand and the young boy, bewildered and lost, yielded. Willie guided them up the stairs to the boys' dormitories. The walls were whitewashed but soiled by hand prints up the rail-less steps. The cold hard steps seemed to be carved out of the stone wall.

"Home," Willie sarcastically announced at the second level. He pointed to the arch door on the left for Sean, who walked deliberately to the darker corner and dropped his bedding without looking at Patrick, who followed Willie to the right of the staircase.

In his dormitory, Patrick took an empty bunk at the end of the row and was glad to have the blank wall to look at. He dumped his blanket on the bed and punched the center to vent his feelings.

"Be smart, Patrick. Shake ye mattress often." Willie scratched his crotch to make sure Patrick understood. Then he pointed to a divided shelf over the bed. "If a boy takes ye things, ye'll do the same." Patrick looked on the shelf— one soap and one comb—and turned to see Willie sitting on the floor in the aisle.

"Comb and soap be gone by supper. Hide 'em or find a way to carry wit' ye." Willie continued. "And ye fife, 'tis a lot to hide.

If they hear your music, count it gone. Not one day pass before it be gone." He touched his shoulder to be sure he had his attention. "Patrick, ye have to show the other lads. What little ye have must be held. Stand up to the them; ye soap and comb be fine on the shelf after ye do. If the lads best you, days be long and yonder shelf be empty." Willie stood to go. "Nay, never the fife on the shelf." His words were ominous and stern. "Patrick Doyle, ye have begun a long road. Me be in the workhouse for a year and two months. Next May me be fifteen. Must choose—go out or stay with me family—which me never sees. At fifteen ye can sign out of Portumna. Alas, there be no work but, me make me way. Are ye fifteen yet?"

"Nay." Patrick did not reach back to Willie in friendship, but he listened carefully. Willie continued.

"Ye will nay see your family. Your da and brother may pass sometimes but nay your mother and sisters. If ye try to meet your father and brother, they will change your detail so it canno' happen. Just the way things be. Tomorrow the work boss put ye to work. School six days after dinner. Sunday, rest-day.

"Da and Sean...thought we be together?"

"Sean—the other side of the staircase. Adults on t'other floor. Not far but not close either." Willie started to leave but turned. "Rest now. Our dinner bell will ring soon. Count the bells; they tell which building eats. Ours be three clangs. Come quickly. Be late and get a rap on the head." As he walked away, he tossed back his final words. "Tomorrow ye start the life ye've been given, Patrick Doyle."

Patrick sat on the mattress edge with comb, soap, and fife in his lap and let Willie leave without another word. He stretched on the bed to contemplate all Willie said and counted on his fingers the months until his fifteenth birthday next March. *Me be gone afore Willie,* he thought. *Make me way, get me family back.* He rolled over to turn his face to the wall. The seam of the mattress by his head was pulled until he had a small opening. The soap and comb were pushed in. Then Patrick moved to the bottom and pulled a tiny opening under the mattress, below the seam. His crafted fife was carefully pressed well into the middle of the mattress. "Have the soap and comb," he told the empty room. "Nay, me fife." The seam breaches were pulled together to hide his only possessions.

Patrick lay back on his bed and shook his head trying to figure out his new clarity. The absence of gnawing hunger cleared his mind. He was able to think—think ahead and think back. It was new, strange and confounding. Over the past months, hunger had interfered with his thought processes. His mind was more alert than it had been for a long time. Raging thoughts came at him like bullets. *Separated. Ma. Food. Da. Work. School. Fiona. Lice. Willie. Fiona. The cottage. Thieves.*

Back at the cottage, hunger had pulled his world into the size of a porridge bowl. This evening his mind expanded, and his larger world befuddled him. It included the workhouse, two floors of this building, two floors of the women's building across the yard, a dining room, a latrine—and fear. Thoughts of saving his family and getting out of the workhouse overwhelmed him. And, he longed for the porridge bowl world of yesterday.

"I would rather eat straw, and sleep with Sean," he told the wall—an easy conclusion after being fed. This bare room and meager distraction were his introduction to loneliness. In this state, Patrick began to understand the workhouse and what it was.

The dinner bell clamored three times.

Patrick was not hungry. The Doyles had eaten only hours ago. How could that be? Yesterday he was starving and today he is offered food twice in a few hours. He remembered the small carrots and bread crust that his starving neighbors shared early this morning. For the first time in a year, he was called to eat without the mongrel desire to get all he could grab.

Patrick felt guilty. He felt disloyal to the strength that had allowed him to face starvation and survive in the cottage at the foot of the hill. Where was his discipline in this place of food—and nothing else? Would he eat food and forget his family, his fate and his determination to move into a better life? Hunger became his ally—food his enemy. Patrick would not eat the meal placed for him in the dining hall this evening. He would wait for hunger. Maybe it would return to him in the morning. He set the first rule for himself.

"Do not eat unless me be hungry." He spoke again to the blank whitewashed wall in the deserted dormitory. "Eat for strength, not satisfaction," he explained to his own shadow on the wall. Once every day that Patrick Doyle lived in the workhouse, he left the dining hall without eating the meal set before him. Thus, he invited hunger.

Patrick would remember starvation—it brought him here, it changed his world, and it would make him all he would ever be.

The first days passed in a blur. Work was a salvation for Patrick. Two weeks passed. Work filled his hours and since it was manual, left his brain for thinking. This week's assignment was mucking out the latrine, Monday, Tuesday, Thursday, Friday and Saturday. It was a bitter job—unending—working from one end to the other, and then starting again at the first. The smell sapped his strength and burned his eyes. The boys that shared this job did not talk. Talking invited the horrible stench into the mouth. Smelling was one thing; tasting another.

Sweeney happened upon Patrick working in the latrine. Patrick backed away as he came in. "Ah, Doyle. Me be seekin' ye." He walked to the filthy pale of water at Patrick's feet and kicked it over. "Welcome to the workhouse." As Patrick danced to keep his feet dry, Sweeney walked away laughing. "Ye be doing a good job, lad," he snickered across the latrine. Then he turned back inviting the boy to challenge. Patrick took one step toward the giant man and stopped.

He wants me to strike out, he thought. As Patrick stepped back again, he saw bitter disappointment on Sweeney's face. *Me not be giving him the satisfaction.* Patrick turned away and resumed pushing the filthy water down the trough. Patrick felt like a winner. Sweeney slithered out murmuring something about *next time.*

Re-mopping was just part of the job. Even while doing the dirtiest of chores, Patrick's mind was elsewhere. His self-discipline was growing with his mental exercises. Patrick concentrated on the beauty of his home and convinced himself that even with Sweeney's threats and every filthy sweep of the latrine and cloud of stink— he would smell the pure soil and green grass of the sod at the cottage—again—someday.

Each week had a good day—Wednesday—when he was assigned to help Willie gather trash for burning. It was such a better assignment that he did not resent being bossed by a boy his own age. Patrick and Willie worked hard to gather all the bins from all the buildings and carry them to the burn site. It was restful after lifting and toting the trash, to stand and tend the fire. The smoky smell was pleasant, and he enjoyed being outside the workhouse walls until everything was ash.

"When me leave here, me be strong. Each day me lift so my muscles be strong. See me carry bins over me head? See me run not walk? When we go, we be strong." Willie spoke and opened the door to friendship again.

"What ye say...we?"

"What be your plan, Patrick Doyle?" Willie stopped raking the fire to ask. "Ye need a plan for leavin'. Ye can no' help yo' family from inside. Haven't ye figured that, smart boy like ye?"

Willie asked again. "What be your plan, Patrick Doyle?"

The fire was ash and the dinner bell clamored. "Eat for strength. And, for God's sake, get ye self a plan." Willie shouted as he ran toward the dining hall. Patrick got up quickly and made a race across the yard.

That night, Willie's words haunted Patrick. He already had a program of reviewing and assessing movement of people through the workhouse. He made a mental list of work details and noted the preferred ones. He quickly became aware of the management of the residents. The Master of the Workhouse was Malcolm Anderson. A tall commanding man. Patrick saw him only once. Stationed at every turn and managing the workgroups were Guardians. They were harsh men and women whose job was keeping everyone in order. Patrick learned quickly, the Guardians were not there to make his life easier.

The first four weeks were for observation. Patrick studied movements through meal, work times and school. He knew when his mother and sisters were in the yard or in the dining hall and when Sean went to school but there was no way he could manage to see them. The only possibility was through a work assignment that might give him a moment of access. His efforts trying to see Fiona got him a cuff across the ear for lingering. These corrections were recorded and could prevent him from getting the best work assignments. Patrick had to decide which would be more important in the long run. Reluctantly, he stopped trying to see her. He would forego immediate pleasures for the long-range goal and strive to gain a favored place in the strata of the workhouse. After so much observation he discovered that Willie seemed to have good work assignments and moved around freely, but Patrick could not discern why. He went to bed wondering about Willie and the freedom he seemed to have.

A plan, he repeated and repeated to himself. Before accepting sleep, Patrick got up from his bed and walked up and down the aisle among the sleeping boys.

The next morning, he waited at the door to talk to Terrance Moran.

"Terrance, would ye trade beds with me?"

"And why would me do that?"

"Me place be good, but from ye bed," he pointed out the high window toward the clock on the tower, "me can see the clock."

Terrance thought a moment about this strange, silly request. "Ye want me bed, to see the clock...and what can ye offer for it?" Every favor had a price in the workhouse.

"Your ash duty for one turn." It was a good offer. Each boy, in turn, had to clean the ash from the fireplace. It was a dirty job and no one relished the task.

"Once? Nah," Terrance refused.

"Twice?" He offered.

"Done. We move after dinner tonight." Terrance accepted. Now Patrick had a spot that allowed him to see the clock and plan his days and nights accordingly.

This was just one step in Patrick's efforts to change the workhouse to suit him, not the other way around. Except on the dark of the moon, when he could not see it, Patrick looked at the clock several times during the night. Each time he got up in the morning before the monitor demanded, each time he stood at the door before the bell rang, each time he was one minute early for school, Patrick felt control. It was power. The clock was his source of power and he was growing stronger. Compared to cleaning ash, this was a great deal.

Gathering the ash was an awful job. It was such a disagreeable job that boys only had to do once in rotation. Now with his commitment, Patrick had to do it twice in two weeks. The downdraft blew the sooty dust up his nose. On rainy days there was no sooty dust, just a muddy mess that took a long time to clean up. Patrick drew the scoop and gingerly poured ash into the bucket, taking care not to create a larger than necessary offending cloud. The broom was old and worn and it took many sweeps to clean the fireplace area. By the time he had filled the bucket, he was late for breakfast. The bells rang and he had to rush, no time to wash up. The guardian looked at the filthy boy and knew why he was late. But he cuffed his ear anyway. The smack was part of the ash-cleaning job. Patrick learned to lower his head as the blow approached to protect his ear.

"Ouch!" he proclaimed so the guardian could be satisfied and not strike again. His breakfast gruel had a gritty, burnt taste and feel. He could not rid himself of the dirt and smell all day. But, at the end of the day, he could see the clock.

Patrick *chose* to check the clock and get up rather than be *told* he had to. It was especially easy to get up on Wednesdays. Luck dealt him one favor—when picking up trash deposited outside the women's building, his mother brought the bin. After the first chance meeting with her as she brought the cans to the door, they met on Wednesdays when the big clock said 5:11. Today was trash day. They did not touch—no hugs. If their plan was discovered, it would be thwarted. At most, they exchanged a few quick glances.

"Paddy, you be alright?"

"Yea. Da, Sean, too." He became the keeper of his mother's concerns. He did not tell her that he never saw Da. Sean passed him as they walked to separate classrooms for the evening schooling.

The next week they had two lines.

"Fiona, Mavis?" He asked

"Yea, fine..." Tears ended that exchange.

The third and last week that he saw her she pressed a note in his hand, allowing her fingers to trace across his wrist. Because he had no pockets, he put the note in his mouth until the trash was loaded on the wagon. It was damp with saliva when he retrieved it during a private minute in the latrine.

Annie was a skilled writer and the only family member who could read well. She was careful with her letters, which were written with dusty soot from a burned straw.

She wrote: "Mavis gone. Study reading. Do it." It was smudged and all he could make out was: *Mav gone Study Do.* It was enough to inspire him. She had always urged him to practice his reading and writing but Patrick never saw the point, until now. If he managed to save his family and move back into the world, he would need the skill his mother urged. He made a plan to work hard in his study time. He would collect bits of paper so he could make notes, in case she got the trash bin assignment again. It would be difficult and improbable because he could lose his assignment at any time and paper was not available in the workhouse. His only chance to get paper would be in the trash from the registrar's office. Willie had the detail that went into the registrar's office.

"Willie, can ye get me bits of paper?" It was hard to ask for a favor, but Patrick was learning to do things he did not want to do. And, he was learning that Willie was a valuable asset.

Willie did manage to get a couple of scraps of paper for Patrick, but after three meetings he never saw his mother again as he gathered trash bins. It was the way things were in the workhouse. The paper was folded over and pushed into his mattress with his fife.

Annie's admonition about *study* gave purpose to Patrick's new-found mental clarity. In class after an exhausting day working, Patrick was ready to improve his letters and numbers. He was sitting erect and holding his chalk and slate when the teacher entered the room. All around were tired boys, totally disinterested in this class. No one seemed to notice Patrick's new stance except Willie, who was sitting behind him with the same purpose. The two boys listened intently and wrote with strong bold strokes as if all that happened in this place had no significance except these study hours.

On the next evening, as luck would have it, Patrick was seated behind Willie in class. He noticed Willie, who held his slate and chalk with determination. He saw the intense attitude and heard the bold strokes strike the slate. Patrick thought, *Willie be like me.*

The third day, Patrick and Willie were seated side by side in the classroom when the teacher entered. They were the students that other boys did not understand. They were avoided and allowed to sit and work at their own speed—side-by-side. It was two weeks before Patrick and Willie spoke to each other. Patrick acknowledged Willie. "Thank ye for helping me family."

"Making friends no be a good idea."

"Aye." And so, the two boys continued to work side-by-side on their studies. They looked at each other's slates and nodded commendations for work well done. Soon their work in the classroom was for each other's approval more than the teacher's. It was important for Patrick to see Willie succeed. It was important for Willie to see the same in Patrick. The workhouse had rules to keep residents unattached and it worked for outward appearances. But ties winding through the letters, numbers, slates, chalks and brains were not apparent. Friendship came unsought and unannounced to the boys, captive in body and circumstance but not in spirit.

Chapter 4

Across the yard, back in a corner of the Administration building, the Master of the Workhouse, Malcolm Anderson, did his job. He made sure the workhouse adhered to the laws and regulations governing this social welfare operation. He made sure the staff did their jobs. He made sure the kitchen and infirmary were staffed and supplied. He kept the walls, doors, windows and floors sound and well maintained. He did all he could while remaining aloof and detached from the residents—with a few exceptions.

Malcolm Anderson spent a portion of every day regretting the events that brought him to the Portumna Workhouse. True, he was in the highest position and made a very good living, but doing a job you hate, is a curse. Worse than that, every day, he faced the reason he had taken the job. When running from the past, the deepest, darkest place can hide the deepest, darkest secret.

Ten years ago, he left his home in the midlands of England to follow his love to Ireland where her father was given Salisbury Manor, a land grant from Cromwell. The English lived well off the backs and land of the poor Irish. They were hated but, because the native people needed jobs on the estates and the land they sharecropped for the manor. Hatred was buried and seething. Malcolm did not understand the history, he was shallow, in love, and enjoying the rich life he would marry into. The estate stretched across the glens where the River Nore runs to the sea from Kilkenny. The pretty dark-haired girl took his hand and brought him to this beautiful country, and they made promises. Like his countrymen around him, he ignored the plight of the cottage dwellers.

One fateful day the men of the estate were hunting upland birds when one shouted, "Poacher! Shoot!" Before Malcolm Anderson knew what was happening, he raised his gun to his eye and caught sight of movement through the morning mist into the brush. His single shot dropped the quarry.

As he moved forward, the first thing he saw was a string of fish thrashing on the ground where they had fallen from the poacher's criminal hands. The fisheyes were looking for help, the gills were struggling for oxygen, and the bodies were flopping up and down hoping for water to take them to safety. Three steps further into the bushes, Malcolm saw the poacher—a boy, maybe fourteen years old, thrashing on the ground, his eyes big with fear, mouth wide gasping for oxygen and legs digging the ground trying to move away from his executioner. In two minutes, the scene was quiet. Malcolm dropped his gun and fell to his knees. The boy was dead. Lord Salisbury picked up the fish without looking at the boy.

"Lunch!" He announced as he admired the fish. Before heading home, he turned to his servant. "Tell the Malloys' to come get their boy."

Malcolm did not move; he couldn't.

"Justice, Malcolm, Justice," Salisbury insisted.

The gunning party moved away. Malcolm was still bent over the boy. "Justice?" He whispered as tears came. He put his gun out of sight and stood vigil. Finally, in what seemed an eternity, he heard the sounds of wheels against gravel. There was no justice in the eyes of the family that came to claim the limp body of the sandy-haired child. Malcolm stood alone while the father, mother, brothers and sisters put the dead boy in their wagon and, with the strength of their combined backs, pulled it up the rutted road to home.

That day ended love's dream. Malcolm walked off Salisbury Manor and away from his planned future and bride. That one shot still rings in Malcolm Anderson's ears and kills his sleep. He is forever burdened. He changed—no longer the man who held a lover's hand, made promises and walked carelessly across glens and by the River Nore.

Malcolm Anderson took the job as Master of Portumna Workhouse to punish himself and find a way to atone for his guilt. He did not know how to emerge from his own desolation, but he knew where he could find boys like the poacher and if he helped them, maybe he could sleep though one good night without hearing the gun shot or feeling fish flopping on the foot of his bed.

Anderson kept perfect records of the boys he had put his magic hand on. Past successes (and failures) taught him how to select his *boys.* It was not a haphazard plan. His system was carefully devised and perfected in the years since he fired that fateful shot. First, he made a selection. Then he observed to see if his choice had the potential he sought. It took special characteristics to survive in the world after the workhouse put its tattoo on a boy. It was easy to evaluate the inner strength of a young boy, but Malcolm had learned it took more than that. Sometimes inner strength caused a boy to fight the world.

That never worked. His chosen had to have good intelligence, a marketable skill and a desire to better himself—not by brute strength but by using his brain and exhibiting self-discipline and a cooperative attitude. He looked for boys who had a *limited acceptance* for where they were now. The boy had to apply himself to school and prepare for the outside world. Lastly, the boy had to be an orphan without family ties in the workhouse.

It was hard to determine if the boy was focused on a better future, but Malcolm Anderson had a good instinct for that. Most of all, his selectee would have to believe in himself.

During his years as director, Anderson had singled out four boys to cultivate for a future outside the workhouse. An unusual turn of events focused Malcolm Anderson on Willie. He watched Willie. If he measured up, the director would help him to emigrate to England or America. Anderson had connections on both sides of the Atlantic.

❖ ❖ ❖

Life had been difficult for Willie, for so long, that it had become acceptable. His tiny family—mother and little sister—came to the workhouse after his father and two brothers died. Willie was twelve. His mother died just a month after they came to Portumna. He marked each day, each week and each month on the calendar he scratched into the wall under the stairs. He would be gone the day after his fifteenth birthday and come back for his sister before she was thirteen. Willie had a plan.

Willie did not know he was being watched for potential.

"One more year and I be gone on the 15th." He spoke aloud

to the calendar as he laboriously scratched the grid for May, in his fourteenth year. "No need to wait for the day after." Then he folded his strong legs, stretched back with his head resting on muscular arms to dream of that day of freedom. On that day, he would go past Sweeney—on the way to his real life. Willie was not sure how, but he would work until he had enough to take his sister, Mary Ann, to America. It was a dream and it kept him going. His dream included sunshine, calm seas, hard work, and wonderful days in America. It was a perfect dream and he was very good at dreaming it.

The perfection and beauty of it lulled him to sleep. His legs unfolded and a turn to his side, relaxed the boy. As his breathing settled into a rhythm, the hated nightmare started. *Sweeney opened the big door and pushed him to the sod inside. Mary Ann came flying through the air to land in his lap. Willie got up and put her on his shoulders and tried to get back to the other side of the dreaded door, but Sweeney's huge hands held him. Then Sweeney's evil laugh came out of his ugly mouth like wet peat bog—black and slimy. Just before the door slammed shut, Willie saw his father disappear and his mother die.*

His arm jerked in his sleep and caused his head to hit the floor. Clunk! The sound and the hurt, inside and outside the nightmare, brought Willie awake. The hangover emotion caused him to call out. "Da!"

Willie slapped himself in the mouth. He was pleased by the sting. Nothing, except a stupid nightmare, would cause him to call out to his father. There was no excuse for the slip of tongue, even in sleep, that spoke his father's name.

The workhouse was just another obstacle and Willie would master it. Days here were easy compared to the event a week before he arrived. After two days wandering the forest looking for edibles, he returned home and found his father hanging in the cottage. He unwound the rope from his father's neck and discovered his two little brothers, dead in the corner—from starvation. His mother sat dazed by the cottage door with Mary Ann tight in her grip. Moving to the workhouse was too late to save his mother. She died in less than a month. Only Mary Ann remained. How hard would it be to survive in this place until he could go on his own? If it weren't for Mary Ann, he would have bolted when his mother died. Willie became an expert at biding his time.

Every institution has its rules and a multitude of paths around them. Willie began by seeking work that got noticed. He wanted to create a job and make himself indispensable, and he was not beyond looking for favors from whoever was in charge. He would study hard, work hard and beat the system—whatever that meant.

Luck would have him passing over the courtyard when Sweeney was *greeting*, in his usual harsh manner, a large family. Willie forgot his purpose and followed the mother, father, grandmother and six children.

"What be your name?"

"O'Grady."

"I be Willie."

"Come, O'Gradys. Follow me. I be helpin' you." With that he picked up the straggling toddler with one arm, grabbed the single sack of belongings and managed to open the door to the big room. Willie put the little girl down and took the elbow of the old woman. "Sit here. It be all right. Soon ye be eatin'" Willie knew there would be plenty of sadness ahead but there was no need to take the smiles away first thing.

He turned his attention to a softly crying boy. “Nay, nay, tears. I be helpin’ you. I live here and doin’ alright.” He picked the boy’s chin up gently and smiled in his tear-filled eyes.

When the registrar entered the room, the family had been sorted to girls on the right, boys on the left. The father stood with his papers as quiet settled over the scene.

The registrar expected the usual turmoil from a family. He was surprised at the presence of Willie, who exuded calm where there was usually pandemonium.

As soon as the formalities of submitting papers, roll call and dormitory assignments were given, Willie stepped forward again.

“I be helpin’ ye get ye clothes changed and ye things stored. That will leave a little time together before ye go to your sleepin’ rooms.” He was kind and helpful. They knew that this young man was on their side and it was a comfort beyond measure. It meant more to the family, at this moment, than milk, potatoes and the possibility of cheese or meat.

The registrar sent a report to Anderson later that afternoon. Willie was summoned to his office. “Come in, boy, and take that seat,” Malcolm Anderson directed, without looking up.

“Good standin’, sir.”

The Master looked up with added interest. “Very well, William Carney. If you want to stand...” He noted the boy spread his legs and took a stance that would support him for a long time, if in fact, this was to be a punishment. Malcolm Anderson stood and made an imposing impression on the young man. “I shall stand too, but as you see, if you take a seat, we will be closer to looking eye to eye." He smiled. Willie took the chair; Anderson did, too.

The smile from the Master and the humor in his countenance was not lost on Willie. He took a deep breath and relaxed in the chair, keeping his back straight for courage. He still did not know why he was called here but let go of fear.

"It came to my attention that you assisted the registrar with the O'Grady family today."

"They be so many... and me two hands...," he raised his hands from his lap, "...lifted bags and children."

"It was a good thing, William."

"Willie, sir." It took a lot of nerve to correct the Master but he did not want the name of his father. "Me father be William. I be Willie"

"It was a good thing, Willie. You were very helpful. The registrar and I have talked. and we think you could be very helpful to others coming into the workhouse. Would you like that?"

"Aye."

"You are now in charge of resident orientation, Willie. Whenever you hear the bell clang at the door, stop what you are doing and come to greet whoever is entering."

"Whatever me be doing, sir? Even if me be in the field?"

"Yes, whatever. If you hear the bell, come quickly from any quarter. I will make sure everyone knows—you are to lend a hand at the entry."

"Anythin' different than the O'Gradys?"

"Just the same, Willie. Helpful and friendly." After the amazed boy left his office, Malcolm started a new folder—Willie Carney. He looked up Willie's day of birth and wrote that on the outside of the folder so he would know exactly how much time he had before the boy's fifteenth birthday. Willie became the fifth boy that Malcolm Anderson planned to put his magic touch on. He would have a future, if at all possible.

That evening in class, Willie asked his teacher about the word *orientation.* He needed to know exactly what it meant and how to spell it. What he learned pleased him—more than pleased him, it exalted him, put a lilt in his step and a strange hope in his heart. He had stumbled into attaining his first goal. He had an important job and made a difference in this terrible place.

Overseeing resident orientation was not a full-time job. He was always busy finding work and doing it without being asked. Willie seemed to be offered every good job that came available. And moving around as he did, he found opportunity to see Mary Ann. She never saw Willie but his glances at her were important to Willie's determination. Soon he was the Master's favorite errand boy and message carrier. Mr. Anderson knew by close observation that Willie was trustworthy and did not engage in workhouse gossip. He did not use his position to lord over the other boys, which could have made him disliked or an object of jealousy. Except for being aware that Willie had free range over the workhouse, within the male boundaries, no one knew he was special in the eyes of the Master. Anderson wanted it that way; Willie wanted it even more. He would do nothing to jeopardize his freedom and most of all his chances to see little Mary Ann.

It was not just Mr. Anderson who made Willie's life acceptable in the workhouse. A new set of allies was building for the boy. First it was the O'Gradys. After that, each family who found a friend in the strong boy as they were oriented, never forgot his help on their most difficult day. As the months went by, more and more families supported him with smiles and favors, when they had the chance. In all quarters, Willie had friends.

Willie's life was one of the easiest in the workhouse until tragedy struck. Mary Ann pined for her parents. Willie noticed she was more and more frail. Willie missed her on his usual rounds and began to worry. He spent a week looking for her, but before he found her, he was summoned to the infirmary.

"Mary Ann, 'tis Willie." She lifted her tiny arms for his neck and bent to her. It was a quick hug for she had no strength to hold up her arms.

Willie took her hot hands and held tight as if he could send his strength to her. He knew in that moment that his heart must have healed from his mother's dying—how else could it break again? His prayers were fervent and faithful. He took comfort in her sinless life and knowing that she would be together with Mama, and Jesus, in a short while. It was his own loss that tore him to small pieces—pieces smaller than the tiny hands that were now growing cold.

Malcolm Anderson needed to give Willie something strong to keep him from bolting from the workhouse after the death of his sister. His plan for Willie's future would be for naught if he left without his schooling and without a sponsor. About this time, Willie's friendship with Patrick Doyle came to the director's attention.

"This could be a good thing. A very good thing."

Chapter 5

Willie had to mourn for his sister alone. He had only himself now. No obligations, no commitments, no ambitions. He saw Sweeney at the door and was tempted to go for one last jeer and pass the devil, laughing.

That night, Willie did not come to class. Patrick was unsettled by his empty seat for two days in a row. News in the workhouse spread in a zigzag fashion, from floor to floor and back and forth across the courtyard. Death was reaping. It did not come in the door, past Sweeney. It reared its ugly head from a corner where it waited with great patience. Death took a wee girl from the second floor of the south building. Patrick feared for Mavis and in his concern for his sister, forgot about Willie missing school. At sundown he searched the returning wagons hoping to see his Da or Sean. He did not. When he finally voiced his fear for his sister, he was told. "Nay ye sister, lad. They tell ye when 'tis your family. Must be 'nother." Patrick took heart.

Willie did not come to school again.

That night Patrick spoke to God and offered thanks that Mavis was not dead. He was willing to utter that prayer but refused to call to God for deliverance from this place. That was a useless prayer. God had no power over the workhouse and Patrick failed to believe that he was that important to the Almighty. Just before sleep, he whispered to the black night, "Where's Willie?" Patrick pulled his fife from the mattress and played silent notes without breath until sleep took him to the hills beside their cottage and gave melody to his fingers. Even silently, the fife brought the possibility of life; God was too far away to do that. He composed symphonies, complex melodies and put silent words to them. They gave substance to his life when all around him lacked meaning. One string of notes spoke of Willie and the need to find him.

Before the morning light entered the workhouse, Patrick was waiting to join the first workers moving with buckets to milk the cows. He was risking severe punishment by not going to the latrines. He knew Willie was working the harvest this week. He was determined to find him.

Patrick's head was down as he walked past Sweeney who was at his post, slapping, kicking and pushing the boys. "Move. Move on."

As soon as they were out, Patrick left the group and fell into a small ditch. Pressing his body to the cool earth, he became part of the yard just thirty feet from the ugly, mean doorkeeper. Discovery would give Sweeney an excuse to beat him unmercifully. Everyone knew the consequence of testing the doorkeeper's vigilance. Because of that knowledge, no one in the group would tell on Patrick. They quietly talked of Patrick Doyle in the ditch as they moved on to the cow barn and pulled on teats that morning.

Patrick was motionless as he waited to check each succeeding group for Willie. That was his plan, but he failed to think about the sun rising quickly, lighting the yard. It was getting riskier by the minute. Four groups moved out and the first ray of light lit his red hair as Willie emerged from the door. Risking everything he rolled to the path and came to his feet before his amazed schoolmate.

"Patrick!"

"Shhh. Me thought ye was sick or dead."

"Nay. Not. Me sister be the one what died. Poor Mary Ann."

"Quiet back there!" The group boss called. "Quiet or everyone'll work extra and have a cold dinner." Willie took Patrick's collar and jerked him into the line going to the hayfield. Neither boy said another word as they walked. This was a large group and the boss did not notice the extra boy as the scythes were pressed into hands calloused from this work—all calloused except Patrick's. A wide golden blanket of hay stretched as far as the eye could see. With steady rhythm and synchronized swishing, the day's work began. The swishing sound covered the quiet talk of the workers. It allowed a social exchange that Patrick had not experienced since arriving here.

"We can talk..." Pause. "...we be careful." Pause. "Wait for swish." Pause. "Softly." Pause. "Ready?"

"Sorry for..." Pause. "Mary Ann." Pause. "School tonight?"

And so, in the gentle sounds of the scythes, the boys gave into their desire to be friends. All day long, using rhythm, they talked of school, family and their plan to beat the workhouse. They agreed that they could survive and escape this life if they did it together. In spite of sound judgment, they became friends. Thus, they forged their partnership; the very thing that the rules forbade. The very reason conversation and routine was avoided. If it became apparent that they were friends, they would seldom see each other in this place.

Between the swinging of the scythes, they devised a complicated scheme based on sequence numbers.

"In school," pause, "sit together," pause, "every two days." Pause

"Next week, pause, "every three days," pause, "back to two days," pause, "next week."

"In the dining room—never together," pause.

It became a game and exciting. "Latrine," pause, "go on hour," pause, "on even days." Between the moving of the scythe they agreed to speak to each other only on Mondays and Saturdays. The scheme might not work but Patrick and Willie both enjoyed the idea that they could bend the rules and make their own way in the workhouse. As the workday was near ending, Patrick presented another idea. "Meet at night?" Between the moving of the scythe, Willie disclosed his secret place under the stair and invited Patrick to join him. "Friday," pause, "midnight," pause, "next week," pause, "Saturday," pause, "every eight days," pause. It was purpose and motivation. It was a way to outsmart the workhouse efforts to keep them from being friends. It took all day to put these plans into short phrases. Many things were not said but understood.

Willie knew the day was nearly over and so he voiced his fear. "Ye will be..." Pause. "...caught." Pause. 'Going back." Pause "Sweeney." Pause. "Ye boss..." Pause. "...will report..." Pause. "... latrine not cleaned."

"I know..." Pause. "He will hurt..." Pause. "...nay kill me." Patrick put his scythe with the bloody handle, in the wagon. His hands burned and the pain prepared him for the gauntlet he would have to pass to get back into the workhouse.

Patrick and Willie were satisfied with the day's work. The hay was cut. The boys had missions. They had motivation. They had a game. They had each other and hope spread before them like the golden field of stubble hay.

The two boys separated and started the walk back. The line

was two by two and Patrick stayed in the middle of the group until Sweeney stepped out to meet them and count. If he did not step to the rear an innocent boy could take his punishment.

"Two. Two. Two…." Sweeney was counting smugly. His work groups were never wrong. Then he saw the odd boy and the monster face turned red. "What's this? Name, boy! Doyle?" Sweeney recognized. "Patrick Doyle," he growled. Sweeney had him by the shirt, lifting him into the air and pitching him to the ground beside the entry.

"Stop! Stop!" Sweeney was blown up by rage. "Boss, why be Patrick Boyle in your line? Did he cut hay today?"

"Nay. I do no' know where he came from. Me line be right all day." He lied. He could not count and would not take any blame.

Sweeney walked over to Patrick and put his foot on his chest. "Move in," he barked at the boss and work line. "Doyle stays."

"Ye be mine," he whispered in the boy's ear. Patrick raised his bloody, raw hands to his forehead to let the salt of his sweat go into the blisters and burn. He wanted to cause his own pain and keep Sweeney from controlling his fear. The ogre lifted the boy by the shirt, drew the neck of the garment tight around his throat and held him in mid-air so the buttoned collar would restrict his breathing and press the collar button into his neck. Patrick was sure Sweeney would not kill him but as the minutes ticked away and blackness swirled, he prepared to die. Abruptly he was dropped into a heap spraining his ankle, but that was nothing compared to the kicks delivered to his legs and torso.

"Get up, boy. Where ye been all day?" Patrick did not answer and so, Sweeney hit him in the face and knocked him to the ground. "Ye want to leave? Go to the registrar and sign out. Don't think ye can go out and in past me...when ye want. Get up! Tell me, where were ye today?" He struggled to his feet and stood to face Sweeney again. "Doyle, which boss lied? Who are ye covering for?" In that instant, before Sweeney knocked him to the ground again, Patrick knew it was better to take Sweeney's beatings than get a work boss in trouble.

"Did no' work—hid out all day."

"Lazy boy. Sweeney'll make a man of ye."

One more, hard slap cut his lip and sent him flying against the door. Patrick got his balance and half fell/half ran through the entrance. He kept on running and stumbling until he could not go another step.

Suddenly, he was pulled up short by the guardian in charge of the latrines. "Doyle! Where've ye been."

Patrick couldn't talk. Blood ran from his mouth.

"Ye shoulda come to your work. I'd slap ye around a bit meself but it looks like someone beat me to it. Six in the morn! Double duty."

Patrick did not go to the dining hall; he went straight to his bed. His swollen lips would not manage food; his stomach could not contain it. His bruised legs and battered chest needed rest. He slept for a short time and listened for the clock chime time to go to class. Sweeney might pull the strength from his body, but he could not tear, bruise, or batter his determination. Patrick was glad he did not go to eat. Hunger felt good. It blended with his pain and gave him strength—as it always did. In the classroom, the teacher's look of surprise and concern was ignored. He felt Willie's eye on him but did not accept his gaze. This was just another day in the workhouse. It was time to do numbers, reading and writing. Patrick was sick with pain and his day had been long and exhausting. He got through his class work but was unable to meet Willie at midnight. Try as he might he could not get his body from the bed as every abused muscle tightened and screamed with cramps. Every breath cut his chest. The boy cried for the first time and it took all his strength to keep his sobs silent. Sleep finally came, wrought with dreams.

Annie walked down between the beds where the other boys were sleeping. "Paddy, I come to find you. Get your fife and be gone." She pushed his hair from his eyes and lightly kissed his cheek. "The Doyle's are a-goin', but no need to hurry; we have all the time in the world."

"Nay, nay, Ma. We must hurry." He cried as he pushed the cover aside, jumped from the bed and pulled on her arm. She stayed put on the side of his bed and refused to move at his beckoning. "Come," he begged. "Come, we be goin'."

"I must stay with Da. Go, Paddy. Go!"

"I donno' want to leave you."

"Here!" She thrust carrots and bread at him. "Go."

The dream was over, and Patrick woke with panic. He looked for his mother in the darkness, but she was not there. He closed his eyes and tried to bring the vision back, to no avail. The blackness invited him to stay somewhere between actual and fantasy. His feeling of her was so real, so strong. He could see her face, hear her voice and feel her presence and so he decided to stay in the dream longer. "Ma, tell me what to do." he asked. "Be a good boy? Me donno' know how to be kind anymore. Donno' know what to do with me insides. They hurt more now than when they was hungry. Ma," he begged. "Let me sit and play my tunes and die. Canno' we go back to the cottage?" Patrick did not know what depression was, but he was deeply into it.

Chapter 6

The morning sun lit the room but not his mood. Patrick would go to his work group without breakfast and trust his old friend hunger to comfort him. Another day without eating and drinking left the boy gaunt and weak. He passed out in the latrine and was carried to the infirmary where nurse Reagan examined him. She pressed her thumb into the calf of his leg and saw her imprint remain. "This boy needs water," were the first words Patrick heard as he began to respond to the smelling salts passed under his nose. "Patrick Doyle, have you been eating and drinking?"

"Nay."

"Have you not been fed in dining hall...and where did you get these bruises? Your rib..." She lifted his arm and touched the bruise on his side. He winced. With gentle fingers she traced the ribs. "They're broken." She ran her hand gently around his torso along his waist. He cried out and sank back sweating. The organs were damaged, no doubt. Notes were made. "Are you fighting with the other boys?" she asked as she examined his swollen ankle.

"Nay."

"Your work boss hit you?"

"Nay." Patrick could honestly deny all her accusations.

"I have to do a report." She left the room and Patrick to his thoughts and the large cup of water. "Drink," she ordered. When she returned, she brought a tray of fruit and milk and worse news. "The Master wants to see you as soon as you are able. First, more water and food. Mr. Anderson wants to know why you are starving and thirsting and how you were injured." He took the nourishment in slow and meaningful bites that gave him time to think about what he would say to the work-house master.

Malcolm Anderson was seated at his desk when Patrick entered his office. When he rose, he towered to over six feet. He stood, not out of respect for the scrawny kid, but for effect. His height was so unusual that it alone made a statement of power.

"Patrick Doyle." He recognized the name. This boy was the key Anderson sought to keep Willie from leaving too soon.

"Aye."

In perfect English, he addressed the cowering boy. "Sit down," he invited as he took his seat. "We need to talk. You have been here almost two months. No trouble reports on you." He looked down at the nurse's report. "You went to infirmary today with injuries and dehydration. Why aren't you eating and drinking? Explain this to me and remember, I am not a fool."

Patrick kept his eyes fixed on the Master but said nothing.

"Where is your problem? Nurse Reagan said you deny fighting in the dormitory or in your work group."

Patrick did not want to lie; he did not know what to say to this imposing man, and so, he said nothing, *Tell on Sweeney?* He was confident he was not the first boy to be slapped around by the angry doorkeeper. He looked up at the man demanding answers and saw his countenance soften. *Could this man be me friend?* It was an astounding thought.

“You are not going to tell, are you?”

“Nay, sir.”

“Are you going to be alright if you go back to your bed and your work?”

“Aye, I be well if I go back to them and school.”

The interview was over. Nurse Reagan came to escort Patrick out. “Let him rest in the infirmary until school time. No work for two days.” At the office door, Malcolm Anderson asked two more questions and, with the answer, knew how long he had to work with this boy. “How old are you and when is your birthday?”

The boy had a strength that was not going to lead to more beatings but instead, would make him stronger. Anderson had seen it in some boys, a few of the many who ended up in the infirmary with injuries. Patrick Doyle would not be back in here in this condition again, he was positive. He would not force the boy to tell what he wanted to keep to himself. If Patrick Doyle wanted to solve his own problems, so be it. Anderson sat back in his chair, lowering himself to the level of most of the world, and resolved to help Patrick Doyle. He asked his assistant to bring the file on the Doyle family.

❧ ❧ ❧

The rumor mill in the workhouse was abuzz with the story of Patrick Doyle’s injuries, his trip to the infirmary and interview with Mr. Anderson. The rumor went to Sweeney and struck terror in his stone heart. Each hour he expected to be summoned to Anderson’s office. He gathered his belongings and counted his few coins. It was a sure thing—he would be put out of the workhouse with winter coming on. Sweeney could not survive in the world. His grotesque demeanor precluded employment. No one wanted him around to remind them of destitution and ugliness. Because of the Doyle boy, he would lose his job—he was sure of it. "The boy be paying before I be put out." Besides anger, the only thing the monster had was vengeance.

Sweeney did not sleep that night. At the midnight hour, he quietly crept through the hall to the boy's dormitory to find the bed where his nemesis lay. Each step closer to Patrick Doyle excited the man. His meager life had few pleasures. It had been a long time, but this was not the first time, his senses were acute with hatred and murder. He had killed before and he paused in the dark to remember that exhilaration. Tonight, he would have that pleasure again.

All the boys, exhausted from the day's work and full of potatoes from the evening meal, were sleeping soundly. He looked in each face searching for the one with blackened eyes and swollen lips. He was not going to lose his job over a simple, deserved, little beating—murder would be worth it. He would kill the boy and leave before he was found out.

This fateful night, Patrick had fallen asleep while playing silent notes on his fife. The fife was still clasped in his hand resting on his chest, rising and falling with each breath the unaware boy took. Sweeney looked at the boy's tattered face and smiled a crooked sneer. The boy was found; the deed could be done. He raised the knife he held in his fat hands and aimed for the victim's throat. As he did the sleeve of his coat brushed Patrick's check and in reaction, Patrick brought his hand up, still holding the fife, just as Sweeney dropped his head forward. The two motions collided, and the finely crafted, sharply honed fife jammed into Sweeney's eye, perfectly fitting into the socket and circling the eyeball. For a split second, Sweeney looked into the shaft. Light spots penetrated the dark where the note holes were carved. Then flashes of white light, red blood and blackness came in quick succession. The assailant fell back in pain, holding his eyeball and catching the blood gushing from the socket. In the confusion, the knife fell to the floor and slid under the bed. The sleeping boy turned his body toward the wall, clutched his beloved fife, and continued his exhausted, unbroken sleep. Sweeney's knife was lost, and the anticipated pleasure was gone. He limped away in a trail of blood, whimpering and cursing.

The next morning, Patrick found blood on his fife, on his bed and on the floor. It was a mystery.

Sweeney had his own mystery. Malcolm Anderson did not call him to his office, nor did he lose his job. Everything seemed to be normal, except Sweeney had to get an eye patch to cover his mutilated eye socket and sightless mangled eye. The blood clotted in the void; a gooey liquid oozed down his face. The stupid man did not credit Patrick Doyle with holding his tongue and saving his job. He did not chastise himself for trying to kill the boy. He only knew the boy punched out his eye. And, if possible, he hated him more today than yesterday.

After about a week, outward evidence of Patrick's injuries healed. He met Sweeney crossing the center yard. The boy walked wide to avoid the doorman, but Sweeney pursued him and, with biting accusations, cleared up the mystery for Patrick. "You punched me eye with ye fife. I be comin' again. Better sleep with one of ye eyes open—every night."

Chapter 7

The day-to-day drudgery of tending to the downtrodden was depressing for Malcolm Anderson. His background, although not noble, was on the fringes of the well-to-do. Poverty and starvation had always been a condition of the undeserving and he had little compassion for them until he watched the Malloy family haul their dead boy home from the Salisbury estate. He had to ask himself what the boy was willing to risk for three fish, as well as what he was willing to do to stop him. It was a harsh lesson. Now, he did penance each day for that lesson. He was a good manager and delegated well but did not like to mix with the residents. Rather, he preferred to stay in his office and administer from afar. He believed in letting people live and work out their problems. The prospect of a new boy with potential was invigorating and the only thing that made this work palatable.

He covertly watched Patrick Doyle. His work history, his discipline and his studies were reported to the director in the weekly staff reports. No trouble. Good schoolwork

"Bring me the reports on Terrance Moran, Patrick Doyle, and Joseph Logan," he barked to his assistant. To be very careful, Anderson requested information with the names of several boys, some of them troublemakers, and some randomly listed. He did not want the staff to know which resident he was singling out. The reports came to his desk, but he read the only name that suited his purpose at this time—Patrick Doyle.

Anderson had ways of knowing what went on in the workhouse. His best tool was good contacts within the system, and he had one on each floor of each building. He had Willie on the floor where Patrick lived.

"Willie!" He called sternly. "My office." Willie came quickly and knew it was the Master's way; it did not alarm Willie anymore. He diverted his path and went straight to the office.

"Master?"

"Sit."

"Nay." It was the usual invitation and refusal. Malcolm smiled at the expected.

Their relationship continued. Anderson did not ask Willie to spy on his fellow residents but paid close attention to things the boy would say in short, but frequent, meetings.

"Did you work in the hay field this week?"

"Aye. Look at me hands." Willie showed the blisters. "By Wednesday, me hand picks up the scythe but not much good."

"Trouble on Thursday past?"

"The count was wrong coming back that day."

"And...?"

"Sweeney hurried us in and kept the work boss." Willie was honest enough to admit he saw trouble but loyal enough to keep Patrick's name out of the issue.

As soon as Willie left, Anderson issued an order to rotate the boys cutting wheat every three days.

Another day, Anderson summoned Willie and mentioned Patrick Doyle.

"Patrick Doyle? Aye, he be in my class. Not friendly type." Willie was quick to protect his friendship from the Master. Anderson took note of that, too. Willie would not betray

Patrick for favor at the top.

Malcolm Anderson leaned back in his chair, smiled. "Go, Willie," he was dismissed. If Patrick had known of Willie's special relationship with Malcolm Anderson, he would understand why his friend had such freedom around the grounds.

❖ ❖ ❖

The information gathered on Patrick Doyle did not disappoint. Patrick did not come to Anderson's attention again with injuries or trouble. Except for efforts to see his family, he got little attention from guardian staff. His friendship with Willie was advantageous. Although Patrick was not an orphan, Anderson considered him a candidate for his program.

Meanwhile, Patrick went about his work and studies independently, making no trouble for himself or his work boss—completely unaware of the reports going to Anderson's desk. The attachment between Patrick and Willie was noted. The boy's relationship was very fortuitous. The Master spent many hours constructing and revising his plans. Now he had one plan that included two boys. The bond between Patrick and Willie gave him a new challenge—two boys co-dependent on each other for success. He liked the idea. No doubt Patrick would be as loyal to Willie as Willie was to him.

Willie was the physically stronger of the two boys. He had a natural muscular build, stamina and he was streetwise. On the other hand, Patrick was brighter, quick-witted, and agile with an unbelievable strength of character. They would make a good team. In the strange order of things among the peasantry, Patrick was of the higher class. Willie was of the lower, struggling, but always successful, caste. After Mary Ann's death, Willie had no family to hold him back. Without attachment, he could bolt and run away at any time. Willie's friendship with Patrick Doyle would be the key to keep him here until his next birthday. He had to develop an attachment to the Doyle family, and it had to happen quickly. Willie was detailed off the farm work crew and reassigned to the carpentry shop.

At midnight the boys met under the stairs to the attic. Willie had news for his friend. "Me be deciding to leave."

"How can that be. Ye no be fifteen, like ye said."

"Run away. No family to worry for. Mary Ann be gone, me too. Will ye come with me, Patrick? We be a team."

Patrick was quiet. The idea of leaving the workhouse was enticing "Canno' go. Me family needs me, and I must have papers so I can work. Best to stay with the plan till we be fifteen. America waits."

"Too, too restless." Willie could not explain how his sister's death left him lost.

"What'll ye do outside?"

"Cut hay. Swish. Swish. Good and strong with scythe." He made the sound and motion.

"Hayin' be done soon. Winter comes. What then? Do no' go, Willie. Wait for me...or at least past winter." Patrick had to admit his plea was selfish; he needed his friend. "Can ye wait a bit longer?"

"Aw, me birthday so long off."

"Mine comes first in March....me waits for ye in May. Together we work and save me family. Ye said ye would help me. Sorry Mary Ann be gone but, it still be our plan to be fifteen. Ye birthday," he begged. "Not now," Patrick ended with a plea.

"Aye, at least not this week." Willie slid down with his emotion. "Me moved from harvest. New work tomorrow—carpenter shop."

"Da there. Should be me goin' there." Patrick fell quiet with the prospect of Willie seeing Da.

"Me wish it be ye. What Willie know about carpentry? Not a nail, that for sure."

"Ye be with Da." Patrick was stuck on the notion. "Should be me."

"Ye know they would never allow that—ye and your Da." Willie shook his knowing head. "Never happen"

"Ye remember me Da? Look for him?"

"Aye. Wood shop not big. Me find 'im..."

Patrick fell silent as jealousy took his thoughts. He could picture Willie and Da and it bothered him in ways he had never experienced before. "Gotta go," he announced, emphatic but quietly. And, quickly began to scoot out from the stair hideaway. Patrick could not stay another minute with Willie and the prospect of him seeing Da. It hurt.

Just before he cleared the tread, Willie grabbed his foot and held him there. Patrick pulled against his friend twice and yielded.

"Paddy," Willie called his nickname for the first time, "...ye can no work with ye Da. That's the way 'tis. But, Willie can... till May...stay till May." Patrick listened as Willie agreed to stay until his birthday. "If ye canno' go in carpentry shop, it best be me standin' in for ye. Just one more thing we do to make the best of life here."

Patrick relaxed but remained silent. He drew his foot away, still not sure what to do with the raging jealousy. "Da," was the only word he could whisper.

Willie took both of Patrick's feet and pulled him back under the stairs to the wall. "Bring ye messages. Take some to him. Use this lucky assignment."

It made good sense, but Patrick could not get past the vision of Willie and Da, side-by-side. Once more with less alarm, he said, "Gotta go," and pushed himself out from the stairs.

Back at his mattress, he brought the fife to his mouth. More than anything he wanted to send his breath though it and make music that would define his feeling. Instead he touched it to his mouth and lifted it. No breath traveled the pipe. No notes went into the air. No music soothed. He could not even imagine the melody. Jealousy took that from Patrick, too.

Reason began to return, as he lay awake until the clock in the yard summoned him to work. If he hurried, he could pass Willie on the way to the latrine.

All he could give his friend was a nod and a warm glance to let him know, in the light of the morning, it was good that he would see Da.

Chapter 8

Andrew Doyle was in agony. He was dying and he knew it. His agony was not his illness, nor the pain, nor the weakness from it. It was guilt—life's only true agony. Andrew had failed his family. He took a wife and fathered Patrick, Fiona, Sean, and Mavis, but he did not keep them nourished and safe. He could have blamed God but instead, he blamed himself.

Shortly after entering the workhouse Andrew had trouble with food. His appetite evaporated and he thought it was because of starvation. But, weeks later, everything nauseated him. Then the pain started—sometimes nagging, other times cutting. His thin frame became skin and bones and his stamina disappeared. The pain remained. Andrew did not have a name for it, but he knew.

Today's cutting pain in his stomach was nothing compared to the stab he felt when Sean punched him on the day they arrived at the workhouse. That pain, delivered by his suffering son, never left Andrew and so, when illness incorporated the emotional pain, Andrew accepted it as just punishment. His guilt was overwhelming, his depression deep and dark.

Early attempts to see his family failed. Andrew never got closer than fifty yards to the woman's dormitory. He managed to see Sean walking to the dining hall once in the last seven months. That was it. No sightings, no news, nothing more. Just frustration and now, pain.

In his former life Andrew could take a piece of wood and bring it to life with tools and nails. He planed, carved, and rubbed a plank until it had life and beauty. He could soften edges, dissolve splinters, and pull grain into line to produce beautiful furniture. Those skills and their rewards were lost at Portumna. Now, Andrew hammered with all his strength driving nails into raw wood to make mattress frames and coffins. His guilt and pain were laid out on a plank each morning as he picked up another nail and drove it straight and true to the center of his plight. Watching a nail break the surface, enter a plank, go straight to the heart of its path and almost disappear into a pungent, sweet wood was his only release.

Lately after two hours at his task, lifting the hammer was difficult. Holding the nail with trembling hands became almost impossible. Andrew could not contemplate the day when he could not pick up a hammer and board and drive a nail. He knew it was coming as sure and steady as the pain.

Then Willie was brought into the shop and over to Andrew.

❖ ❖ ❖

Willie walked into the carpenter shop wondering why he was there. The activity, tools, and smells were all foreign to the boy who had spent most of his life tending animals and crops. His first job was lifting and stacking wood and sweeping sawdust. It was not difficult and gave him the opportunity to move around the whole shop and see what was being done with hammers, nails, and saws. Willie hardly admitted to himself that the tools looked interesting. The work boss addressed him after the noon meal.

"Ye will learn to build bed pallets. Doyle will teach what ye needs to know." Willie's interest sparked at the mention of that name. He followed the work boss into the back of the wood shop. "Doyle," he called and pointed to the man bent over in the corner. "Here be the boy; I told ye." Andrew looked up but did not move. He waited. Willie recognized Andrew Doyle. He was so changed it was difficult to believe he was the man who came in only months ago.

"Willie," he introduced himself and hoped Andrew Doyle would remember him.

"I teach. Do ye want to learn?"

"Just another job," was Willie's less than enthusiastic answer. Andrew understood. There was no enthusiasm in the workhouse.

"Pick up that hammer, lad. We begin."

Andrew looked again at the boy. "Willie... ye helped me family." The connection was made and a softening in attitude encouraged Willie. He needed no further introduction; Andrew Doyle would remember and repay Willie for those first difficult hours. "Come, I be your teacher." Their relationship started.

They started immediately. "Willie, have ye ever hammered a nail?"

"Nay, not one."

The first day tools were introduced, and then skills were taught and practiced with very little conversation. Willie did all the lifting and toting. Boards were stacked. Tools were carried. If anything needed moving, Willie did it.

Initially, the mystery of tools and tasks scared the farm boy. Saws, hammers, planes, and measures were passed to his hand. He looked into the gentle eyes of Andrew Doyle and thought kindly of his own father—something he had not done for a long time. Then he held each tool and felt the promise of what he could do with it. He grasped the saw by the handle while his fingers ran gently over the teeth. He gripped the hammer with his right hand and, slowly but firmly, lowered the head into his left palm. There was power in it.

Andrew noted the connection between the boy and the metal tools. He saw possibilities in the boy and had new energy to teach him the very basics. Obviously, Willie had never tried to drive a nail or contemplated affixing two pieces of wood together. Soon, the obvious question had to be asked. "Ye never did this before, why're ye in the carpenter shop now?"

"Mr. Anderson's doin.'" The answer did not satisfy either questioner. "Me think it be good."

Willie drove the first nails; it was a good day. He went to dinner and school with his mind full of new ideas. It was one of his best days in the workhouse. Surely the best since Mary Ann died.

Willie came to Andrew in his greatest hour of need and turned him into a teacher at the very time he lost his ability to continue his work. It would not be easy to turn this farmhand into a carpenter, but he was a strong, willing, and able boy.

Andrew Doyle went to his bed at day's end less exhausted, and his pain was manageable. Andrew could not have asked God for such a blessing. He would not have been able to voice it. He slept.

❖ ❖ ❖

The next day, Andrew was ready for Willie. His hammer and saw were oiled and nails were assembled. This was the very first day that Andrew had looked forward to since coming to the workhouse. Willie was on time. He went straight away to lift and bring the planks to their work area.

"How many?" he called to Andrew.

"Six for now."

"Today, I will teach the best way to drive a nail and then—sawing."

Thus, the teaching and learning began. Teacher and student went through the motions. They made mattress frames all week. Willie drove lots of nails and learned the hard way about fingers and hammers. Mastering the saw was more difficult. Willie was diligent and willing to make mistakes and correct them.

"Ye canno' saw good without knowing about the grain in the wood," Andrew admonished. They sawed and nailed all week.

Willie was surprised to enjoy, even relish, all that he was doing. Andrew had a way of presenting tasks so that Willie got a real appreciation for wood, tool, and product.

The days passed quickly that first week. Andrew looked better. Being relieved of the heavy lifting helped. His strength was rationed.

Willie sensed immediately that sawdust presented a problem for Andrew. He took the broom from Andrew's hand, and assumed the tasks of cleaning up—sweeping gently so very little dust rose in the air.

The first week was almost over and much had been

accomplished. More than the six bed frames stacked in the corner. A miracle had happened. A bond was made in the workhouse. Despite all the rules and designs to inhibit trust and support—unexpected, unsuspected, undetected—it happened for the carpenter and novice.

Monday morning Andrew awaited Willie.

"Now, we make coffins for the poor souls who left this place. Not a sad task, Willie. We doin' the last good thing for 'em. Me coffins are smooth on the inside. Time to learn the plane."

Willie watched Andrew push the sharp blade that pealed a thin curl of wood. He saw his teacher test the path for smoothness with his fingers. "Willie this is what ye learn to make fine furniture. There be so much more to carpentry than beds and coffins." Then the student took the plane in hand for the first time.

"We have to work quickly. The work boss does not allow fine work on the insides. Sees no point...but, me does." Willie understood and thought, *perhaps me Mary Ann has one of ye coffins, Andrew Doyle.*

Work and learning mixed well together. Willie loved the steady slicing of the wood and the fine smell of the tool cutting wood. He struggled to learn the proper pressure. Sometimes pushing too hard, sometimes not hard enough. Andrew showed him the carving knife he had honed from a dinner fork. He brought out four stones that had been laboriously shaped to smooth grain and knots. Willie was fascinated. The sharp implements softened wood edges. He slid his hand inside the coffin. He had never felt a piece of wood so fine to the touch. He looked up and Andrew smiled—his student was pleased with today's work. Pride was new to Willie.

Willie swept sawdust ending their first day making a coffin, Andrew rested on a stack of planks. "Willie," Andrew beckoned. He touched the boy—the only time he had touched a human since the day, months ago, when Patrick went out the north door.

"Ye can put together two pieces of wood with four nails and be done...or ye can take a real interest and learn so much more. Tell me now, what's ye here for?"

Willie had no answer for his teacher. Two weeks ago, he knew Patrick's father was in the carpentry shop and he came anticipating meeting Andrew Doyle. He never expected to *like* doing the work. And, it is hard to know who was more surprised at the seemingly natural ability of the young student—Andrew or Willie.

"There is much more to carpentry than what we have here. Today we put boards together. Maybe...someday, ye will do more."

"Teach me."

In that statement, Andrew saw future in his student. The very idea lifted the sick man's spirit. "I'll do all I can but must be careful. The work boss'll watch us." Andrew continued, "Ye must be near fifteen. Are ye biding your time or do ye want to learn how t'make a thing of beauty from wood?"

"I be fifteen in the spring. Can ye teach me by then, Andrew Doyle?"

"I be trying if ye be willing."

"I be willing."

The report went back to Malcolm Anderson from the work boss. Willie was doing well in the carpentry shop under his teacher Andrew Doyle.

❦ ❦ ❦

Conversation was suspect in the shop, so Willie and Andrew worked in unison, in silence. Each day it became harder for Willie to keep silence about Patrick, almost a burden. It was time to tell Andrew.

Willie stopped sweeping sawdust in front of the place where Andrew was resting. "Andrew Doyle, me needs to tell. Ye son, Patrick be me friend. It's time..."

Andrew's head jerk up, interrupting Willie with an astonished expression. His eyes flashed and his hands fell useless to his sides.

"It's time you knew, Patrick be fine. We meet secretly. Tonight, I see him again."

Willie watched Andrew try to stand and fall back to his seat on the stack of lumber. His mouth opened but no words came forth. He looked up at Willie and began to cry—silent sobs and generous tears. Months and months with no word, no sightings, no contact welled up and spilled out of the dying man.

"Are you two finished?" The work boss barked from across the room. "Dining hall, Doyle. Willie—to the exercise yard."

Willie put the broom away as Andrew Doyle wiped his face, turned, and left the shop.

Chapter 9

It was not a coincidence that Patrick started painting dormitory walls at the same time Willie went into the carpentry shop. Malcolm Anderson sought to get Willie and Patrick marketable skills, not knowing if Willie would do well with carpentry or Patrick would become a painter or....if his plan for the boys would ever work.

Patrick was given his assignment along with four other boys—each in a different room. Paint all the walls on both floors of the north dormitory. It was a job he could do and he worked alone. That appealed to Patrick. He got a bucket of thick whitewash paint, a bench to climb for high places, a swab of rag on a stick for a brush and a warning—the lye in the paint will burn the skin. The work boss left him, facing the long, seemingly endless, walls. Patrick started lathing the thick whitewash paint on the rough stone wall of the dormitory. He worked with diligence sometimes writing a word on the wall before coating it over. In his own way, practicing what he learned in school. He had to be careful. The work boss would not look favorably on such frivolity.

One day while he was painting, his mind settled on Fiona. Patrick worked and thought of every line in her face, her eyes that used to smile and the curl to her hair. His thoughts went back to the cottage when she looked at him to take care of her. His promise came back to haunt him. Before he realized it, he had moved the paintbrush over the rough walls in a mysterious way. Among the textured stones, the grey unpainted wall, the newly applied white and the movement of his brush, his sister's face appeared on the wall. Through subtle shading with ash from the fireplace in his pocket for striking accents, her troubled smile and begging eyes appeared. At that moment, the work boss returned to the room and Patrick drew his brush across and erased Fiona's face.

Was she there? Patrick wondered as his brush resumed back and forth motions. *Fiona?* The rest of the day Patrick was careful not to dally with his work. It would not be good to have the work boss catch him doing more than back and forth motions. But just before dinner, he was in the lower back of the dormitory wall. He quickly dipped his brush, pulled it across the lip of the pail to control the paint and with gentle strokes, began pulling Sean's unhappy face out of the wall. It was a very small likeness but undeniable. The same textures, shading, and accents made Sean's angry eyes and intense hatred stare at Patrick. Before he swiped the brush over it, Patrick sat down in wonder. *Now, Sean,* he thought. *How did me do it?* He questioned himself.

Patrick's childish ability to draw simple things was never noted. He remembered the dirt road to the cottage and all the times he drew pictures with a stick and his father admonishing him to move along and stop dallying. Only now did he recall how he loved to create pictures and erase them with his bare foot only to draw again later.

Patrick could draw. His intense desire to see the faces of his family pulled his natural talent into focus. He did not know how he did it and on this first day thought maybe it was his own imagination. *Me mind playin' tricks,* he concluded. It was the only logical conclusion. Tomorrow it would be grey stones painted white; nothing more.

The next day, Patrick could not help himself. He had to find out. Did he imagine Fiona and Sean on the wall? He painted along the wall until the work boss left. With his mind on his mother, he lifted his brush on a dry place at eye level. He pulled a straw from a mattress to add detail. Soon Ma was looking back at him. During his ten-hour painting day, Patrick managed to paint and erase Mavis and Da. When he was alone, his brush flew. A crude but identifiable portrait could be finished and erased in less than ten minutes. He did not know how he did it; he just did. The painting job gave him his first real pleasure since coming to the workhouse.

The report from the work boss went to Malcolm Anderson and stated that Patrick Doyle was doing well painting the walls. There was nothing in the report about the portraits he painted and erased each day. Patrick Doyle could paint walls. That was all that mattered.

❧ ❧ ❧

In mid-week, the two boys planned to meet under the attic stairs at midnight. Patrick had played the silent pipe for an hour before he dozed in his bed and waited for the appointed time. He watched the clock and listened for it to strike the midnight hour. He had one shoe suspended on an exposed foot. It would fall if he should go into deep slumber and relax his ankle. The trick had kept him awake for every meeting; it would work tonight. The shoe dropped and brought the boy awake early. He did not want to fall back to sleep so Patrick decided to go to the stairs to wait for Willie. He dropped to the floor and felt for the shoe, slipping it on his bare foot. Patrick reached up and pulled his pillow under the covers so the silhouette would be identical to the many sleeping boys in the room. Then he began the slow crawl along the wall to the door.

A slight movement ahead caught his eye. He froze. A figure moved toward him. It was massive, bulky, and lumbering. Light from the single window reflected on a bald head. *Sweeney!* Patrick rolled under a bed in time to see the muddy familiar boots— the ones that had kicked him weeks earlier—pass within inches. The wheezing breaths were unmistakable. Lying on the hard, cold floor, his senses were acute. He heard a dull *thunk* and muffled footsteps fading into the black night. Patrick took time to make sure the evil man was gone. He crawled back to look at his bed and then hurried to meet his friend at mid-night.

When Willie arrived, Patrick was trembling in the corner. In unison they said, 'I've somethin' to tell."

"You first."

"Nay, Patrick, Ye." Willie felt his friend trembling in the dark. "Ye have trouble to tell. Good news can wait."

Willie could not see the look on Patrick's face, but his voice told Willie he was frightened. Words did not come; the pause seemed endless "Come on, tell me. Are ye cryin', lad?"

The terror of the night would not let Patrick utter Sweeney. Thoughts of the man froze the boy. He took another path to get to the story. "Me be ready to leave here. Be no good to me family dead."

"Dead? Did ye say dead? Ye no die. What's happened?"

The words finally began to spill as he told what he saw. "...and there in my pillow ... a large kitchen knife. Stabbed in as if me body still be there. I be dead if not for this meeting. Sweeney set to get me—one way or t'other. No help to me family if I be dead. 'Tis time to leave here."

Before the story was finished and the teller exhausted, Willie moved to cradle his friends shaking frame and trembling head. Even as he held Patrick, and digested the story, a plan was hatching. "We, ye and me, settle this thing with Sweeney." He soothed Patrick with quiet assurances and promises of loyalty. On the very day that Willie moved into the carpentry shop and found reason to stay in the workhouse, Patrick suffered terror and found reason to leave. Most of this night would require serious problem solving. The frightened boy, spent by terror, fell asleep on the hard, stone floor under the stair. While Patrick was breathing heavy and deep, Willie took an hour to work out a plan.

"Wake up. Patrick, we need to talk. Feeling better?"

"Aye. Better. I be hungry and that always makes me stronger. Hunger makes me mad, too." He pounded his hand. "That same cold knife should be in Sweeney."

"Ah, 'tis good to see ye changed. It will help with me plan if ye be mad."

"Plan?"

"We no run from the workhouse before we be fifteen. We fix Sweeney to leave you alone. Now. Tonight."

Willie had an elaborate plan and they had several dark hours to put it in motion. First, he went to his bed and brought a sheet—not white, but light enough. Then he stole into the kitchen and returned with a boiled beet. While he was doing that, Patrick went to his bed and retrieved the knife from the pillow and his fife from the mattress. Willie went into the chapel where he *borrowed* one more item, pausing to ask God to forgive him for taking it. When all the props were gathered, they sat and finalized the play they would put on for the swine, Sweeney.

The door to Sweeney's room made an awful squeak as the boys slowly pushed it open. The smell of whiskey put them at ease—the doorman would not hear them or the noisy door. There was time to set the stage. Willie went to the far corner of the dark room as Patrick advanced to the foot of the bed. Willie pulled Sweeney's black hat over his face and began blowing lingering notes on the fife, stopping intermittently to call, "Sweeney. Sweeney." He did this three times before the ogre opened his one eye.

Sweeney saw a ghost, dressed in a sheet holding a candle for weird effect. A knife was plunged in his chest (actually tucked into Patrick's arm pit) and blood (beet juice) gushed down his body.

The terror-stricken drunk froze.

The ghost spoke in eerie slowness. "Patrick ... Doyle ... be ... dead. Patrick ... Doyle ... be ... dead."

He had the drunken man's attention.

"See me fife floating there? It wants ye other eye." Willie dressed in black and hidden in the dark moved the fife toward the man who sunk in the bed at the approaching eyeball-snatching flute. "Beware ... Patrick Doyle be a boy in daylight ... be a ghost at night. Comin' for ye other eye." The floating flute gave a loud one-note blast.

"Beware!" A deep foreboding voice came from another dark corner of the room. "The devil wants ye, Sweeney. If ye comes close to Patrick Doyle, the cross will come out of the hole in his chest and God will take you to Hell." With Patrick's hidden hand he pushed the contraband cross out of his robe into the candlelight. It was just enough religion, sorcery, horror and alcohol to impress the cowering man. Patrick blew out the candle and the two boys evaporated into the night. Dawn was approaching as they hid the evidence and fell exhausted into their beds.

Willie's last words to Patrick were, "Keep the cross. Ye will need to flash it at Sweeney ever so often. Pray to God about stealing it, maybe He'll understand the need." They did not finish discussing leaving the workhouse. Willie did not get to tell Patrick his about his time with Andrew Doyle. That would have to wait until next week.

Chapter 10

Willie and Patrick got up the next day and went about their business as if Patrick had not, barely escaped death. They were tired when the morning bell rang but elated by last evening's escapade. Patrick ran to the dining hall for breakfast and noticed Sweeney take a step back as he approached the door. The old man's eye was as big as a saucer when he saw his *victim* alive and bounding across the yard. Willie saw it too and, with a slight smile, nodded to his friend.

Both boys ate a hearty breakfast of gruel and went to their work—Patrick to the latrine—Willie to the carpentry shop.

❖ ❖ ❖

Willie stepped back and admired the pallet he had just built.

"Well done," his teacher proclaimed as he examined the tight joints, well driven nails, and smooth surface. "Well done." Andrew repeated as he retreated to sit on the planks Willie had piled near the work area for just that reason. "If me had some tar or oils ye could learn the pleasure of bringing up the grain color. Still lad, 'tis a job well done."

Malcolm Anderson read the latest report from the carpenter shop and leaned back in his chair for a good moment. Willie and Patrick's birthdays were again noted. Five months for Patrick; seven for Willie. He had to tie them together so neither would leave without the other. Orphaned, family less, Willie was forming the attachment Malcolm had hoped for and acquiring more than just carpentry skills. The likelihood that he would become hardened to life, impulsive to leave and doomed to failure, lessened considerably.

Reports that Willie applied himself were almost more than Anderson hoped for. His connection in Philadelphia expressed interest in a good, young carpentry apprentice. Malcolm was so confident that he took pen and paper to write to Alexander Childers.

> *Dear Alexander,*
>
> *I would like to recommend a young man that I am prepared to help emigrate. He is being prepared for carpenter apprenticeship. His teacher is an expert craftsman here at Portumna Workhouse. The young man has learned much and still has much to learn. William Carney, known as Willie, will leave the workhouse on his fifteenth birthday in May. Would you consider taking him on and giving him a chance? He has no family and no future here in Ireland. I will provide the usual stipend directly to you for his room and meals for six months. At the end of that time we will know if he has what it takes to make a good apprentice and a life in America.*
>
> *I await your reply.*
>
> *Malcolm Anderson*

On the day he posted the letter, he bedded for the night without fish thrashing at his feet.

Malcolm Anderson got up the next morning refreshed. He was satisfied with plans for Willie Carney. Now, he was determined to decide what was best for Patrick Doyle's future. Just as he pulled out his notes, he was interrupted by a guardian pulling Sean Doyle into his office by the collar. Sean had joined ranks with some ruffians who bullied other boys and generally caused trouble. Most infractions were handled by work bosses or guardians, but more serious infractions were brought to the Master.

The guardian jerked him into the office. Less than a month ago, Sean got a three-day confinement in the punishment cell for stealing from the kitchen. Obviously, he did not learn from that experience.

The guardian held Sean's collar as they stood in Anderson's office and waited.

"Stand tall, boy."

Sean, ever defiant, slouched as far as he could. "Up!" the guardian jerked on the collar as Malcolm Anderson entered the room.

"Sean Doyle set his mattress afire with coals from the fireplace," the guardian charged.

"Sean Doyle. Did you set fire to a mattress in the dormitory?"

No answer.

"Will you own up to your actions?"

No answer.

"This is a serious matter. You have threatened the safety of the entire workhouse." Anderson addressed the monitor. "Take him to the cell. Seven days."

As Sean was led to the door, he pulled back to face the director. "Can me leave? Now? Be gone from here? Out of

Portumna?" It was a plea.

Anderson walked to the boy and removed the monitor's hand from his collar. He stooped down to look Sean in the eye. "Sean, your family is here until they can make a better life. You are part of that family—your Ma and Da, brother and sisters. You need to stay here, take your punishment, and make the best of it until all the Doyles leave for a better life."

Tears came to Sean's eyes and spilled to his face. He did not turn away; he fixed his watery gaze on the Master. "If me believed that....," his voice trailed off and he began to sob. "Niver happen. Me family together again? Out of here?" He cried with abandon. "Ye know. Ye know ye be lyin'," he accused, backing away. "It be lies. Lies." Sean's eyes flashed hatred, anger, and accusations. He ceased crying, wiped his face with his fist and turned away to go with the guardian. His angry demeanor and defiance went out the door first. "Liar." Sean's last word washed back over the Master of the Workhouse.

Malcolm Anderson stared at Sean's back. He saw a ten-year-old child with knobby elbows and a cowlick in his hair. Then he returned to his desk to wipe his only tear. Two things were certain: Sean Doyle was going to have a short, troubled life and what the boy said was true.

❖ ❖ ❖

Malcolm Anderson's perception of residents of the workhouse began to change after Sean Doyle was led away. Now he realized that children in the workhouse were, for all intents and purposes, orphans. Previously his selected boys did not have a mother or father. Patrick Doyle was his first selectee with parents. He had never thought of it before. Boys may not want to leave their family, but here at Portumna Workhouse, the family did not exist any longer. His criteria—selecting orphan boys—was a moot point.

One truth remained. A boy with potential could not help himself or his family by staying in the workhouse. His limited program of rescue and launching still made perfect sense.

Malcolm Anderson was not sure if Patrick Doyle saw things as his younger brother proclaimed. He leaned back in his chair and wondered. *Will Patrick Doyle leave his family to find his future?*

❖ ❖ ❖

A door opened in Malcolm Anderson's mind. He needed and wanted to know how a family made life in the workhouse—not only because of his interest in Patrick, but also because Sean accused him.

He picked up Patrick's file and resumed his morning agenda. Now, more than ever, because Sean probably could not be helped, he would help Patrick. Malcolm was initially impressed with the boy's determination to take care of himself after he suffered that beating. He recalled Patrick's words, *back to work...and school, too.* Malcolm discovered later that Sweeney was most likely responsible for his beating and there was a rumor that Patrick was responsible for Sweeney's eye—just workhouse rumors but, intriguing.

Patrick was more complicated and very different from Willie. Physically, he was taller and less muscular. In contrast to Willie, he always appeared groomed— a difficult standard in this environment. That led Malcolm to believe that Patrick was perhaps artistic in nature. He was smart, no doubt. His schoolwork was excellent. Anderson got reports and noted that Patrick maneuvered around the workhouse rules to see his mother occasionally. He managed to know where his brother Sean was, too. Efforts to see Fiona were futile. For obvious reasons, separation of teenage boys and girls was the strictest. It did not matter that they were brother and sister. He never had the opportunity to be near her. Patrick was reprimanded twice for his effort to get in the yard when the girls were there. After that, he wisely made no further effort.

Anderson saw in one of his reports that Patrick had traded bed space in his dormitory, so he had a view of the tall clock tower on the administration building. Patrick Doyle was precise in his motives and actions.

Malcolm made a list under Patrick Doyle:

Intelligent
Regimented
Dedicated
Well grounded
Independent
Strong Character

Chapter 11

Both Willie and Patrick were anxious for their next meeting under the stairs. Neither had trouble staying awake until the midnight hour although they had worked hard all day. Willie had eaten his allotment of potatoes at dinner. Patrick passed his to the boy next to him and looked forward to being hungry all night. Their stomachs and tired muscles did not command sleep. They had not talked since the night of their escapade with Sweeney. Each had news to share.

Willie arrived and squeezed back under the lowest stair to scratch the date on their makeshift calendar. Then he tallied the number of days he had been in the workhouse and the number until his birthday with two more etchings. He was busy with this when Patrick arrived.

"Just finished," he whispered. "Ye turn."

Patrick slid low under the stairs and, in the light of the candle that Willie *borrowed*, Patrick did his own tally and blew out the flame on the precious candle.

The candle was stashed in a small crevice they had carved between the stones, safely hidden until the next meeting. The boys had devised a way to bring an ember from the fire to light the candle.

Then, as was their habit, the two boys stretched out side-by-side so they could whisper in each other's ear. If they were discovered, not only would they be punished in solitary cells, their meetings would be over. They spoke very low and listened carefully. Words were precious in the night also.

"Have ye seen Sweeney again?"

"For many nights, me could no' sleep, expecting him. Nay, he did no' come."

"Me thinkin' he leave ye alone, now.'

"Me thinkin' he frightened of the night ghost but not the day me."

"Ye be done with him." Willie offered assurance.

"Nay, Sweeney waitin' for his chance with Patrick Doyle. Trouble do no' just go away." Patrick spoke with authority and conviction.

"Watch ye back and me be watchin' for ye, too."

After the usual black-of-night pause to think about the words spoken, they began again.

"New work. Painting walls in the dormitory," Patrick announced. "Me practices words on the wall, then paint over. Me also paints pictures and paints over."

"Pictures?"

"Faces of me family."

"Ye paints faces?"

"Fiona, Sean, Ma, Da, and Mavis. 'Tis like me family waiting to see me on the stone walls. Tomorrow, paint again and sees me family."

Patrick went quiet to enjoy his new happiness and pleasure—such a rare thing in his life.

"Ye?" It was time for Willie to share.

"Me work, the carpentry shop. Ye Da, Andrew Doyle, be me teacher. Making beds and coffins with him all week." He told it all at once in quick words

Patrick jerked, almost spasmodic. The need to be quiet almost caused the boy to stop breathing. Willie felt his friend's jolt.

"Da? Ye see him, and work with him all day. Me Da? Me Da?"

"Aye, ye Da."

"Every day?"

"Yah. Learning carpentry. Ole Willie learning to take a piece of wood and make it smooth and part of a bed or coffin. With ye Da." Willie shared his own happiness.

Patrick trembled. He shuddered. Finally, he turned away from Willie, whimpered and drew himself up into a ball of arms and legs. Pulling his body tight was the only way Patrick could accept that Willie was seeing Da every day—working with him. His mind screamed with emotion that hurt. *Willie and Da!* He scooted away from his friend, not wanting his closeness or another word whispered.

Patrick would give all he had to be in Willie's shoes tomorrow—his fife, his faces on the wall, his hopes and dreams—for one day in those shoes. He traveled back in time to the cottage, remembering Da making Mavis' cradle. Da invited him to watch and help him build but Patrick was not interested. Now he chastised himself for not doing with Da what Willie was doing every day. Guilt came in to gild his jealousy. For this moment, Patrick was totally alone in the world, rejecting his only friend. He was left isolated and with feelings of animosity. Patrick moved further away from Willie in the black silence under the stair. He uttered the only word spoken aloud—without whispering. "Da."

Willie waited.

Patrick pulled his sleeve across his wet face and runny nose. Sanity seeped back into his being. He crawled back to

Willie's side and whispered, "How be me Da?"

"He be sick. Sorry t'say."

"Sick?'

"If I no' lift the boards, he could no'. Me totes the beds and coffins. And the tools."

"Da, sick?" Patrick was having trouble imagining his strong father unable to lift a board.

Willie put his hand on Patrick's shoulder. Into his ear went the last words this night. "Ye Da be dying."

Chapter 12

Malcolm Anderson had never seen Andrew or Annie Doyle. Today he would. He cleared his desk and took an unusual walk out of the administration building. Residents and guardians all looked up in surprise and the tall imposing figure strode by with purpose—down the south side to the carpentry shop.

The shop foreman approached. Malcolm waved him off and proceeded into the work area. It did not take him long to find Andrew Doyle and Willie amid a stack of planks making bed pallets.

He saw an emaciated man, skin and bones, obviously in pain—a clear picture of failing health— not the result of previous starvation—undoubtedly disease. The wasted body, dark-circled eyes, the trembling hands and difficult breathing were signs Malcolm had seen before. Andrew Doyle was dying and there was little or nothing anyone could do for him.

"Is Andrew Doyle able to do this work?" he asked the work boss.

"The man be sick but, with Willie's help he can. We was about to take him out before. He a good teacher for the boy... and they make pallets and coffins."

"Good. Keep him with Willie as long as possible. Let me know if you need to move him out."

Malcolm left the shop knowing Andrew Doyle would not be alive when Patrick's birthday came in the spring. He had seen the wasting disease many times before and this was the late stage of the illness.

For the first time since he came to work at Portumna he recalled the day of his father's funeral. Andrew Doyle will die, in the next so many weeks. It was as if he died to his children on the day he entered the workhouse. *What is worse?* He thought. *Burying your father? Or knowing he is just over the wall and might as well be dead?*

Malcolm went to see Annie Doyle next. She was in the laundry with six other women, all working over the hot tubs—lifting heavy wet bedclothes and sweating. "Who are these women?" He asked the work boss, being careful not to single out his interest. Then he turned and walked away. He knew which woman was Patrick's mother.

The one important thing he could do for her, he did. He assigned her to care for the little girls in the two-to-five-year-old's dormitory every Monday. If she was careful to spread her time among all the girls, she would have some time with Mavis. At the very least, she would see her little girl. Women assigned to the nursery were not allowed to work there all the time to prevent attachments to a child. In Annie's case, as well as others, the attachment already existed. For these reasons, mothers of the children would only get one day in the nursery each week.

As requested, a report came back to the Master. Annie Doyle was a good worker with the children. He even had a chance to see Annie in the dining hall and noted an occasional smile. She was lovely, actually. Small wisps of curls worked out of her single braid and circled her face. Light freckles accented her nose and cheeks and her gold and auburn hair and blue/green eyes. With renewed health, she stood out among the others.

She would need protecting from guardians and staff. He had never before concerned himself with problems women had with the male staff members, but he knew. For the first time in his years at Portumna, a woman who likely had to protect herself from male staff advances, had a face and had a family.

"Annie Doyle. Come to my office." He met her after her mid-day break in the yard.

Annie entered with head bowed and trembling. "Master?"

"Sit." He took time to think and allowed her time to relax.

She gathered her courage and asked, "Be my children or my husband?" Annie knew family members were called in under dire circumstances. "Tell me, please."

"No. All is well. Sorry to say, Sean is in confinement for trouble."

"Oh, my poor Sean."

"Can I ask about my husband, Andrew and children Patrick and Fiona?"

"I can only say they are going about their work assignments."

"Thank you."

"I have questions for you, and you must answer honestly."

She nodded and trembled more.

"Have any of the men on staff....," he searched for the word. "...bothered you?"

She looked up, questioning with her eyes.

"You know what I am asking. Have they *touched you* or more?"

Annie found it very difficult to answer Mr. Anderson. She knew how things were in the workhouse. She had been defending herself and careful never to be alone where unwanted advances could be hidden or worse. Talking to the director could mean harsh repercussions.

"Answer. It is important for your safety to trust me. Touched you or more?" He asked again.

Annie Doyle lifted her head and look directly at Malcolm Anderson. Her old spirit surfaced. "Yes. I have been touched, pushed against the wall, talked to in vulgar ways. I learned quickly never to accept any of that as friendly or in exchange for favors—as others do. Now, I never walk alone." She blinked twice. "I will fight to keep what they want from me."

He was right about the lovely Annie Doyle. Each day as she became again the woman she was before starvation; she was in greater peril.

"There is only one way I can help you. I will call you to my office a couple times a week. Rumor will spread through the workhouse. You will have to ignore the rumor. As long as the male guardians believe you are coming to me, they will leave you alone."

Malcolm stood. "You must trust me. I will not be touching you or pushing you against the wall. Come when you are summoned. Sit quietly there." He pointed to the chair in the corner. "After fifteen minutes you will leave with my shield protecting you." He walked to her chair and invited her to leave with a gesture. "I know no other way."

Annie left without a word.

Anderson ascertained that Annie could read and write. He could tell by her language that she had some formal schooling. She was assigned to the registrar's office two days and only two days in the laundry. It was the best he could do for Annie Doyle. It was a lot.

After a day of studying Patrick's file, dealing with Sean and seeking out Andrew and Annie, Malcolm thought about the family as a whole. Before, although they were required to enter the workhouse as complete families, they had always been fragments, individuals, or sole entities—split and placed in their own quarters.

Malcolm Anderson saw things differently now.

❖ ❖ ❖

"Annie Doyle, what ye doing for the director. What's he doin' for ye?" Snickered remarks came from the other women and the guardians.

"Getting a bit from the Man?"

Vulgar gestures flew in the laundry, dining hall, and dormitory. None got a response from Annie. She held on, hoping they would stop, always confident in her position. Annie had nothing to be ashamed of and it did not matter if anyone else knew it. She was not touched or pushed by the men, although she was sometimes tripped or bumped by the women.

She was a smart woman and took advantage of Anderson's protection and her assignments. In the laundry, she worked to get her physical strength back. Of course, her days in the nursery sustained her. Annie Doyle got some color in her cheeks. Her face relaxed. Her body began to rebuild into the athlete she used to be.

Anderson put a Bible on the chair he assigned to her. He moved the chair out of the corner and into the light so she could read. Later, he put paper and pen there with the admonishment that she was not to take any out of the office.

Annie began writing her memories and putting her notes

in the back of the Bible. They were always as she left them when she returned. As she wrote, Annie focused her mind on her family's situation. The scattered loved ones were like specks inside the workhouse walls. Patrick and Mavis were the only ones she had seen since coming in.

She thought about Fiona and her budding beauty. Sean worried her. He came to the workhouse with hatred in his heart. That could only bring trouble. Her longing for Andrew was an every-day, every-nighttime longing. Thinking of him brought her comfort. Thinking of the children brought her anguish. She could not fathom rescuing them all.

In her little corner of the registrar's office Annie wrote on a scrap of paper.

"Andrew will save Sean".

"I will save Mavis."

"Patrick will save Fiona."

She failed to make a note on who would save Patrick. Her confidence in him was boundless.

Her appreciation and trust of Malcolm Anderson was total. He was a man of his word. She had no fear coming to her place in the corner. He never stepped close to her and rarely spoke to her from behind his desk. In her appreciation, she stopped wondering why he was helping her. Annie took advantage of her good fortune, as any resident of the workhouse did when something unexpected eased their life.

Annie began to believe she could find a way to save her family. A small thread of hope bolstered her.

As her confidence grew, she quietly spoke a greeting to her mentor. "Good day, sir," and went straight to her chair to read. One day, she took all her strength to ask a question on her mind.

"Mr. Anderson, please, how is my Fiona?"

Malcolm looked up and paused. "Fiona? I'm sure she is fine. I have no report otherwise." His tone of voice told Annie that she had overstepped her place. She dropped her head and pretended to be reading.

Malcolm walked to the door, turned to answer Annie's question about Fiona. He did not step back so Annie could see his face.

"Fiona is being prepared for her future. She is being trained into service. I hope you will be wise enough to accept whatever that may mean. Fiona will have housekeeping skills that will give her opportunities beyond the workhouse—most likely out of Ireland."

He came back to the center of the room. "Do you want your daughter picking Oakham until she is old enough to do laundry?"

Annie knew picking Oakham was *busywork* for girls. It had little purpose except to keep the girls occupied. Large baskets of old ship rope were brought in for the girls to separate the fibers. Some of the fibers were woven into mats but mostly it was busywork. The fibers were harsh and hard on young fingers. Annie got the vision of Fiona spending her hours and days, bent over the baskets, pulling the ropes apart.

"Annie," he spoke her name gently to soften the blow. "Fiona needs a future out of the workhouse."

"Will me know if she be gone?" She reverted to her cottage vernacular. She knew when she asked, The Master of the Workhouse would not tell her. She would not know when Fiona was gone.

Annie could not think. She could not challenge. She could not process this information, so she said nothing. She knew young girls left the workhouse to go to work in service—some in England, some in Ireland for the English. She also knew they were emigrated to be married off. She refused to accept it would happen to her precious daughter.

"She be thirteen. Thirteen, by Christmas." It was a whisper spoken to herself.

Just as Annie was beginning to gather strength and seize hope, this tragic news brought her down. *Would Fiona be gone? Forever?* Then she let her mind go back to the cottage—something she rarely did any more. *Patrick!* Her mind screamed. *Does he know his Fiona is goin' somewhere?* She saw her two children, so close in age, with their special bond—preparing to face the world together—now, possibly separated forever. *Does he know?* Annie wept silently as Malcolm Anderson left the room.

She opened the Bible and found a blank paper and wrote:

> *Fiona Mary Doyle. Thirteen, December 1851*
>
> *Lovely beyond words, hair of red, eyes of blue like her father. A girl for running and skipping. For singing and dreaming. Picking flowers for the cottage. Following Patrick walking the walls. Washing Sean's hands and picking up our baby, Mavis. Listening to her father's words and picking up wood curls from his work. Around my knees holding my yarn. Growing into a woman. Saying teach me, show me, help me. I have missed you since we came here. I pray to set my eyes on your beautiful face again.*

She slid the paper into the Bible at Psalm 23, closed the book, left Anderson's office and returned to the laundry. She lifted the heavy, wet, endless sheets and thought of her family as it used to be.

Chapter 13

Stories of Annie Doyle and Malcolm Anderson reached every corner of the workhouse. It was delicious gossip. No one failed to repeat it. No one tried to deny it.

"Anderson's whore," was the worst name she had to bear.

"Two, three times a week. Both be smilin' like cat that got d'milk."

"Wonder how good she be?"

"Tell us, Annie. How good dat big man?"

One fateful day it reached the sick man in the carpenter shop. Willie came in that morning and found Andrew bent in half with pain.

"Andrew!" Willie quickly came to his side. "To the infirmary?" he asked.

"Nay. Stay here. The infirmary— no coming back. Help me, Willie." He put his hands out reaching for Willie's shoulders. "Straight."

Willie grasped his torso and helped Andrew to stand straight. He stacked two more planks on the pile so Andrew could almost sit and yet look upright to the work boss. Willie knew what to do. He started immediately making it look like Andrew Doyle was working.

"Willie, a story about me Annie. Do ye know?" He could hardly put it into words.

"Me hear."

"D'pain worse with it."

"Not be true, for sure."

"Ye sure? Anderson, top man here. He do what he want to Annie."

"Canno' be sure. Me see Annie Doyle in Anderson's office last week. She be readin' Bible in corner. Canno' see harm in that." Willie touched his shoulder to reassure. "Workhouse gossip."

Andrew relaxed a little and let the tension go from his gut which eased his pain. Willie drew another plank, marking it for cutting. "Here?" He asked his teacher as he picked up the saw.

❖ ❖ ❖

Under the stairs four days later, Patrick had the same questions. "Me Ma, no take to Anderson. He be mistreating her." Patrick was enraged, even more than at Sweeney last month. "What can me do? Time to take the Doyles out of the workhouse. We be starvin' out there but we be together. Willie, ye must tell Da. The Doyles are a'goin'. Get Fiona, Sean, and Mavis. Be better to sit by the road and die—than this."

"Do no' believe it." Willie did all he could to assure his friend "Wait, gotta think. Ye can no' get the Doyles together to leave. Sean in cell. Ye Da too sick to walk out t'door."

Patrick was too disturbed to stay under the stairs. "Doyles a'goin'." He scooted out to go.

"Stay," Willie asked as he took his arm. Patrick was too upset to lie on his back in the dark. His agitation required movement. He smacked the hand that tried to hold him.

"Goin', Willie, goin'."

"Meet next week. Me be getting some truth. Talk to ye Da

tomorrow. Be here?"

Patrick melted in the darkness and yielded to his friend. "Me be here," he replied, totally forlorn. "What's one more week?" Willie released his hold and Patrick slid away.

Willie stayed under the stair to think. *Talk to Andrew,* was his first thought. *Talk to Mr. Anderson,* was his second, better thought.

"Anderson," he said aloud to the black night. Willie had no idea what he could say to the Master of the Workhouse that would help his friend.

❖ ❖ ❖

The opportunity did not come right away. Willie had to wait for Mr. Anderson to summon him. Finally, the call came. "Willie, in my office."

Annie Doyle was sitting in the corner, as before, reading the Bible. Willie advanced to her chair and stood there looking at her.

When she looked up at him, there was immediate recognition of the boy who helped at orientation. She smiled.

Willie continued to stand, holding her gaze.

Annie returned his gaze at first quizzical and then understanding. She nodded and gave him a reassuring, understanding, all is well, look.

They were locked in wordless conversation when Mr. Anderson entered.

"Willie," he turned around. "Have a seat," Malcolm invited.

"Nay," Willie declined as always.

"There was a scuffle in the dining hall last evening. Did you see it?"

"Yea."

"Patrick Doyle?"

With that question, Annie looked up.

"Me heard an insult about Patrick's Ma. He no let it pass."

"You may go now." Malcolm dismissed Willie and walked him to the door where he placed his hand on his shoulder and turned him around.

"Willie, that is Annie Doyle." He pointed to her. "She comes here to read the Bible. Annie Doyle...," he addressed her before opening the door for Willie. "...are you safe here?"

She looked up and nodded.

Malcolm Anderson knew that Andrew and Patrick Doyle would soon know that no matter what rumors flew across the yard, in the dining hall, and around the workstations, Annie Doyle, wife and mother, was not a victim of The Master of Portumna Workhouse.

Chapter 14

Sean wanted Patrick to join him in his righteous, rebellious shenanigans. He soon realized that would not happen. When he passed Patrick going to school, Sean stole a moment to entice him into his group. Patrick stood firm.

"We be turning over tables in the dining hall tomorrow."

"Why?"

"For the hell of it." Sean's countenance became animated.

Patrick shook his head. "We need to do things to make life better until we get out of here."

"Nah. Me fight." Sean was adamant as he pointed his thumbs into his expanded chest.

"It no' be good for us." Patrick took his brother firmly by the shoulders. "Ma and Da did no' teach us to fight."

"What did they teach? Eat dirt? Work endlessly. Me walk the Capstan wheel day after day—crushing stone? Work boss pushing, pushing. Me push back." He recited thoughts that went through his brain hour after hour with his *busywork*. Sean's eyes flashed with passion. "Me niver learn anything to make me live like this." Sean waved his arm in a big circle outlining the workhouse.

Patrick grabbed Sean's arm and tried to hold it. "We be makin' a life someday."

Sean pulled away and spat. "Someday? What 'bout t'day?" He became angrier. "T'day!" He pulled from Patrick's grasp. "Ye be like Da." He shoved his brother in the chest as he spoke. It was not a compliment; it was an indictment. Sean's face and countenance went from angry passion to blank and hard. Patrick saw his brother withdraw and he had no way to reach him. He was helpless. Sean moved on to class while Patrick leaned against the stone wall for support.

News of Sean's latest punishment in the isolation cell traveled through the rumor mill. It was, too often, Sean's life, depending on his latest trouble. Last month he had three days in the cell. This week, seven days for setting the fire in the dormitory. In the cell, boys like Sean lived in darkness, amid their own filth, to be taught to follow rules. The lessons were sometimes learned but not by Sean. He became more and more rebellious—more and more hardened. His body was now ten years old, but his face and attitude were way beyond.

Sean sat in his cell mindless of all that was happening outside. All he could do was brood. He saw himself as abandoned and did not want to see his brother or his father. He was convinced that one, or both of them, could have kept the family out of the workhouse. His mind was full of accusations, recriminations and rebellion. It was easy, with this mindset, to join with a band of troublemakers who replaced his family. Sean enjoyed his reputation as a ruffian. He fought the system, other boys, shadows and demons—as well as reality. When he was bullying or making mischief, he got reassuring glances from his fellow troublemakers and it felt *good*. They were the only good feelings he had.

Sean soon became familiar with the punishment cells. The stone box, 4 by 6 by 8, sat on the north side of the yard next to the latrine. Inside, the stench, the stone bench, and floor gave no comfort. The only light slithered in the observation hole high on the door. A slat at the bottom of the door was for food passage. Potatoes, boiled and dry, were pushed in each day.

Patrick was on the grounds on the cold rainy day when Sean was released from his seven-day confinement in the cell. He went to the doorway to wait for his weakened, filthy brother and offered his hand.

"Are ye a'right?" Patrick asked his ragged, dirty brother.

"Are ye a'right?" Sean fired back as he slapped the helping hand. "Ye be one of them! Out me way."

"Sean.... Sean...." Patrick's call went unheeded as his brother stumbled toward the washroom in all his fury and filthy degradation.

Patrick Doyle would not give in to the circumstances that required defeat. Before Sean reached the washroom door, Patrick was in his face.

"Sean Doyle, ye have much to learn and me be feared ye will learn the hard way." It was a soft and gentle proclamation.

"Out me way, Paddy. Get t'school. Away from ye brother, else ye be cuffed. Follow the rules or see the cell."

Sean averted his eyes, but Patrick would not allow it. He took hold of Sean's filthy head and insisted that his brother acknowledge him with his eyes. "Ye be a Doyle. Son of Andrew and Annie, brother of Fiona and Mavis....and me. Deny ye family and have nothing. Nothing." Then Patrick wrapped his arms around his defiant brother. For one short moment, Sean yielded and let his head fall to Patrick's shoulder. For one short moment, Sean was just a boy—nothing more. Patrick felt his brother's heartbeat, the slow rising of his lungs drawing life, the thin ribs and quaking body He was as close as he was in the cottage when they shared a bed. Both of Patrick's arms circled Sean's narrow body. His hands went up the bony spine. He inhaled deeply, seeking something he could hold on to, a fragrance or an essence of his brother.

Then, the guardian forced his hands between them, pushing bodies apart. Sean stepped away, and went into the washroom.

Patrick's heart broke. He did not feel the scuff on his head and the barking of the guardian. "Sean," he whispered and cried as he went on to school.

Two weeks later, Sean and two of his pals walked out of the workhouse. He was on his own in a starving world.

❖ ❖ ❖

One of Patrick's daily chores—looking for his brother and trying to ease his struggles, was over. Willie brought the news under the stair.

"Sean be gone."

"Out?"

"Sean, Kevin O'Leary and Michael Turney. Gone."

"Sure'n he did no' check out with the registrar. Poor Sean." Patrick's voice was low and forlorn.

"They watched the door and when Sweeney went to pee, zip, gone."

"He canno' come back..." Patrick took time to grieve.

"Maybe when we go, we will find him. Eh, Willie?"

"Don't hold out for that. Sean no stay around the workhouse the next months. Nay. If he be smart, he go south. Cold winds coming soon off the sea."

"Sean not showing smart thinking. No thinking at all."

Willie reached out in the dark and patted Patrick's head. "Sean be as gone as my Mary Ann." The two boys were very quiet in their thoughts until steady breathing signaled their slumber. They were still asleep under the stair when the first morning bell tolled. By the second clamor, they had scrambled to the dormitory to protect the secret place under the stair.

Patrick agonized about getting word to his mother about Sean. *She has to know,* he decided. Patrick had three turns picking up trash before she got his message. At last she came with the bins. "It's Sean," he managed to say. "He be gone out." With knowing, sad eyes she looked at her remaining son. Anderson had already told Annie as she sat in the corner reading the Bible the day Sean left. Annie knew her prodigal son was gone, and she knew what that meant. By the time Patrick and Annie had their moment of grieving at the trash bins, Sean had been gone a month, never to be heard from again.

The struggle to save his brother was over. The occasional passing near the classrooms was over. Hoping to see his mother bring the trash bins out every few weeks was all he had. It was a thin line of connection. It was his life. Annie could report that Mavis was well, but she could not bring herself to tell about Fiona. There was absolutely no chance he would know about her. Patrick's favored sister seemed to float further and further away. Annie and Patrick had no idea how far.

Willie brought more and more distressing reports on his

father.

"Wasting disease, he has. I'm sorry t'say." Patrick did not share this news with his mother.

Nevertheless, Patrick kept his dream to save his sisters and his mother. In the silent notes he played on his fife and the passionate songs he wrote in his mind were his lifeline. He recalled his father beating the drum. When he concentrated, he could almost hear him. The most dramatic, demanding beats he put to his words.

Don't grow old here
Fiona, Fiona
Nay, Nay. Thump, thump
Don't grow old here
I say. I say. Thumpity, thump
Young and bright and beautiful
The day after today Thump, thump
The sun will shine even for thee
Aye, the sun will shine for me. Thumpity, Thump
We will see the horizon again, again
And walk or run all the way to it. Thumpity, thump thump.

His music sustained him in the darkest hours. He stayed in his dream because reality gave him no clue. There was no clear path to saving the Doyles. His silent music always ended with a one-word prayer to God. "How?"

Chapter 15

After Sean left, Patrick wanted to see Fiona desperately. He was consumed with the need. There was absolutely no opportunity to see her—in passing or by chance. Truly, Patrick missed Fiona most of all. They were *Irish twins*, only eleven months apart, raised together in the cottage. He thought he could look out for her in the workhouse but learned immediately, he could not.

Since the first weeks when he got in trouble trying to see her, he stopped trying. But today he would try again. He hid under the table in the dining hall as the boys filed out. When the cleaning crew began cleanup for the girls' shift, he joined in the work. No one paid him any mind as he swept tables and floors. When the crew left, he went under the table again to wait.

"Boy! What ye doin'?" The guardian had him by the shirt-tail. She did not give Patrick time to get up. She was a strong Amazon of a woman and pulled him across the floor, bumping tables and chairs. "Think ye can hide out her to see one of me girls? No chance. Ye not see ye girlfriend on my watch." With that she swung Patrick through the door.

"Nay. Me sister, Fiona Doyle." Patrick rolled over to his knees and raised up in a prayerful position. "Please, just see her?"

"Fiona Doyle?" She paused to get her thoughts. "Ye nay see Fiona. She be in prep." She walked away and left Patrick there to think about what she said. *Did she say prep?* He could not imagine what she meant.

Patrick hurried back to the supply room to get his bucket of whitewash, where he got the second scuff on the ear of the day.

"Late! Where ye been, Doyle? No mid-day, boy. Get to it." His words accompanied by the usual slap aside the head

Patrick went to the dormitory where he finished yesterday and started his back-and-forth work. As soon as he had the chance, he wrote the guardian's words on the wall. *In prep.*

His failed effort to see Fiona made his day torturous and long. With no break for lunch it seemed endless. He did not mind being hungry; it was his preferred condition. The clock turned slowly until it was finally time for supper and school.

Willie came in and took his seat next to Patrick. They worked on numbers until finally it was time to write words. Patrick turned his slate so Willie could read. **Fiona prep??** And then, erased it.

Willie nodded and shrugged. He understood the question, but it would be days before they would meet under the stairs where he could give the answer.

Patrick settled into a kind of acceptance that allowed him to get by day to day. *For now,* he told himself as he did what he had to do. Avoided Sweeney at all costs. Worked his assigned job. Studied hard at school. Retreated each night to his silent fife. And, waited for the night when he would rendezvous with Willie. He needed to understand where Fiona was and to get news of Da.

School was his comfort zone. He went to each session eager to learn. Reading came easy. Soon he was reading everything he could, but resources were limited even in the classroom.

"Help me?" he asked his teacher. "Why is the language me read so different from what we speak?" Patrick became aware that he did not speak the verbs he read. "Be? Is? Are?"

"The verb *to be,* Patrick. Look." He conjugated the verb on the slate. Then he wrote, *Be* on the right side of the slate.

"No need to practice the correct way." The teacher mimicked. "Ye Irish speaking, be good enough for you." They were insults and Patrick felt it. The teacher did not think there was any value in the boy speaking properly. Patrick spent the rest of the class reading for the words that should substitute *ye* and *be. Nay, not good enough for me,* he thought.

Suddenly, he recalled how at times, Ma read words put together like this. She knew the right pronouns and verbs although she did not always use them. It was two languages—and Patrick was advancing in his schooling to see the difference and the value in it. He would practice. He missed his mother more than ever.

Patrick looked forward to school even when he was dead tired from painting walls. He was most anxious for the next meeting with Willie under the stairs.

The mild early winter days were good. The nights were cold. Soon the winter months would bring some snow, lots of rain, and constant dampness. The boys felt it most when under the stairs, far from the heat in the dormitory and warm bodies. Some heat rose from the floor below but when Willie and Patrick crawled into their stone box under the stair, the chill set in quickly. Willie managed to smuggle in an extra sheet, which he folded twice. It insulated the stone floor and helped.

"Gettin' colder at night and dark before dinner time."

"Too cold for us?" Patrick asked.

"Nay, we be good at least past Christmas."

Willie did his calendar. Patrick waited with his long agenda. Finally, Willie stretched out and whispered in Patrick's ear.

"Fiona or ye Da?" he quietly gave the night to Patrick.

"Fiona. Tell me, where she be? What's prep?"

"They takes girls out of the workhouse. Gets 'em ready to leave."

"Leave? Go where?" Patrick's mind raced ahead.

"Girls no stay here much past thirteen years. They be valuable in d' world."

"Valuable?" Patrick scooted to the edge of the space where he could sit up. He could not take this information on his sister lying down. "Valuable?" he repeated.

"Well..." obviously, Willie did not want to tell. "They be old enough to give men pleasure and have babies...they be servants or wives." Patrick reached over and took hold of his friend. He shook him. The news, without details, was beyond awful.

"Turn me loose and listen. Me tell you about girls of age—thirteen. Be Fiona thirteen?"

"Thirteen the day after Christmas."

"This be what it means for girls in prep. Me not saying what happens for Fiona. I be around the workhouse but me not know about Fiona." He paused for Patrick to let go of his arm and settle down. "Be ye ready to hear it?"

"Aye."

"Girls have a future out of the workhouse because they can

go in service or be married off. That's good for landowners. They no longer taxed for girls in workhouse. They taken out to learn maid work or kitchen work. Ye know. They be learning wife-y things. Some go in service. Some sent to colonies to marry English there."

"Fiona be goin' somewhere?" Patrick tried to keep alarm from his voice.

"It be like this. A few girls go in service for the English in Ireland. Most who go in service work in England, but some go to the colonies. Ye need to know—many girls go to Canada or Australia to marry blokes who work the mines. Either way, there be no choice to keep their bodies to themselves.." He took a breath after spewing out these difficult facts for his friend.

Patrick let an animal sound escape from his gut and pulled his arms tight across so his dinner would not come up.

"Me do no' know about Fiona. Those things kept very quiet to keep families from knowin'. Willie gets no chance to get to south building. Me have lots a chances here in north building. One thing me knows...if Fiona be healthy, she be leaving the workhouse. May be gone by her birthday."

Patrick went flat to the hard floor. "Fiona." All was quiet for a while. Finally, Patrick was ready to process what he had learned.

"The guardian said she was 'in prep'. Me thinks that means she no be gone yet. Ye must find out. Me be beggin' ye." He turned in the dark and took hold of Willie again—this time gently, pleading. "Ye can. Ye can, Willie. Me must know. Remember *Mary Ann.* Fiona be my *Mary Ann.*"

"Me be trying all week. This be the hardest workhouse secret. Me be tryin' again for ye, Patrick Doyle."

"Me seein' what the workhouse does. Doyles no more a family. No more since Sweeney opened dat door. No more."

"'Tis a hard lesson and it has taken ye months to see. Ye can no' hold Ma, Da, brother and sisters. Sean gone. Ye Da failing fast. He no' here much longer. Fiona be sent out. Ye Ma stay for Mavis—many years." He waited for Patrick to respond but none came.

"Ye and me, Patrick Doyle, go looking for a better life. Together. We work. Me be willing to help ye and someday Annie Doyle and Mavis Doyle will come and be with us."

Patrick turned; Willie felt his breath.

"Ye me brother, Willie. The workhouse take ye family away. It be trying to take mine. The workhouse gave me a new brother, Willie Carney. Ye, and me. We be a new family that the workhouse can no' destroy." As Patrick spoke, he became animated and had to concentrate on keeping his voice down. He wanted to shout the challenge to the stone walls, dreary buildings, and desolate atmosphere. "Brothers, Willie and Patrick—a new family."

"Willie and Patrick—a new family," was echoed in the dark.

"A good carpenter."

"A good painter."

"Good carpenter and painter in America. Send for ye Ma and sister."

"Find Fiona, too."

It sounded good. It sounded possible. It sounded believable.

❖ ❖ ❖

Patrick and Willie became quiet in the dark. They, who

were no longer boys, rather fourteen-year-olds forced into manhood, had to consider the important commitments they had just made. They were *going-forward* thoughts. Willie had to let go of his treasured independence and Patrick had to abandon the idea that, in and around these walls, he would save his family. They did not think profoundly. They just did.

"We are brothers," Patrick spoke again—quietly and sincerely. He lay still another minute and started to leave.

Willie took his arm, held tight and said, "Da be dying, soon."

Patrick could hardly remember returning to his bed. Willie's words, "...dying, soon," echoed in his brain. He was emotionally drained and not sure how or what he felt. He crawled into the bed, retrieved his fife and played without sound. He wanted to sleep but it did not come and when it did, it was a fitful sleep full of fear and doubts. Twice he turned on his hand holding the flute. It dug into his skin and awakened him. Finally, close to daybreak, he tucked his instrument into its hiding place and yielded to sleep...just in time to get up for another day.

Patrick's first thoughts were, *Da, can't.* His second thought was Willie with his father in the carpentry shop. Both tore at him. He went to his job in the dormitory conflicted. Fiona gone? Da dying? All joy was gone. No pleasure would come in his painting. No words or portraits would appear on the walls. He dipped the makeshift brush and began lathering the whitewash on the wall. Anger and jealousy drove his motions. He pushed and pulled the brush as if answers were in the strokes. The only person he could vent at was Willie. *Damn Willie.* All the brotherhood thoughts of last night were squelched by Willie's bad news and recurring jealousy. Willie was, at this very moment, where Patrick wanted to be—with Da. Especially if Da were as sick as Willie said. Suddenly, Patrick dropped the brush into the bucket, splashing whitewash over his feet. *Willie don't know. He can no' know. Da no' be dying.* His brain screamed with excuses. He did not know why Willie made that story. He just knew it could not be true. Besides that, Patrick could not deal with his painting job while Willie was with his father. For the first time since coming to the workhouse, jealousy, anger and fear brought confusion. Patrick felt beaten, defeated, utterly lost. He could not see past the wall he was painting or the walls surrounding his life. Patrick wanted to run.

He picked up the brush and dropped it again. "Can no' do this." Patrick walked away from his work and bumped into Guardian Jones at the doorway.

"Hey Doyle!"

Patrick felt the tug on his shirt. He jerked loose and began running—the surprised Jones in pursuit. Parker, the guardian at the yard, joined the pursuit and tried to stop him with words. "Back. Back, I say!" Patrick was running with purpose and gaining speed with determination. Now he was chased by Jones, Parker and one other guardian. Patrick and his pursuers were across the yard and headed for the far exit. By the time they reached the carpentry shop on the south perimeter, six monitors were chasing the boy who was running like mercury.

"Stop him!" A warning was shouted to the work boss at the door to the carpentry shop. He reached for Patrick, who had lowered his head and proceeded like a battering ram. The surprised work boss was knocked to the floor. Patrick was in the carpentry shop.

Willie heard the commotion and looked around a stack of boards in time to see Patrick put his head into the work boss's stomach and literally bounced into the shop, landing flat on his back.

"Oh, Patrick, no." He whispered under his breath.

"Da! Andrew Doyle!" Patrick yelled. "Da!" From the floor, out of breath and losing steam, He cried once more. "Andrew Doyle!"

The angry work boss and Patrick's pursuers arrived at his feet just as his father came to his head. Da went to the floor and lifted his son's head. Jones jerked Patrick's feet to pull him from his father's embrace.

"Up! Get up!" The work bosses and guardians screamed.

Andrew threw his full body over his son. Wrapped his arms around and received Patrick's arms. The workhouse team tried to lift them both but for an instant—that felt like eternity—Patrick and Andrew stayed—wrapped together.

"Da, Da, Da..."

"Paddy, me Paddy."

"Are ye sick, Da?"

"Me be dead... soon."

Andrew drew Patrick's face to his. Everyone went into slow motion. Did the workhouse staff soften in the presence of the boy and his dying father? Who can say? It was not their nature, but Patrick and Andrew had their moment.

"Son, ye must take care of ye self." Andrew pulled a breath from deep within. "Has ye still got ye fife?"

"Aye, me fife."

"'Twill take ye home again." Talk was exhausting but

Andrew had more to say. “Take care of Fiona and ye fife. Let nothin’ happen to them. Mavis, a baby. Sean lost. Ma and me had our life.” Da continued. “Be wise in ye choices. Comin’ t’me was foolish but me not fault ye for it.” He squeezed his son. “Let it be ye last foolishness. Be strong. Find ye way.” Patrick said not a word as his father took his face in his hands and looked into his eyes “Find a way, Paddy. Your fife and Fiona,” he managed to put emphasis on his words although his breath and strength were gone. He hugged Patrick and fell away exhausted. “Fiona and fife. Me love ye, Paddy.” His last words came out soft and caressing, like a prayer.

Jones and Parker took Patrick’s arms from his father and pulled him from under the paper-thin man. Andrew remained face down as Patrick dragged from the carpentry shop. Willie bent down to help Andrew Doyle.

Guardian Jones ran ahead to the Master’s office to give a report. Parker followed with Patrick in hand. Cardinal rules had been broken. Malcolm Anderson took Jones’s and Parker’s account without response. He had to make an example of the boy and support the actions of the guardians. The punishment would be solitary confinement in the cell.

“Bring him in. That is all,” he dismissed them.

The accused stood defiant and straight before Anderson. His eyes looked into the face of the Master. Tracks of dried tears traced down to his chin, full of saw dust. Behind the eyes and dirty face, Patrick stood strong.

“Did you leave your work and go into the yard and carpentry shop?”

“Aye.” Patrick had no remorse. “I did.” His voice was clear and unapologetic.

"The punishment cell—three days." It had to be done but it did not have to be too severe. Malcolm Anderson watched the boy leave with his spirit intact—no excuses, no whining.

Patrick saw the inside of the cell for the first time. Three cold potatoes were tossed in with him for the meal he had just missed. His only regret was he could not have his fife with him.

Chapter 16

The guardian of the second floor of the south building approached Annie Doyle's bed and gently touched her shoulder.

"Ye are summoned to the infirmary, Annie Doyle."

She hastened into her overgarment and followed the guardian. The air grew colder as they walked further away from the hearth. Annie shivered from the winter night and emotion. She had no clue which of her family needed her, but she had a feeling. "Andrew," she whispered as she walked. He had been so strong on her mind the last two days.

The infirmary attendant met her at the door and led her to Andrew's bed without a word. She knelt and leaned over to kiss his cheek and took his hand. He was warm, very warm. "Fever?" she asked, looking up at the nurse

"Nay, he be finished wasting away. 'Tis the end."

Annie let her tears flow. Without crying or sobbing, a flood came from her eyes, across her cheeks and onto the bosom of her clothes. She did not wipe them; she let them run, unchecked, silent. For all these months in the workhouse, Annie had not cried. There was so much to say good-bye to, here beside her beloved's deathbed. And, so she cried copious, abandoned tears for all that was lost. Hope that she would someday have Andrew again was slipping away as she felt him cooling down.

"Andrew, Andrew," she begged. "Open your eyes. See, it's me."

He trembled and lifted his eyelids. "Annie," his silent lips moved. "Annie," he tried again.

"Don't talk, Love. I'm here." She moved onto the side of his bed. She lifted the blanket and slid her body against his. It was easy. They were both so thin that Annie and Andrew could lie together on the narrow bed. He was so far gone that he did not react to her embrace. Her arm went over his chest. Her hands caressed his arms and head. She smoothed his hair and pulled her fingers slowly across his soft yielding lips—almost a kiss.

Tall and strong, Andrew came into the cottage with a basket of rich, fat, brown potatoes. He put the basket down and lifted Annie from the floor. His smiling eyes were lovingly caressing her as his strong hands swirled her around. His mouth went to her ear and she felt his breath. The moments were Annie's. The breath she felt was his last. She held him until his eyes closed and a cough brought blood from his mouth.

Annie took her sleeve to wipe the blood and hide his death from the nurse. She would hold him until he was cold. The last of his warmth was all she had.

Later that night Anderson got a report from the infirmary on the latest death in the Portumna Workhouse—Andrew Doyle. It was not hard to figure out why Patrick tore out of the dormitory and made his way to the carpentry shop. Malcolm could guess how Patrick knew his father was dying.

Willie was summoned. A monitor from the carpentry shop escorted Willie to the Master's office. With usual malice the guardian pushed Willie through the door. Malcolm Anderson pointed to the chair.

"Nay, sir." Willie declined the seat and stood mid-way into the room.

"Did you see Patrick Doyle force his way into the carpentry shop?"

"Yea."

"Do you know why Patrick did that?" It was a precarious moment. Willie hesitated; Anderson went on.

"Andrew Doyle has been teaching you. Right?" Willie nodded.

"Did you tell Patrick his father was dying?" Willie nodded again...and fidgeted.

"At school last night. Wrote on me slate." A lie that did not give away their secret place and meetings.

"Now Patrick is in a punishment cell. Did you know he was going to break the rules, run into the yard at forbidden time and out to the carpentry shop? Were you part of this?" If so, it must be punished.

Willie's composure slipped. Confusion reigned as he tried to decide if the director put blame on him.

"Yea...Me mean, Nay." The truth. Willie moved forward to emphasize the truth. "Never want Patrick Doyle to be in the cell. Me ne'er do that urging. Me only told of Andrew Doyle."

"Come sit down, lad." Anderson invited again with insistence.

Willie took a seat. "Me not want Patrick to break rules, run to the shop or go to the cell, Master Anderson."

Man and boy took a moment to compose themselves; each needed to breathe and reflect on the results of the sparing.

"About another matter..." Anderson changed the subject

and relieved the tension in the room.

Still, Willie sat on the very edge of the wooden chair tendered to him.

"Andrew Doyle made that chair."

Willie instinctively ran his hand over the smooth seat and slightly down the leg.

"He was a master wood smith. He could make more than bed frames and coffins. You could have learned so much from him."

"Me already learned much in the carpentry shop and wanted to learn more."

"There you will stay." Malcolm proclaimed as he stood to end the meeting. The residents will think Willie was properly chastised.

Malcolm walked with Willie to the door. "Learn all you can, Willie. It will help you when you leave here."

Patrick sat on the stone seat and ignored the potatoes. He found the small ray of sun that came in the crack in the door. He followed its path from side to side until it disappeared with the setting sun. He searched the wall for a place to do his tally. It was traditional, all incarcerated made their marks. Down close to the floor he found a small whitewashed stone that had not been scratched. Patrick made his first mark and wondered where Sean's tallies were. Just before dusk gave way to dark, Willie came to the cell door.

"Patrick," He called through the open slat. "Ye alright?'

"Yea."

"Three days; ye can do it."

"Yea."

"Da died. Ye mother was with him."

"Thank ye, for tellin' me." Nothing could have been harder than this news in the cold dark cell where he sat. It seemed appropriate.

"Move on. Move on." Patrick heard Sweeney's voice chasing Willie. He could not see the large stone Sweeney threw at Willie. He could only hear Willie's taunting call.

"Ye missed, ye ole one-eyed goat."

Then ten hot potatoes slid under the door for the evening meal. Patrick used them for heat until cold and hard. Then he pushed them aside.

Patrick had no appetite with the news Willie brought. He took small comfort in knowing his mother was with his father at the end. He spoke aloud, almost a prayer: "Thank God, I saw Da." Then he went over, word for word, what his father said to him. "I'll niver forget."

There were no tears. Tears would be giving in to the powers that did not allow him to feel loss or express mourning. Patrick understood—his family was lost to him.

His head went back to rest on the stones—his eyes wide open in the black cell. *Da said, Fiona,* he sat up quickly. *Only Fiona?* It just dawned on him that his father did not commission him to look after Ma or Mavis. *Only Fiona?* He pondered. *Only Fiona and me fife.*

It would be a long sad of grieving. The December air chilled to the bone. He twisted to the fetal position on the stone bench, pulled his arms into his shirt for warmth and caressed his hungry stomach. Hunger was the only comfort he had as it took him back to the cottage. He did not have to close his eyes. In the blackness, he could see the green hills, grey and white stone walls and the home he loved and missed. He could see his family, each in his own spot in the room. Tonight, those thoughts challenged him. His father had given Patrick an unexpected gift with his last breaths. After months of wondering how he would save his whole family and somehow get them back to the cottage, Da had, through some strange wisdom, told his son the fife was the way to save himself and only Fiona. He did not know how or why. But he imagined lifting Fiona and releasing the other burdens. His mind narrowed down from the impossible to the possible. "When time be right, Fiona goes with me." Patrick grasped his father's words and began immediately to believe that he could do what Da told him to do.

Suddenly ready to eat, he felt around the cell until he located the potatoes Sweeney had thrown in. Patrick took one bite and spit it out, coughing and sputtering. Bitterness filled his mouth and assaulted his tongue. No doubt, Sweeney had flavored the spud. "Thanks, Sweeney," he announced sarcastically

Patrick would stay hungry and embrace the empty gnawing in his gut as he often did—to help him believe he was strong and invincible.

Each time Sweeney brought the potatoes, Patrick gingerly tasted them. Sometimes, he got one untainted—surely by accident, not by Sweeney's generosity. Sometimes Sweeney was not the one who brought them, and Patrick ate one or two. A tally was made on the wall to count the days.

Twice in the three days, Sweeney came with a long hot poker and tried to get Patrick through the opening. The first time the poker hit Patrick's ankle, he screamed.

"Akkkk," cackled Sweeney. "Did me poker get ye eye, ghost? Soon, an eye for an eye."

Patrick heard Sweeney's laugh go off in the distant darkness. He was muttering his constant warning, "Next time." Thereafter, Patrick slept where the long poker could not reach.

On the morning of the fourth day, the door came open and painful light assaulted his eyes. He had endured. Patrick came from the cell with clarity, determination, confidence, and hunger. The last potatoes were left in the cell. Patrick was stronger and better equipped to find his way because he was hungry and because of what Da had said.

Patrick would survive his sentence in the cell and life in the workhouse would resume as if nothing of significance happened in the carpentry shop. The lesson was made—do not break the rules and cross the family divides.

Chapter 17

Christmas made promises to the residents of the workhouse. Amid the hard walls, the arrival of Christmas brought anticipation and even a feeling of joy to the men, women, and children entering the dining hall. Residents who had been here for Christmases past told of the expected meal. Citizens of the county, out of Christian charity, brought gifts to the workhouse. There would be meat, puddings, fruit, even cake. In this dismal place, colors dressed the one-day holiday.

The Crib, a rough stable with straw and an empty manger, appeared in the dining hall. Each day, starting on the twenty-second, half-life-size figures were added. The animals—cow, horse, goat, donkey—then the shepherds carrying white sheep, and wise men, dressed in robes of red and gold. Anticipation grew as Joseph, and Mary, dressed in blue, were set in place. The manger remained empty until Christmas Eve, when Baby Jesus would come to the stable and the Crib would be completed.

Patrick and Willie were under the stairs the week before Christmas.

"December twenty-first. First day of winter. Christmas—four days." Willie announced. He was doing his calendar. "Seventy-nine days to ye birthday, March tenth." he continued counting. "One hundred thirty-five t'mine, May fifteenth." He slid out from the wall.

Patrick slid into his calendar and verified. "Aye. Ye can count." They smiled in the dark and punched each other jokingly.

"Ye has to wait fifty-six days for me."

"'Tis agreed, brother." Patrick looked again at his calendar before the candle went out. He touched December second, the day his Da died, two weeks and two days ago. "Sean be gone one month, three days. Christmas is Tuesday. Fiona's birthday on Wednesday." He blew the candle and put it away.

Willie could tell that Patrick had more to say. They had established camaraderie under the stairs that was hard to explain. Partly because the black night allowed the boys to express themselves. Beyond that, they understood each other very well. Much went unspoken yet heard. They waited for each other to find their words. Tonight, Willie waited for Patrick.

"I be thinkin' about Christmas in the cottage with me family. All together. We made gifts for each other." He paused to enjoy the memory. "Each year Da made a wooden toy for us to share. He made us a perfect ball one year. Beautiful. Smooth. He handed it to me and said, 'play with each other. Find ye a way to play with it and care for it.'" His sentimental journey closed him down for a while.

Willie continued to wait.

"Find ye way. That's what he said to me in the shop the day he died. Find ye way." Patrick paused again. "He not be talking about playing, he be talking about living."

Patrick could feel Willie agreeing.

"We traded the ball for food—a poached rabbit from Angus McGrady."

After just the right amount of time, Willie took his turn talking.

"Christmas on Tuesday....and then the New Year, 1850. It be

our year. We be finding a way—our way—making a life. This damned workhouse canno' be it!"

"Will Ma, Mavis and Fiona have Christmas dinner with us?"

"Nay, Paddy. Not happen, not even on Christmas. Two evening meals—one for men and boys, one for women and girls. But, ye will enjoy the chorus and music makers of the parish church. They come with the priest and bring some instruments for us to use—fiddles and drums for anyone who wants to play. 'Tis a surprise how many of us *downtrodden* can make music."

No doubt the coming holiday brought the boys to this melancholy frame of mind. A season, be it only one day, of promise, renewal, hope—with one timeless family, set up in a manger set in a makeshift stable, waiting for the little babe to make a difference—in Portumna Workhouse dining room.

❧ ❧ ❧

Christmas was a mild day. The sun warmed and the breeze was from the east—warmer than usual. The sky dawned clear and blue. There would be no work or school today. Extra time was allowed in the yard. At both morning meals, Malcolm Anderson ceremoniously walked into the dining hall to put Baby Jesus in the Crib. Every person stopped eating and watched his passage through the tables with the precious symbol. As soon as the doll was in the manger a cheer went up to the rafters. Christmas had arrived at Portumna Workhouse.

The evening meal was all that Willie had said. Unbelievable treats, in abundance. During the meal the chorus and musicians played wonderful music. Some sang along with *Lullay, Thou Tiny Little Child* and *God Rest Ye Merry Gentlemen.* Patrick was spellbound. The music caressed his soul and satisfied his palate more than the food.

Malcolm Anderson stood. "Our guests invite you to come use these instruments and make music." He pointed at the fiddles and drums set aside for this evening. There was a mumble and shuffling among the residents, hesitant to come forward. Anderson was reiterating the invitation to urge them to do so when from far back in the dining hall beautiful lilting notes from a piper floated forward. The mumbling and shuffling stopped. The player was lost in his music. It had been a long time since Patrick had let his breath travel up the pipe. He heard notes from his fife, and they lifted him. The workhouse melted away and the only thing in the world was his music. He had not meant to go to the center of the Christmas celebration. He only meant to blow the scale to see if his fife was still true. But those eight notes set him free. He could not stop without hearing more. His fingers had to move. His breath had to blow. His ears had to hear. The music he had composed in the dark came to light. He was a hungering boy who had found a feast.

The sound grew in volume and the notes wound through the room. A traditional Irish beat with recurring melodies enticed memories of home, hills, and happier times. The piper's music was full of green grass, white sheep, and blue skies. Several fiddle and drum players joined. Then the song became somber. The audience swayed back and forth to the notes reminding them of the sad days away from family and home before the notes picked up a new, lively beat. Sudden exuberance and joy required dance and many residents got to their feet. Unbridled Celtic spirit lifted to celebrate Christmas and life remembered. Hands clapped to the beat. Men and boys danced in the aisles. Heels and toes. Kicks from the knee. Straight backs. Faraway looks. Tentative smiles. The music brought people, who could not reach out to each other, together to dance. Pub life was remembered. On this Holy Day, at Portumna Workhouse, a national identity resurfaced—in sick and troubled Ireland.

Everyone looked to find the source; some stood. Fingers began to point at the boy at the corner table, playing a beautiful home-made fife. "The piper," they shouted and pointed to Patrick.

"Patrick," uttered Willie

"Doyle," spat Sweeney, nearly choking on his cake.

"Patrick Doyle!" quietly exclaimed Malcolm Anderson.

❖ ❖ ❖

As the men and boys trailed out of the dining hall, Patrick lifted his fife again. They softly sang as he played the old familiar carol—*This is our Christmas Day*—some in Gaelic, some in English—altogether lovely.

Willie waited at the door for Patrick to pass. "Give me the fife or it be gone before the sun sets tomorrow," he whispered as he fell into the crowd beside his friend.

Patrick slid the fife out of his sleeve and into Willie's.

Malcolm Anderson left the dining hall, went to his office and fell into his chair, still disbelieving what had happened. Patrick Doyle was a Christmas miracle. After weeks of wondering if painting walls was the boy's future—this! Music, pure, sweet, and beyond ordinary, told Anderson that Patrick was very talented. He needed to be launched differently.

The next night, Patrick returned to his pallet after school to find it pulled apart—totally rifled. His comb and soap were still there. The thieves did not find what they were seeking.

❖ ❖ ❖

When the excitement of Christmas settled down, Malcolm Anderson summoned Patrick Doyle to his office.

"Sit," he invited

"Nay, sir." Patrick declined

"Sit," he commanded

Patrick sat on the edge of the chair in the center of the room. He looked around and noted another chair by the window with a Bible on it. He brought his head around to face the Master of the Workhouse.

"Patrick Doyle, I want to talk to you about your flute."

"Me fife?"

"Yes, your fife. Where is it?"

He shifted on the chair and turned his eyes from the Master. "Hidden. Could be stolen from me." He looked up with pleading eyes. "Me never disturb with it, sir. Please, do no' take from me. Please." Anderson walked from the desk toward a chair near Patrick, as the boy continued. "'Twas Christmas that made me play in the dining hall. Me never do it again. Please..."

"Where did you get the fife?"

"Me made it. No more playing in the workhouse. Me promise. 'Twas foolish...."

Anderson could see that his questions were making the boy nervous.

"Easy, lad. I would only take it to keep it safe for you. It would be safe in this office where no one else could touch it." He required Patrick to look at him. "I would not like for it to be taken from you either. Where is it now? Is it safe?"

Patrick was frantically thinking while nodding his head. He did not want to tell the Master that Willie had it and reveal their relationship. He could not deny an answer. "I bring it soon. 'Tis hard to part with—even for safe keeping."

"I understand. Bring it quickly before something happens to it."

Now, tell me about making your...um.... fife—the making and, who taught you to play it."

"Me Da brought me a good straight maple branch and give me a sharp, short knife to carve wit. It took all winter carving it smooth." Suddenly, talk about work on his fife came easily. "When it came time to hollow it, me Da sharpened his awl and stayed with me to be sure I did no' work too fast. Finally, the light came through from end to end." Anderson encouraged him with his attention and occasional nods.

"Putting note holes was scary. Could have ruined all me work but Da kept me careful. I mark one hole, near the middle." Patrick traveled back to the time. "Work be slow. Cutting through the shaft." Patrick paused in thought—recalling work with Da. "I blew the note."

"A good sound?" he asked.

"Aye, good."

"More holes?"

"I did holes up and down the shaft."

"Now it is finished."

"Nay, sire. Needed to smooth, rub, smooth—inside, outside, around the note holes. Each time, notes get better. Da went to the coast to find pine trees and bring back pine tar."

"Pine tar?" Anderson asked.

"Da know. Ye boil tar into pine oil. Rub fife wit' pine oil so no warp or dry."

"Who taught you to play?"

"No one. I just blow, listen and play. At the pub me hear Wally McFadden play his fife. Then, come back to cottage and do same." Patrick began to fidget as soon as he finished the story. He came back from his reverie and remembered where he was sitting and became anxious to leave.

"You may go, Patrick, but bring the fife to me as soon as you get it from the hiding place."

Patrick left the office conflicted. He wanted the fife safe, but he also wanted the comfort it brought. It had been difficult giving it to Willie but at least he had it during their meetings. Now it would be unattainable for--*how long? How long?* He asked himself. Patrick was not happy that his foolish impulse to play at Christmas has exposed him, his music and more importantly, his fife. Da warned him not to do anything foolish and he had ignored the warning. *Me fife in Mr. Anderson's office.* It was a terrible thought.

At school that night Patrick managed to give Willie a message on the slate. *Meet tonight. Fife.*

Willie came at midnight. "Trouble?"

"Mr. Anderson make me bring fife to him. He say *safe keeping.* Got t'" Patrick told the whole story, leaving nothing out. "I did no' tell him ye had it."

"Good." Willie pulled the fife from his sleeve. "Ye can trust Mr. Anderson."

❖ ❖ ❖

Patrick slept the rest of the night with the fife in his hand. The next day he painted with it tucked in his pant waist. His plan was to take it to the Master after the evening meal, which he barely tasted, passing most of it to the boy seated next to him. He would take his fife to the Master, still hungry.

Patrick hurried from the dining hall and ran rounding the dark corner toward the Administration building just as Sweeney stepped into the path. He started to let the boy pass when he recognized him. "Doyle! Get ye to school."

"Let me pass," Patrick demanded, trying to move past him and out of the light from the open door.

"Ye show-off at Christmas dinner. And...," noticing the fife in his hand, "...that ye fife!"

Patrick tried to move further away but Sweeney again stepped in front of him. Patrick backed away and stepped to the side. Sweeney came forward and raised his arm to strike. Patrick ducked to avoid the blow. In the ruckus, the fife went to the ground. Sweeney's huge hand swallowed the fife before Patrick could move.

In that moment, Patrick decided to fight for what was his. He had let Sean go—had let his father die and soon Fiona would be gone, too. "Lost too much," he hissed to no one in particular. "Me fife!" he exclaimed. Patrick drew his strength and forgot the size and danger Sweeney represented. He lowered his head and rammed into Sweeney's stomach, ready to meet his goliath. The fife flew into the air and landed several yards away. Sweeney forgot the instrument and went for the boy's torso. He lifted Patrick into the air and whirled around. When he finally tossed him, Sweeney and Patrick were both dizzy and disoriented. The boy landed on the hard ground.

At that moment, from the dark along the wall, two long lingering notes came from the fife, which was floating in the night, played by a ghost.... and moving toward Sweeney. The one-eyed, enraged, confused ogre, could not see Willie in the moonless night. He turned and ran.

❧ ❧ ❧

Malcolm Anderson answered the timid knock on his door without noticing the trembling boy. He received the fife that Patrick Doyle pushed through to him, without words, and watched him run off toward the schoolroom.

Chapter 18

Dead of winter could not be more dead than in the workhouse. Fingers, cold and stiff, still picked the Oakham, pushed the heavy grinding wheel, made coffins and painted stone walls. The latrines had to be swabbed, the trash had to be collected and burned. Darkness rolled over the walls by late afternoon. Rain laced with ice came off the sea.

Each day there were fewer workers as infections compromised chests, lungs, joints and muscles. Often boys were taken from the wheel to dig graves. The infirmary was busy. The carpentry shop concentrated on making coffins. Just as coffins were needed for the dead, beds became empty, new families came in hoping to live through the cold, barren season. New bed pallets were not needed. It was almost ironic. The numbers seemed to stay the same. As beds emptied, they were filled again with barely a shaking of the mattress. Infection and disease waited just eight inches off the floor.

Willie was often called to help at the registry. Patrick's painting day was shortened by lack of light. All they had was their weekly meeting under the stair. It was time to scratch January 1850 on the wall.

"'Tis a new decade," Patrick noted.

"Aye, our decade," Willie assured. "The new year." He made a day count. "68 days for ye; 134 for me."

"Seems a lot of long cold days." They agreed but, always the optimist, Willie added, "Soon spring'll come."

It was hard for them to dream and plan when cold robbed

their sleep and made their workdays so difficult. The classroom was smaller than the cavernous dormitory and dining hall, so the hearth did a fairly good job, but fingers remained cold and stiff. After a day of working in the cold it was hard to stay awake in the warmth. Desks were gathered closer. Fewer boys were attending—so many were sick. Patrick and Willie were always relieved to see each other walk into the classroom.

❖ ❖ ❖

One week later, Tuesday, January 8th was a day Patrick would never forget. He was painting the walls in the south building facing the yard when Willie tore into the dormitory—panting. "Patrick, quick here!" He demanded as he ran to stand under one of the high windows. "Here! On my shoulders," he said as he pointed to the window and squatted for his friend. "Fiona be leaving today." Patrick's shoes cut into Willie's shoulders as he slowly raised him up.

Patrick took hold of the windowsill and wiped the dirty glass with his sleeve. He could see Fiona and three other girls with a guardian escort, each carrying a small cloth bag, crossing the yard. The sun caught her hair as the breeze lifted it. She brushed it back with a familiar movement, tucking it behind her ear.

"Fiona!" he cried to the solid window atop the high stone wall. No sound left the room. "Fiona..." he prayed, ".... look back, Fiona, look up." He did not blink his eyes. The sun shone bright on his face, but he could not break his gaze. Patrick continued calling as she walked. "Fiona, look back. Fiona, look up. Fiona, look back, look up."

The group moved toward the Administration door. At the very last moment, Fiona stopped. She looked back. She looked up. She saw Patrick in the window. Her bag went to the ground and she began to run back across the yard toward the face in the window. Her hands were waving frantically when the guardian caught her.

Fiona yielded to the guardian's strong arm, still looking back and up. The sun lit Patrick's green eyes as he forced a smile. He could not let her go without that. It said, *courage.* It said, *I promise.*

The scene imprinted on Patrick's brain. Fiona, so beautiful and so young. Golden red hair lit by the sun shining behind her. A small patch of green beneath her feet. Excitement at seeing him lighting her eyes. Could he really see the color in them or did he just know they were blue green? Drab brown stone wall backdropped the scene as the Administration door opened creating a black rectangle that his beloved sister walked through and disappeared.

Before Willie helped Patrick down, he had one more prayer. "Oh God, help me find a way to Fiona, someday."

Patrick sat on the floor at Willie's feet. So Sad. So grateful for this gift. "Willie, me need to know where."

Fiona was gone. Gone from the workhouse. Gone. It hit Patrick harder than he could imagine. The goal he had for himself—to take Fiona from this place when he was fifteen—was totally unrealistic. Even if she was not sent away, he could not take her out the gates of Portumna Workhouse, hand in hand, and provide for her. They were not children any longer. They were not the same as when they had walked down the dirt road nine months ago. As Patrick came down from Willie's shoulders he stepped into a pit of reality.

As he grew into manhood in this year, Patrick could not assess the marker in his growth. But, surely the loss of his family, Sean, Da and Fiona, required him to grow up or dissolve. Patrick would grow up. Unless he wanted to waste his life away setting blame—God or the potato blight—he had to become a man. That night, without his fife to comfort him, he spent his thoughts on the future.

Patrick became more and more dedicated to his mission—Fiona. He would never give up on her. Da's words came back to him. *"Fiona needs ye. Take care of Fiona. Be strong. Find a way. Find a way, Paddy."* Maybe he could not stop today's event, but he would find her. Someday. Some way.

The next evening in class, Willie wrote on his slate so Patrick would know where Fiona had gone. He tilted it so Patrick could see. Just one word: *Canada*.

❖ ❖ ❖

Just as Patrick set his mind to get to Canada, Malcolm Anderson set his to get Patrick to the United States. After hearing Patrick play the fife, he knew *the place* for this talented boy had to be New York. Malcolm's interest in him, was different from the others. His efforts to launch boys had been almost selfish before. He did it to relieve guilt. Never before had he thought so clearly that Patrick Doyle, or any of his selected boys, had a destiny more important than his own penance. Many waking hours were spent deciding how he would proceed.

He looked over at Annie Doyle—so innocent of her son's potential. He checked the calendar again. Not much time before Patrick's birthday. While Annie sat in her corner, Anderson sat at his desk writing letters on behalf of her son

Stories of the Irish pubs in New York were well known. Stories of their numbers and character came across the Atlantic. On the west side of Manhattan, starting around 39th Street and stretching to the river, Irish pubs dotted the neighborhoods. Anderson was making shots in the dark. He had never been there and had no first-hand information, but he was determined to get Patrick in a good place.

The next day Malcolm Anderson went to see Jacob Brennen. Brennen Steamship Company had ferried six boys across the Atlantic for Malcolm. He had already arranged passage for Willie and Patrick, but he needed to talk to Brennen again today

The Master of the Workhouse's relationship with Jacob Brennen was a strange one. They were from different sides of the universe—Englishman and Irishman. The differences in their backgrounds, religion, and political view made a close friendship impossible. However, they liked each other and enjoyed small pieces of time together.

The contrast between Malcolm's and Jacob's height was an outward sign of their differences. Brennen was a big, little man—five feet, 4 inches of strength and power. His belly sat over his low belt. His boots appeared to rise to his waist, especially when seated. Brennen always wore boots; they were needed on the dock and on the ship. The fact was—he did not own any other footwear. He was powerful because of his confidence. He was arrogant and accepted no blame for his actions or shortcomings. Brennen looked one straight in the eye and spoke with honesty—as he saw it. Dirty blond hair surrounded a boyishly handsome face and fell to his collar because he did not take time to wash it or get it cut. Twice a year, Easter and Christmas, he took a pair of scissors and carefully squared it off at the top of his collar, shampooed with soap, and went to mass. His green blazer finished his signature look.

It was two weeks after Christmas when tall, dark, Malcolm Anderson came to see Jacob Brennen, a short, shiny, dressed-in-green, leprechaun.

"Jacob, I have two boys sailing with you in May."

"Right." Jacob rustled some papers and came up with the contract. "Half passage already paid." The most important fact to the shipper.

"One of the boys is special."

"He needs special care on my ship?" His voice rose to question. "Whoa, Malcolm. Not possible." He was a businessman, not a caretaker. "Passengers are a bother to begin with. Me profit is in cargo." True, his profit was in cargo but the money that lined his pockets came from passengers. Brennen was not a businessman nor a caretaker; he was a wheeler dealer.

"No, not special care on board—after he gets to New York. I need some information." He smiled at Jacob Brennen to lighten the discussion. "You are in New York a lot. Go to pubs, right?"

Brennen leaned back in his chair, relaxed, and invited the conversation. "I know pubs," he proudly proclaimed as a true

Irishman. "Me happy to talk pubs, with ye." He reached in his desk drawer for a bottle of whiskey and two glasses. A small amount of the dark elixir was poured. It was for hospitality, not to influence the discussion or the day. Each man drank his swallow down.

"Pewter Mug," Anderson announced.

"Ah, yes; the Pewter Mug. Dunlop. The ole man died and the wife runs it now." He took a moment to go there. "A great pub. Lots of me Erin folk enjoying a beer or whiskey. A little piece of Irish paradise across the sea."

"I'm interested in the music. Any thoughts on that?"

"Always music, always. She has it goin' every night and locals sit in wit' her group. Sometimes not so local—famous ones. Me heard Michael O'Rourke sing there one night." He recalled with a smile. "Now, that was somethin' special."

"I can imagine. I heard him once in Dublin. Special, alright."

Jacob poured another short swallow to enjoy the thoughts coming with this talk.

"Drinks, food, music and in the back room, politics...for sure, at the Pewter Mug." Jacob lifted his glass, nodded to Malcolm as he drained the vessel.

"Do you know Mrs. Dunlop?"

"Me goes in and speaks a greetin', but not so well. Why ye askin'?"

"I have always placed my boys where they can apprentice a trade. Now I have selected a boy, Patrick Doyle, on the May voyage, who is a talented musician. I'd like to get him a job in a pub like the Pewter Mug and give him a chance to play his flute. I don't think the boy would be paid for his music, but if he could get work in a pub, he would have a chance to play."

"Well, Anderson, me can recommend the Pewter Mug but, me has no in wit' the management. What kind of work can the boy do?"

"He paints walls at the workhouse. He is a strong and willing worker. Not a troublemaker. He would do whatever work asked."

"Dunlop owns a tenement that me knows. Kevin Brennen, me brother's boy, lives there. Who knows, maybe there be work for the boy. The most I can do for ye and the boy is tell him exactly where it is."

"Do you have an address for Mrs. Dunlop and the pub?"

"Aye, here somewheres." Jacob opened a wooden chest and fumbled through some papers, coming up with the tattered piece with addresses of eight or ten New York pubs. "Copy what ye wants." He handed Malcolm a piece of paper and pen.

"Thanks. The other boy, Willie, is placed with a furniture maker with shops in New York and Philadelphia. I have to get a job commitment for Patrick before he sails. Can`t get past Ellis Island without the promise of work and the sponsorship it gives. Both boys have to have that. Meanwhile, keep their places on the May nineteenth crossing."

"Ye have it." Jacob stood to end the meeting. As they walked to the door, he promised, "Ye boys be in good hands wit' me. Seem ye are more tied to these two, eh?" Then Jacob shook his head and thought, *foolish English.*

❧ ❧ ❧

Two letters from Portumna Workhouse were posted to New York.

One of the letters went to Mrs. Daniel Dunlop, owner of the Pewter Mug on the lower east side of Manhattan. The other letter went to a construction company in Brooklyn. Maybe they would hire Patrick to paint if all else failed.

Chapter 19

Just before Patrick's March birthday, the Master of the Workhouse summoned Willie to his office. As was his custom, Willie looked in the corner for Annie Doyle. Her chair was empty. Malcolm sat at his desk. A chair was centered in the room for Willie.

"Sit," the Master commanded. Willie sat. Anderson needed to know if Willie would leave when Patrick turned fifteen.

"Are you planning on leaving the workhouse?" Malcolm waited anxiously.

"'Tis in my mind. The boys tell me I need a work permit when I leave."

"There is no work permit, Willie. What you need is the paper from the registrar. You must be fifteen before you can get one. You can decide to leave your family when you are fifteen."

"Me has no family."

"Yes, I know, but no one will hire you unless you prove you can return to the workhouse and not be a burden to those who hire or house you. These are hard times. Getting work and maintaining a life is not easy. Getting your paper from here makes it easier, but not much."

"Aye, me needs the paper. Me has to make me way out of the workhouse,"

"You see how important it is to take the right steps, waiting for your birthday and going through with the registrar's office." He waited to let Willie digest his words. "Is there an uncle or cousin who will help you? Work is hard to find. What is your plan?"

Willie was quiet and unsettled. He shifted in the chair and pushed his hair back. He started to speak and hesitated. It was difficult to decide how much to tell Anderson.

"Not sure. No uncles. No cousins. Not leaving until the weather is warmer and dependable." It was a safe, sensible answer. And, it gave both a little breathing room.

Malcolm had to accept that much from the boy. "I understand. Let me know when you decide to go."

"Thank you,"

Anderson had to trust that the information given to Willie would go back to Patrick. All his intelligence gave him confidence that one would not leave without the other.

❖ ❖ ❖

Two events happened on March tenth, Patrick's birthday—a long-anticipated piece of mail for Malcolm Anderson arrived from New York—and a severe storm.

In the small hours of the morning, the worst storm of the winter pounded Ireland's western coast. Ice coated the landscape and budding trees. High winds and snow followed that accumulated two inches on top of the ice. Crews of men and boys worked to clear paths across the yard and bring in extra firewood. Meals were delayed. Work details were canceled. It was bitter cold in the workhouse. Fires could not warm the rooms against the blasting wind. The infirmary was overtaxed—too many sick and not enough medicines. Not enough staff made it through the ice. Influenza raged. Six died on this day alone.

Malcolm Anderson got to his desk after an exhausting night dealing with the storm. There on his desk was a letter from Alice Dunlop, proprietor of the Pewter Mug, New York City.

As anxious as he was to open and read it, he could not—not now. He had to deal with the dead, the sick, the dying and the freezing. He placed the letter in his top drawer and donned his storm attire and headed to the infirmary.

❖ ❖ ❖

Willie and Patrick were given shovels and sent to work in the yard clearing paths. They immediately moved around until they were working side by side. "Like the day cutting hay, eh?" Willie whispered as they began scooping snow.

"Happy Birthday. The world is one big white cake for ye."

"Me wish."

They worked side by side all morning. It was better shoveling snow than sitting in a cold dining hall or dormitory. They even worked up a sweat.

"How's it feel to be fifteen?"

"Me likes the idea that I can go anytime now. Feels free." Patrick smiled.

"Ye still waitin' for me?"

"Aye, brother. Waitin'"

"Midnight?" Patrick asked. Willie nodded agreement.

It was almost three o'clock before the mid-day meal bell rang. Both boys were starving by then. The potatoes were warm and the dining hall felt good. By the time the meal was over the sun had come out and began melting where the paths had been cut. The boys were sent to their beds, exhausted. Willie stumbled as he climbed the steps and complained of pain in his chest. They parted at the top of the stairs with a reminder from Patrick. "Midnight."

Sleep came quickly to his fatigued body and Patrick had only a few minutes to miss his fife before he slept.

Willie fell immediately to sleep but was awakened in less than an hour to vomit. Chills racked his body and he was burning with fever. Noise of his heaving alerted the guardian. Willie could not lift himself and began to choke. A guardian got to him in time to bend him over the side. He was wrapped in his sheet and carried to the infirmary where he went into convulsions.

Patrick waited at midnight for his friend. He slid under the stair, lit the candle and marked his calendar. Willie still did not come. To pass the time, he counted the days to Willie birthday—as he had many times before. The number tonight was fifty-six. Still no Willie. *First time he be sleepin' through,* thought Patrick. *Snow shovelin' wore him out,* he rationalized.

It was such an unusual night. The spring storm left and took the cold wind. Patrick could hear the ice melting. The moon was almost full and because the snow reflected, there was plenty of light. He made his way back to his bed and decided to pass by Willie's.

Willie's empty pallet shocked him. Patrick wanted to run in every direction to find Willie, but he merely turned a complete circle in his indecision. *Where?* His mind questioned. Back in his own bed he spent the night half sleeping, half awake. The morning bell rang. Patrick was already at the door as the other boys passed. He heard the chatter.

"They carried him to the infirmary."

"Poor Willie"

"Influenza everywhere."

"Dead."

Patrick's knees buckled. He leaned against the wall to let every boy pass. "Willie dead?" Patrick asked the filing boys. Their answer was a shrug.

It was an awful feeling—not knowing, no one to ask, no right to inquire. Patrick knew the guardians would not answer. He hated the rumor mill that would pass from breakfast bowl to breakfast bowl. He walked in a daze with the other boys over the cleared path to the dining hall. The room buzzed with stories of Willie's rush to the infirmary. Most distressing was the way he was carried out.

"Wrapped in the sheet like a bag of potatoes."

The word *dead* traveled back and forth over the dining room. Patrick's meal was passed to hungry boys at his table. He could not eat and could hardly breathe.

The weather, following the snow, was pleasant; the sun was warm.

Somehow Patrick made it through the next day in mourning. The other boys in the dormitory lost interest in Willie's fate. So many were dying in the workhouse, it was better to concentrate on staying alive than agonize over one death.

Work assignments were called out. "Patrick Doyle." His name rang out along with five others. "Follow me." Patrick knew what the work group was—digging graves. The guardians never announced grave-digging like they did other assignments. It became known...the unnamed work group would dig graves. Patrick accepted the shovel and followed out to the barren land beyond the west wall. Rectangular plots of newly turned soil told the story of previous days. Most of the snow was gone. The earth was soft and easy. The guardians had marked three places with stakes where the digging would begin. Patrick and his partner, without talking, began lifting at opposite corners of their rectangle.

"Pile it here," the guardian pointed and instructed. "Neatly, so it can go back easily." He left the boys to the quiet sound of shovel against earth and gentle thrusting of dirt to the pile.

Willie's grave one of those or be me diggin' it today? dogged Patrick's mind. As hard as he tried, he could not stop his mind. Doubts flooded with each push and lift of the shovel. *Me needs ye, Willie.* He began to pray, first to God: *Do no' take Willie.* Then to Da: *Save Willie for me, Da!* His passion drove him to work hard and fast. The more he put into his work the higher and louder his prayers would soar. Patrick got the grave-digging assignment for two more days. The rectangles he dug the day before were all filled in, the tops smoothed over. Patrick refused to cry as he stood beside the five new graves thinking, *Willie?* Then he went to work, digging and praying. Two hours later, Patrick began to sweat and cough. He could not breathe. When the mid-day bell sounded, Patrick went to his bed. The thought of food turned his stomach. He felt his forehead and knew. *Fever,* he thought. *What did Ma do for fever?* He challenged his aching brain. Patrick went for water and wet his shirt, which he stripped from his hot torso. He removed his pants and laid the wet shirt over his head. Soon he heaved from his empty stomach. Twice he retched before he fell asleep. It was the middle of the night when he woke up. The fever had broken. The muscles of his torso ached from heaving. He was weak and thirsty. Water. Patrick drew on his now almost dry shirt and pants and went for a cup of water. As he walked back through the deserted dormitory taking the path by Willie's pallet, the eerie light of the moon lit the room. He looked twice to be sure. The sleeping boy on the pallet could be new to the workhouse or he could be.... was—Willie! Patrick went to the bed to be sure. Willie! It was Willie, sleeping peacefully. With immeasurable relief, Patrick sat on the cold floor beside the bed. Only then, as he attended his brother, did Patrick admit to himself that he would be lost if Willie was not with him when he left the workhouse. "Me could no' make it without ye." He whispered.

"Not to worry. Ye could, Paddy, if ye had to." came a quiet answer from Willie.

Chapter 20

Willie was an exception; he escaped death in the infirmary. From the moment he regained consciousness, he remembered Andrew Doyle's words. "No coming back from the infirmary." He drank water when it was offered and ate food, even if he had to force it. *Me comin' back,* was his constant thought. As soon as he could pull himself out of the bed, he stumbled to the dormitory and fell onto his pallet. Getting away from the teeming germ mill saved him from secondary, deadly infections. Willie was a survivor.

❖ ❖ ❖

Malcolm Anderson was relieved not to see William Carney on the daily death list. He slept in the office many nights while influenza revenged the workhouse and people were lined up at the door to come in. The workhouse had the only doctors and nurses available in County Galway. The winter tested them, famine starved them, and disease stalked them. Resistance to the workhouse diminished when they became ill. Many came past Sweeney just in time to die.

Anderson was exhausted but another winter—the darkness and the doom—had passed. Spring would come, the days would be longer, the hills would bloom, and life inside and outside would go on. However, spring did not reduce the numbers of sick and dying, the brightness and warmth only gave a false feeling of hope

The Master of the Workhouse had forgotten the letter

tossed in his drawer weeks ago. It awaited his attention. He rediscovered it on a bright, warm day. He took it in hand with a strange clairvoyant feeling that it had good news. Malcolm Anderson needed good news desperately. He smiled as he read it.

> *Mr. Malcolm Anderson,*
>
> *I read your letter with interest. It is not often that an appeal for an immigrant's sponsorship lists two very different skills. I could use a worker in my tenements and a musician in the pub. I will rely on your assurances that his music is worthy and that he is a good worker and not a troublemaker. Please complete the necessary papers and let me know when he will arrive. Your appeal comes from my late departed husband's home county. He would like to help one of his own.*
>
> *Alice Dunlop*

Malcolm slapped his hip in joy and took his bottle of whiskey from the drawer to celebrate with one hearty pour. It was a good day, after so many bad ones.

A place was secure for Willie in Baldwin & Winston's furniture shop, New York or Philadelphia, and Patrick at the Pewter Mug, 49th Street, Manhattan. Forty-one days to go. It was time to get the papers ready for emigration and a few other details. Willie and Patrick were going to America. Malcolm Anderson had it all arranged.

The calendars under the stairs were etched *April* by Patrick before they were strong enough to meet again. Their work details exhausted them and after school, they slept without plans to be awake at midnight. Finally, they were well enough to resume their rendezvous.

Willie opened the conversation with what was on his mind. "Mr. Anderson asked what my plan was. Me did no' what to say. Patrick, we donno' have a plan." Worry spilled out of his words. "We be comin' close to time to leave..." There was fear, too. "It gonna happen."

"Aye, it gonna happen. I been thinkin' and waitin' for our time to talk. This be the time." Patrick rose up on his elbow. His thoughts demanded a stance. "Willie, me fife be our plan. I know..." he gave assurance, ".... people puts coins in ye hat when ye play good. We start in Portumna, then Galway, first pub we pass on the road. There be a coin or two by night. Da take me to pub to hear the music. Every hat had a coin in it. Maybe we get a bit of food, if the music is good enough." Patrick talked slowly, trying to improve his language. Applying what the schoolmaster thought was *too good* for him.

"That fife of yourn may feed ye, but nay, me too."

"All be shared. If only enough for one, we get by on half. We hungry before. We hungry again."

"Willie," his voice whispered intensely, "I am going to every pub across Ireland and America until me has enough money to go to Canada. I am going for Fiona." Patrick's words brought optimism and excitement. It was a reversal of outlook for the boys. Willie's goal was to get away from something, the workhouse. Patrick's was to get to something—Fiona.

In their usual manner, the boys lay quiet and thought

about the few precious words they could share. Willie broke the silence.

"Paddy," he said, using the name used in important personal moments, "Willie promised to go with you to find Fiona. Me has no other thing to do."

"Canno' go without speaking to Ma. Before ye birthday. How?" Patrick had one more goal in the workhouse. "Gotta speak to Ma."

"Let me work on that." Willie crawled away quietly.

❖ ❖ ❖

One day at mid-day meal, Willie walked past Patrick and said, "Go see Mr. Anderson. Now!"

There was no one in the office outside Anderson's so Patrick advanced and tapped on his door.

"Yes," barked the Master. No answer. Tapping again. Silence

Patrick tapped again. "Confound it. Stop that knocking and come in," the response came in aggravation. Annie Doyle looked up from her corner at the commotion at the door.

Patrick turned the latch and slowly opened the door. Even if he wanted to, Malcolm Anderson could not have prevented the emotional reunion in the center of his office as Patrick and Annie Doyle ran to each other and slowly drifted to the floor. She took his head in her hands, ran her fingers through his ruddy hair.

"Paddy. Paddy. Paddy." He yielded to her touch and allowed silent tears to wash his face.

The Master of the Workhouse got up from his desk and left the room, closing the door behind.

Annie was strong. She did not cry and took her hand to wipe her son's tears. "No crying, Patrick. The Doyles are past tears. Our time is short, son, let us not cry.... but talk of family."

They talked of Sean and Da. They talked of Fiona and he told her, "Canada." Annie did not know until now, where she was sent. "Canada," she repeated.

"Willie's birthday May 15th, Ma. We are leaving the workhouse. My fife will help me to earn a way to get to Canada and find Fiona. Da told me, afore he die, 'take care of Fiona.'"

"He told me, with his dying breath, that you would find a way. Paddy"

"Aye, Fiona." He took a deep breath for the next words. "I have to leave ye and Mavis."

There was a pause before Annie said what she had to say to her child/man. With a deep breath she began reverting to the cottage vernacular. "Paddy, go. Go wit' me blessing. Ye mother and little sister willingly stay behind while ye do as ye must." She settled back on her heels and continued. "Mavis be fed and taken care. I see her once a week and work in the laundry other days. I have protection from Mr. Anderson. When things get better outside, we will make a way for us. Ye job is Fiona. My job is Mavis. Ye do as ye must. I will do the same." With her exhaling breath, she said, "Here." She pointed to the floor in the Master of the Workhouse's office.

Patrick was silent. He had no words to answer his mother.

"Play your fife. Go, where it takes ye. With my blessing, go!" She held him tightly, kissed his cheeks and forehead. "Go. God be with ye." Holding his hands, she said, "Go," one more time in a whisper. "Hunger is gone. Your strength renewed. My boy," she cried softly. "My boy."

"Hunger not gone, Ma. 'Tis my strength." He kissed her bowed head. "Your son will never yield hunger, never forget our cottage without potatoes. 'Tis who I am. 'Tis what took our family apart." Patrick lifted Annie from the floor and stood tall before her. "Pray, for me, and me for ye and Mavis." He gathered all his strength and walked away from his mother. At the door he turned back to gather one more picture of his lovely mother.

Annie stood tall in the center of the room. She set her shoulders straight and pulled a wild curl from her face before returning to her place in the sunny corner of Malcolm Anderson's office. She was still staring at the space where Patrick stood when the Master returned and dismissed her.

Patrick skipped his meal and went to his work with the other boys who were satiated with bellies full of potatoes.

Chapter 21

Patrick and Willie went to see Malcolm Anderson after the morning meal on that fateful Thursday.

"Come in," he greeted as the invitation to sit was declined by both.

"Master, we have come to let ye know we be leaving." Patrick took the lead. "My fife?"

Malcolm Anderson went to the shelf and returned the instrument to its owner.

"Thanks for taking care of it." Patrick was grateful as he caressed his fife. Anderson acknowledged him with a nod.

"Today?" He asked.

"After the evening meal." Willie announced.

"You are determined to go today?"

"Yes, sir. We waited for Willie's birthday. Today is the day." Patrick affirmed.

"I see." Anderson took their news as matter of fact. "Go to the registrar after eating. Your papers will be ready to sign, and your belongings will be there." He stood and walked over to the boys. "Willie," he took his hand, "you have been a great help to me. Good luck." He turned to Patrick. "Good luck," he turned to Patrick and took his hand, too. "You can return, you know."

"We not comin' back, Mr. Anderson. Like brothers, we make our way." Willie spoke. Patrick nodded agreement. Conversation was difficult. Fear and doubt crept in the longer they stayed in this office. They had nothing else to say.

They had nothing, except Patrick's beautiful, handcrafted flute.

❖ ❖ ❖

The rumor mill at the workhouse buzzed over the boys' trip to Mr. Anderson's office and their plan to leave before the day was over. To most of the residents it was a passing item of interest. To Annie Doyle it had greater significance. She lifted her apron and pressed her eyes firmly to keep back her tears. With stoic fortitude she resumed her work in the laundry. No one saw her anguish, and no one heard her fervent prayers for her son.

The news traveled to Sweeney.

❖ ❖ ❖

Patrick and Willie ate hearty at dinner. They ate every allotted potato before they went to the Registrar's office to sign themselves out, receive a parting bag of potatoes and the clothes they came in with. The boys had grown, and their clothes looked comical—short sleeves and short trousers. They looked like the poor boys they were. Without fanfare or farewell, Patrick and Willie headed for the door. No one watched them go. No one cared if they left.

It was nearly dark by the time they left the registrar's office. The May evening was moonless and noisy with croaking spring peepers. The only light came from the high windows on the front wall. They were out from it in a few steps.

Patrick thought he would be elated to be going out, but he felt nothing. He did not know what to put in his mind during this passage. At last the thought he needed claimed his attention. *Don't look back.* Ten steps into the world, he spoke to Willie.

"Don't look back. Pretend the workhouse disappeared. Gone, Willie. Gone."

Neither would voice their fears. They advanced to pillars that marked the entrance to the property. Although their eyes had become accustomed to the night, they did not see the monster-man crouched behind the post.

Sweeney was upon them in an instant. He went for Patrick, throwing his arm around his neck and bringing a dagger up to cut. "An eye for an eye!" He shouted as he moved his knife up to take Patrick's eye and life.

Sweeney was huge but not fast.

Patrick was quick. In reaction, he brought his bag of potatoes up to hit Sweeney's face as he pushed away from his attacker. In one crazy instant, Sweeney grabbed the fife and slashed out with the knife, as the bag of potatoes came toward him. The knife connected with the bag, spilling potatoes. Sweeney lost his balance and fell forward, still slashing out to connect with any part of the boy. In his effort to get away from Sweeney, Patrick stepped on the potatoes, slipped and went down, too.

Willie rushed over to help Patrick. "Sweeney, you goat." He stepped between Patrick and the dagger. Willie jumped and came down with both feet on Sweeney. The knife found a target. Screaming in pain, Willie fell back doubled over. The villain could not get his breath. He had lost his grip on the knife but still had the fife.

Each—Patrick, Sweeney, and Willie—rolled away from

the centered scene of the attack. Patrick struggled to his feet, unharmed. He picked up the knife. Sweeney began to get up, searching for the knife. Willie lay motionless on the ground.

Patrick took a breath and looked at Sweeney, who had risen to his knees—an unbelievable sight—exactly Patrick's height. His huge, ugly face full of anger and revenge. The ogre had one last chance to hurt Patrick. He lifted the fife over his head with both hands spread from end to end. "Ye fife, Doyle," Sweeney cackled to taunt. "In two," he threatened as he prepared to break it.

Without thinking but feeling all that had happened in this past year and believing Sweeney had killed Willie and was about to take his future away, Patrick yelled, "No! No!" He plowed toward Sweeney with all of his strength and weight. He fell on Sweeney's chest. The knife, still in Patrick's hand, wedged between the boy and the man. It did not go easily into Sweeney's coarse jacket and fleshy body but with Patrick's full body weight, it moved in. All the sharpening Sweeney did on the blade, preparing for this attack, made its course easy. Before the knife stopped, it found its way between his ribs. Patrick lifted himself from the motionless man as everything flashed in his mind—the cottage, Sean, Da, Ma, Fiona, Mavis, hunger and music. He reached over and pulled his fife from Sweeney's unresisting hand.

Patrick jumped off Sweeney and came to Willie's side as a shadowy figure emerged from the darkness. Without a word, a large man in a cloak, carrying a lantern, advanced to the scene. He threw back his hood. The boys exclaimed, in unison. "Mr. Anderson!"

"Willie. Patrick..." then he saw the blood. "What....?"

"Me leg, me leg," Willie cried.

Anderson grabbed the cloth bag that had held potatoes and made a tourniquet. He swirled his cloak from his shoulders and wrapped it around Willie.

Patrick began, "Sweeney attack me with his knife from behind that pillar. Willie tried to help me. Then..." Willie interrupted, quickly and loudly to stop Patrick.

"Me tried to fight him off. He tripped and fell on the potatoes. That be when he got me and fell on his knife." Finishing Patrick's story exhausted the injured boy.

Mr. Anderson did not miss any detail of the scene and the boy's words as he continued to tend to Willie. "Is he dead?" He asked.

"Donno' know. He groaned and rolled over."

As soon as Anderson had the tourniquet held in place on Willie, he went over to Sweeney. "Well, that's that," was his comment as he returned to Willie.

"This is serious. I must get you to the infirmary." He picked up the injured boy. "Patrick, you cannot come back in the workhouse. My carriage is over there." He pointed up the road. "Go, get in it and wait." He looked into Patrick's white face, demanded his eyes, and commanded. "Do not leave. Get in my carriage and wait—no matter how long. Stay down so no one sees you. Be there when I come back. Understand?"

"Aye," Patrick weakly answered.

Willie managed a small smile of encouragement to his friend. Patrick could not smile; he looked blankly and forlornly at Willie.

"Mr. Anderson, me needs to talk to Patrick. Please." Anderson placed Willie carefully on the ground. "Hurry, we must hurry." He stepped a few feet away.

"Paddy, ye are not the boy in the workhouse any longer. What ye were and what happened here is left here. Forget Sweeney. Forget what happened here. Forget it all."

"Me never forget, ye saved me life. Me wait for ye, Willie."

"Aye." He looked away. "Mr. Anderson, now."

Malcolm Anderson gathered Willie up and looked at Patrick Doyle. "Go to the carriage as I said. You cannot go back, and Willie must." Anderson gently pushed Patrick's shoulder toward the carriage. "Go."

He did not watch Mr. Anderson carry Willie back to the workhouse. He would have had to look at Sweeney to do so.

Patrick slowly walked toward the carriage and climbed in. Suddenly he was chilled and shivering in the warm May night. He wrapped himself in the blanket found on the seat and cried.

Chapter 22

It was midnight when Anderson returned to the carriage. Patrick had exhausted himself with emotion and fallen into a fitful sleep.

"Patrick," Anderson gently touched his shoulder and offered a drink of water from a jug.

Patrick reacted violently as if Sweeney had finally gotten to him. He jerked to an upright position and lashed out, pushing against Anderson's chest.

"It's alright, Patrick. Easy, lad," gently, calming, as he grabbed the defending hands. "Sit up and take a drink. I have things to tell you."

"Willie?"

"Willie is resting now. He has a serious injury to his leg." Malcolm drew his finger across his thigh to show where the knife had traveled. "It'll heal but it will take time. He lost a lot of blood. The artery was nicked, not severed. It will be months before Willie can leave the workhouse."

"I be goin' back and wait for him." Patrick moved to get out of the carriage.

"Stop. You will not return to the workhouse. Patrick, listen to me. The details of what happened here are settled. Willie will answer all questions and that will be that about Sweeney. You..." he touched Patrick's chest, ".... cannot go back. Willie understands. That is how it is."

Patrick melted back into the seat like a blob of soft clay. No strength. No center core. No shape or purpose. Whatever he needed to do at the moment, he did. He settled into his blanket nest and listened to see how Mr. Anderson's words could possibly help this situation.

"I came out here tonight to intercept you and Willie. This thing with Sweeney...." He had to address *that* before he could help Patrick to move on. "He came out here with that knife and got what he deserved. Thank God I was here to tie up Willie's leg. Forget Sweeney."

Patrick was not sure he could forget Sweeney or what he did with the knife. But he pushed the monster from his mind and tried to concentrate on Mr. Anderson's words. *Me canno go back in the workhouse? Because of Sweeney?* He was confused.

"Are you listening, Patrick.?" Obviously, the boy was having trouble concentrating. "I said forget what happened here...." –the exact words that Willie had said. Anderson waited for Patrick to accept what he said. "As if it never happened, lad." He reached over and put his arm around the boy. "I came out here tonight to intercept you and Willie. For a long time, I have worked on a plan for both of you. This past year, I sent him to the carpentry shop and you to painting so I could find work for you both."

Willie carpentry. Me painting? Patrick leaned forward to listen.

"There is a plan in place for you and Willie to emigrate to America."

America!

"It's all arranged." Anderson looked into Patrick's eyes and demanded his focus. "Now, Willie can't go, but you," he paused and waited for Patrick to understand, ".... are leaving in four days."

In four days.

"You will stay with Jacob Brennen, the ship's captain, until you sail on Monday. There will be provisions for the trip as well as a place waiting for you in New York City. You will be living and working in a pub. I wrote to the owner, Alice Dunlop at the Pewter Mug pub. She is sponsoring and hiring you. You will be painting in buildings that she owns. What you do with your life there is up to you. Do you understand what I am telling you, boy?"

Patrick was astounded. It was more than he could take in. "Me leave without Willie? For America? In four days?"

"Yes. Someday Willie will come...hopefully."

"America, without Willie....," was all Patrick could repeat. He sat very still and finally voiced the only truth he knew. "Mr. Anderson, me canno' go without Willie. We are brothers."

"It is your chance, boy. You must go. Captain Brennen will take you to the Pewter Mug."

"Will he be alright, sir?" Patrick could only think about Willie.

"Yes, Willie will recover."

"Me wait." Unaware of his action, Patrick ran his hand over the fife; he caressed it. "Me wait," He repeated as he pushed back the blanket and started to leave the carriage. "Mr. Anderson, thank you for your plan and for coming in time to save Willie. But, me not sailing in four days. I wait for Willie."

"Do you understand, lad? You cannot stay here, and Willie cannot come for a long time. This is *your* chance."

"Me understands. Willie saved my life right here, tonight. Sweeney came for me, not Willie." He pointed out into the black night. "He is my brother. Canno' leave my brother behind. We find a way.... together." He took a moment to think while the astounded Anderson waited. "Tis my plan to play this fife for food and money. Tell Willie, me be in pubs from here to Galway. He find me when he be healed. Tell him, Mr. Anderson, please tell him." Patrick ended with a plea.

"It is admirable that you be so determined, Patrick. This is a hard time for you. I will take you to Jacob Brennen tonight as I had planned to take both of you." Anderson lifted the reins. The carriage lurched forward; Patrick fell back in his seat. "We are going to Clarinbridge. That is where Captain Brennen lives and keeps his ship. We are starting out much later than planned and it will be almost dawn before we arrive. You have four days of food and room with him. It is my hope that you will reconsider and get on that ship on Monday." Anderson looked back and pointed to the stain neither could see in the dark, but he knew was on the boy's shirt. "There is a clean shirt in that bag and use some water in that jug to wash the blood from your hand."

Patrick was exhausted but he could not sleep. Each time he closed his eyes Sweeney's face, contorted in death, came to him. When he finally dozed, he felt the knife cut through Sweeney's shirt, slide through soft tissue, and grate against rib bone. The blade suddenly ceased its journey and jerked Patrick awake.

Jacob Brennen was aggravated to be disturbed at this hour. He had expected Malcolm Anderson earlier with two passengers. Now, he had arrived late with only one. He opened the door and invited them into a dimly lit foyer, smelling of stale pipe smoke, last night's dinner, dog and the sea. Brennen gently pushed his dog aside and re-lit his pipe to reward himself for being awakened.

"So late, Anderson? One boy?"

"Only one boy. You are over-paid to keep him three nights. Bed him down and we'll do our business."

Patrick was led to a stair and told, "Go...." Brennen pointed up, ".... take a bed."

"Mr. Anderson, please don't forget. Tell Willie where I be." Patrick was on the first step. "Please."

He gave the request a nod and said, "To bed, Patrick."

The men went into the kitchen. Brennen learned from Anderson the barest details of why he did not bring two boys.

"Ye gets nothing back on the other boy. Money paid is money paid," Brennen made his point.

"Willie Carney is in the infirmary and could not enter at Ellis Island injured. You know how that works."

"I shoulda never made this bargain wit' you, Anderson. Takin' young boys wit'out family only trouble and I be sailin' one passenger short. Every fare counts in this business." Brennen was sour about the whole deal.

"I'll pay the balance for this boy to go and you can hold on to the money for the other boy. I want him to sail when he is healed from his wound."

Brennen put out his hand palm up, to receive the balance of Patrick's fare. As Anderson put the money in his hand, the captain said, "Sure, when he be ready, I takes the other lad."

It was a weak promise. Anderson knew it was probable that Willie's passage to America would never happen with Jacob

Brennen.

Then he told the sea captain about Patrick's hesitancy to go. Brennen's eyes lit up. His attitude improved. He *might* have two passenger spots to fill by Monday—both spots double paid when he finds other passengers. The truth is there were many people on the dock wanting passage to America. He walked Anderson to the door and bade him a friendly farewell with a pat on his back and extra money in his pocket.

"The boy will sail wit' me on Monday. No problem. Jacob Brennen knows just what to say to the hesitant immigrant. Me talked many onto me ships."

Malcolm Anderson wanted Patrick Doyle to have this chance so bad that money was unimportant. He spent it on the chance that Patrick would go.

In the attic room, Patrick lay on the bed. It was warm and musty but not frightening. At last he could think about the predicament he was in. He did not want to think of Sweeney but could not help but remember his arm around his neck and the dagger coming toward him. Then he went to the moment Willie screamed in pain. In all the midnight plans they made to leave the workhouse, he had never considered the possibility that Willie would not go with him—that he would go alone. To clear his mind, he lifted the fife, which had been clasped in his grip since he got into the carriage. His hand was cramped. He flexed his fingers. It was only natural that the fife went to his mouth and the flexing fingers brushed over the holes. He did not have to hold his breath back. He played the scale. The spell was broken. He did not have to be silent any longer. The notes, the beautiful lilting notes were his friends, his comfort and his soul in this dark attic.

Patrick played the fife. He was the piper and did not have to silence his notes. He was out of the workhouse, he had escaped death, he had a chance. It crossed his mind that Jacob Brennen would put him out, but he did not care. It did not matter. He would leave this attic now if Mr. Brennen put him out—or in the morning. He was not sailing on Brennen's ship. He would play the fife now—tonight, before dawn's light.

Patrick played for himself, because he had been denied music for too long. He played for his family. He played for his cottage life, the green hills beyond, Ma's love, Da's care. He played for Fiona. Softly and tenderly, Patrick moved his breath through the smooth shaft. Gently and rhythmically his fingers danced over the holes. The music maker was not tired, he was not hungry, he was not afraid, he was not lost. He and his fife survived. He was so completely engrossed in his music that he did not see Jacob Brennen and his dog take a seat on the top stair. It was the infusion of pipe smoke that got his attention.

Patrick lowered the fife and prepared himself to be reprimanded.

Brennen was overcome with emotion and could hardly address his young guest. "Me son be a piper. Since he be gone, me never hear the fife such again… until now." He raised a gnarled hand that was used to pulling rope, to wipe a tear.

"Sorry to disturb but me couldno' play in the workhouse. Now me play." He got up from the cot and started for the stair. "I be leaving. You can sleep." Brennen did not move for him to pass.

"Sit back, boy," Brennen ordered.

Patrick backed up to sit on the edge of the bed. "Anderson tells me ye not intend to sail wit' me on Monday. What ye goin' to do?"

"Ye know about me hurt friend, Willie?"

"Aye."

"Me waiting for Willie t'heal and workin'. Play me fife in the pubs round about here with my hat on the floor. Sorry to bother. I be leavin' now. The side of the road better'n the workhouse." Again, Patrick started for the stair.

Brennen remained steadfast with his hand indicating stop and sit. "Ye absolutely, positively not sailing to America on Monday? Ye mind is made? Passage paid by Malcolm Anderson."

"Me mind made. Absolutely. Not wit'out Willie. Can no'."

"Ye haven't slept all night. Go to sleep. We will talk again tomorrow."

Jacob Brennen sat awhile on the top step, smoking his pipe and thinking, before he and his dog went down the stairs. Patrick was asleep before they reached the bottom step.

Chapter 23

Patrick awoke to bright sun that had finally filtered into the attic porthole. He sat up with a start and questioned, "Where's the morning bell?" Then he realized—no morning bell, no work, no workhouse. *Out of the workhouse!* He sat straight up in bed. The next thought, *No Willie,* caused him to flop back. His emotions went up and down with each realization. *On me own.*

Patrick was scared. He entertained thoughts of going back to the workhouse before the last terrifying thought came. *I killed Sweeney.* He could not go back.

He quietly headed down the stairs intending to leave without being seen. All was settled here. He would not sail on Monday, might as well leave now. The squeaking old stairs gave him away. Jacob Brennen was waiting when he reached the bottom step.

"Do ye know me name?"

"Brennen"

"Jacob Brennen. Call me Captain."

"Thanks for the bed. I be leavin' now...Captain."

"Eat," he pointed to the kitchen as the dog came to befriend him.

"Leavin' now. Not sailin' wit' ye so me be goin' straight away." Patrick continued toward the door.

Jacob Brennen, not used to having his orders disobeyed, flashed anger. "Eat," he demanded and took Patrick's collar to turn him around. He marched the boy to the table, as he would have handled a swabbie on his deck. Not too gently, he pushed him into a chair. A small cut of bacon, some cold thick oats with milk, and a slice of brown bread lay before him. Brennen's finger pointed his next command and Patrick began to eat.

The Captain took the seat across and laid his gnarled, strong hands on the table. He was formidable in bulk and demeanor and he knew how to use a silent pause for emphasis. Obviously, Jacob Brennen had something to say. Before he spoke, the dog's and Patrick's eyes were set on him and they were ready to listen. "Are ye still certain—not sailing on Monday? America, lad. Think of it."

"Not sailin' for sure. Me waited this long, a bit longer..." He shrugged his shoulder.

"Ye wants to go to America?"

"Aye but can no'. Not without Willie. "

The Captain re-lit his pipe. "If ye intend to make ye way in the world—be smart. Every choice ye make has consequences. This may be the first time in ye life when no one stands by to tell ye what to do. Free to do what ye want, lad. Sca-rrry." His voice rose in pitch. "Three nights wit' a bed and meals. Here! All paid for by Anderson. Ye walkin' away? Stupid! Worse than stupid, foolish." Da's words came back to Patrick, *let this be ye last foolish thing,* he remembered. Brennen's hand slapped the table bringing Patrick back from his reverie. The dog backed away; Patrick stopped eating.

"When someone offers ye a foot up, for God's sake lad, take it. If there be an opportunity, grab it. Me not talkin' bout stealing..." he paused to think his words, "....ye aren't the lad for that." He took a long draft of his pipe and continued. "Smart thing be—eat and sleep here. Plain and simple." Brennen stood up and began pacing. "Use the brain God gave ye. Do nothing wit'out thinkin' it through." Patrick pushed the brown bread into his mouth and watched the captain. "Me expects ye at d'table in the morning tomorrow, not when half the day is gone like t'day..." He almost smiled, ".... and at this table at low tide today and in bed each night till me sails on Monday. Wither ye goes wit' me or nay."

Brennen leaned back and watched the smoke rings cloud the kitchen. Then, with a different tone in his voice—almost sad—added, "Someday ye will regret the choice to stay when me sails. It not be a lesson, it be life." It was his last effort to urge Patrick to go.

He commanded the dog, "Stay", and went for the door. "Be smart," He shot back at the bewildered boy at the table.

The breakfast tasted wonderful. Patrick could have eaten it all but instead he ate some and fed the rest to the dog. He washed his dish and his face, slid his fife into the waist of his pants, and went out to his first day. The sun was already way past mid-day. Freedom was overwhelming. He had nothing to do. He had nowhere to go. From the front doorstep the sky and road stretched endlessly. Through the trees, Patrick could see Galway Bay sparkling in the sun. If he could see far enough, America and his dream of finding Fiona was beyond the horizon. He only knew one thing for certain and he thought it, *no Willie.*

Patrick was tempted to retreat back up the stairs and play the fife, but he didn't, he took his first step toward the village. This first step took more courage than he thought he had. *Why so hard?* he wondered as he took another step and started down the road, always noting landmarks to find his way back. Patrick had been into villages before, but he had no experience. His head swung from side to side as his eyes tried to survey Clarinbridge—houses and trees—sounds and smells. His feet stumbled on cobblestone and his stomach tumbled and his hands began to sweat. Patrick took hold of a fence. The solid wood supported and calmed him, so he let his hand lightly follow it along it as he continued down the road and turned a corner. A church, small shops and few people further unnerved him. A large shade tree offered him place to sit while he dealt with his panic.

"No time for fear. This be the start," he gave himself a sermon. One long sigh, and he was on his feet again, feeling better. Moving very slowly, he divided the scene into small segments and focused his eyes and attention. Patrick looked at each house, each shop and walked very slowly. He saw small patches of gardens between the houses and there were no black, odorous potato vines and none of the people he saw were emaciated with grey skin and red eyes. Patrick looked for starvation but could not find it.

What he saw was *color*—painted houses, painted window boxes, dresses and shirts of blue and red. The brown on brown or grey on grey of the workhouse was contrasted in his mind. "Me be missing color," he exclaimed as he moved on into the village. On the far corner, beyond the church, a building painted bright yellow and green, flanked by window boxes filled with May flowers, was ***Biddy McGee's Pub***, shining like a star. Patrick approached and watched several men file in. Chatter and a lilting female laugh came out to the road to greet him. He lost his nerve and started to retreat. Suddenly a push against his back startled him and his father's voice said, *find a way*. In utter confusion and dismay, Patrick entered the pub.

Biddy McGee was a tall woman, almost six feet, with huge blue/green eyes and dark curly hair, which was capped by a red bandana across her forehead and tied at the nape of her neck. Her complexion was light and pristine—no freckles. Biddy had become owner of this pub on the death of her boss. She managed it with character and good humor. She claimed to be a descendant of Blackbeard after seeing a drawing of him and decided to wear the bandana to look the part. It was a *good story* and it helped keep patrons in line after too many whiskeys. Her laugh matched her size.

The generous, happy owner behind the bar called to Patrick. "Lad, are ye lookin' for someone?"

All he could manage was shake his head and answer with one word. "Work?"

All in the pub laughed, but not unkindly. Youngsters coming in from the hills looking for work was not unusual. "'Tis not that easy to find. Are ye hungry?"

"Nay."

"I have no work but ye be invited to sit and drink." She drew him some water. "Ye be welcome."

The patrons went back to their conversations as Biddy McGee came to sit with Patrick. "What's ye story, lad? Where were ye afore ye came into Biddy's?"

"The workhouse, Portumna."

Biddy went to tend to her customers. As soon as she could, she returned to sit with the boy. "Name?"

"Patrick Doyle."

"Patrick Doyle, me knows of workhouses. For two years

Enniskillen Workhouse be my home. We share no good memories of those times." She left him to draw a pint for herself.

"What kind of work did ye do in the workhouse?" She tried to get him to talk but he could not relax. His answers were short and did not invite conversation.

"Whitewashed the stone walls."

"There be no spare money here for hirin'..." she paused, "... times have been hard as ye knows. We beginning to feed each other again, but still scraps." She just could not send him out the door without helping. "The back outside wall needs doin'. Me can give ye a bed for tonight and a meal in the morning."

"I be painting for ye but..." It was hard for Patrick to barter; he had never done it before. He thought of the Captain's advice and took a minute to think it through. "Miss Biddy, me needs a bed for Monday. Nay afore Monday. A bed, Monday."

"'Tis a deal. Ye paints on Saturday and ye has a bed for Monday and breakfast, too. If'n ye calls me Biddy."

"Thanks, Biddy."

"All will be ready for ye." She tendered her hand to shake. Patrick took it strongly. Biddy smiled.

"Be there music here?" He used all his courage to ask.

"Aye, when Angus and Davis come in, music happens at Biddy McGee's."

She waited for him to continue but he closed down. "Now, Patrick Doyle, ye can sit here as long as ye likes." She went back behind the bar and when she looked up again, he was gone.

Patrick painted the stone wall that wound around Biddy

McGee's Pub on three sides. He came ready to work on Saturday morning and a bucket of whitewash and a brush awaited him. It was good to let go of the uncomfortable feeling of freedom and take up responsibility. The wall was broad and rough. Patrick was happy to have a brush—much better than a rag swab—as he diligently painted into each crevice. The wall was not finished when the sun dipped low, the tide was out, and Brennen expected him at the table. He walked down to the water to wash the brush and then stepped in the pub to speak to Biddy.

"No' finished, Biddy. Tomorrow."

"Sunday 'tis a day of rest. Ye can sit and be idle like us all. And lad, ye wanted music? Tonight, the boys be here."

Patrick nodded and ran out the door. Biddy was left shaking her head. Efforts to befriend the boy were to no avail. "Be figuring him out—soon." she said to no one at all.

Patrick ate his evening meal alone. Hearty fish chowder and bread. It was warm on the stove but no Captain to be found. The dog sat at his feet waiting for crumbs. He ate the soup and spent his time organizing his mind for his new life. He thought of the next two days but could not go any further. These days with Captain Brennen were much too easy. He did not have hunger or hardship to motivate. Patrick finished his portion of soup but decided against refilling the bowl or eating the bread. Instead, he went up to the attic, shined his fife, cleaned the holes and tube and blew the scales. "Tonight," he uttered. The notes floated around the room until he took a breath. "Tonight," he repeated.

A warm glow emanated from Biddy McGee's Pub. Music drifted into the warm May evening. Patrick, with his fife tucked in his pants, was excited and scared. He wanted to quietly sneak in and take a seat. Biddy saw him hesitate at the door.

"Patrick." Biddy called. "Come, come." She came over to take his arm and insist. "Ye be hungry?"

"Had me dinner." Patrick took the seat she offered and turned his attention to the fiddle and drum, playing an old Irish tune.

"Soon we be dancin' but not until the whiskey softens," Biddy tried to engage him. "Do ye dance?"

He shook his head.

"We be singin' too. Soon. Do ye like to sing?"

He shook his head again. Before she could quiz him more, he pulled out his fife. It was the easiest way to communicate. The lantern light hit the polished wood and made it shine.

"Glory be! We see no such an instrument here."

"Me, and me Da, made it." Patrick drew his shirtsleeve over it to make sure no dust had settled on it. His fingers traveled up and down the holes as they naturally did whenever he took it in hand.

"Play that fife, Patrick Doyle," she asked, cajoled, urged, and required—all in five words.

He immediately picked up the melody that Angus was playing. The fife took the high notes and complemented the boldness of the fiddle. His pure notes gave the music fullness, richness and, as the tempo increased, fun. He got up, still playing, and walked toward the other musicians as Biddy drew a chair into their corner for him.

A dream came true for the young piper. He was making music with his fife, with other musicians, in a pub. It was not a high dream but to the Irish country boy, the village pub was the place for music, and Patrick Doyle made it this far. Finally, Angus, the leader, gave a signal that meant Patrick would play a solo part. He took the melody and made it his. The pub went totally quiet—no talking, no laughing, no whiskey ordering. Not even the sound of a glass landing on the bar or table. Silence. Truly rare in such a setting. When he finished, applause, loud and steady, filled the air. Angus slapped his back with shouts of praise. Something astounding had happened Saturday night, in Biddy McGee's Pub, Clarinbridge, County Clair, Ireland. The village would long remember Patrick Doyle's first solo performance and they would come to hear him tomorrow night, too.

That was when he thought, *Me needs a hat.* He did not have a hat to collect pennies and shillings that might be offered.

Jacob Brennen came in the pub unnoticed that evening. He took a seat at a table in the back to listen. The Captain lifted his glass, and toasted Patrick Doyle, unheard. He was Biddy McGee's only patron who was not surprised by the boy and his fife.

The music, the fun, and the drinking went on into the night. Patrick loved every minute of it. Finally, totally worn out, he put the fife away and quietly walked back to Brennen's while the other musicians were on break. Not even Biddy saw him go.

Jacob Brennen was waiting for him. "Lad, ye needs a hat." He handed him a fine woolen cap. "For tomorrow and every day after." It was a gift, not a loan. The Captain wanted to have a part in Patrick Doyle's future.

"Thank ye, Captain." He went to his bed wishing he could talk to Da, to Ma, to Fiona and to Willie. But there was no one to share this night.

On Sunday Biddy McGee's Pub was full. Most of the village turned out to hear the piper who was talked about in church and all around the town. Sunday was usually family time at the pub, so women and children came with the men.

Patrick came down the stairs ready to go to the pub and found Jacob Brennen waiting. "We goin' to the pub together, lad," he announced. "Donno' forget ye hat." Patrick picked up the hat, wrapped it around the fife and headed down the hill to the pub.

Jacob Brennen walked into the pub and greeted, "Diaduit." Then he stepped aside so Patrick could enter. It was almost like an introduction, a presentation. All eyes were on the Captain and the piper. Biddy pointed to Patrick's seat in the music circle. Brennen with flourish took Patrick's hat from his hand and jauntily placed it on the floor in front of the boy. There would be no mistaking its purpose.

"Paddy Doyle, the piper of Clarinbridge." Captain Brennen announced. Patrick had a new, less formal name.

Two additional musicians came today, a melodeon (small accordion) player and a cruit (small harp) player. Patrick's fife provided the melodies and feeling. He was blending with the group and careful to be a part of the performance. He declined the solo offered. Patrick seemed to have an uncanny knowledge of the music and how his fife fit in. And, he grasped the importance of not taking the spotlight. It might be his natural reticence or the realization that he had a lot to learn from the pub musicians. No matter, both the patrons and the fellow musicians appreciated him. Every tune was magical. Dancing and singing filled the village of Clarinbridge, spilling from Biddy McGee's into the night air.

Patrick had twelve pence in his hat at the end of the evening. It was his first money ever and seemed a fortune. Again, Jacob Brennen came to his aid. He changed the one penny coins into a shilling. He also gave him a small pull-string pouch that would hook over his pant button and ride to the inside. There was something comforting to have the coins resting against his stomach.

On Monday, Patrick went down to the bay to watch Jacob Brennen sail away on the morning tide. He was sorry to see the Captain leave. He watched the boat move away and waited for the *regret* that Captain promised he would feel. It never came. He patted his belly where the money patch rested and went to Biddy McGee's Pub to finish painting the wall.

Chapter 24

Biddy McGee gave Patrick a pallet in the storeroom and the morning meal she promised. Patrick came into the pub to sit with the musicians that night. He was greeted as, "Paddy Doyle, the piper." A chair was in the circle for him.

After the music ended, Biddy pointed to the storeroom and invited him to sleep there again. "We be talkin' in the mornin'." He found a square of cheese, three roasted carrots and a cut of bread on his bed. Until he tasted, he did not realize he was hungry. Before he laid his tired, happy head down, he ate it all. Five more pence jingled in his money pouch.

Biddy was cleaning the bar when Patrick found her the next day.

"Ye finished the wall. Good job."

"Thank ye for the extra night and meal. I be goin' now."

"Sit." She pulled up a chair and put a plate before him. "Eat."

"In the evenin' ye be Paddy, a mighty fine musician. At day, ye be Patrick, a troubled boy." Patrick took a bite of bread and looked up. "'Twas ye paintin' that got ye bed and food. Ye knows that, right?"

"Me knows." Again, his short, unrevealing answer frustrated Biddy.

"There may be other walls round town needin' paint." She was trying to get him to talk.

"No thanks."

"Lad! Canno' ye see? We in Clarinbridge be tryin' to friend ye. What ye gonna do? Wander off, down the road? Maybe another pub set a place for ye in the circle. May even get a few coins? That ye plan?"

"Aye."

"'Tis a poor plan, lad. Not one boy playin' in Biddy's can live off coins in a hat. Each has other work. Have ye a place to be?"

Patrick was lost. He did not see how or why he should talk to Biddy. She was kind but she was like the Captain. In a matter of hours, they would be oceans apart. Why admit to his doubts? Why tell her about Fiona? Why tell her about Willie? Why tell her about Sweeney? These were his burdens and putting them down here, with this woman, in this pub, in this village, would only make it harder to pick them up again. It was Willie who could guide him in who to trust, who to talk to, where to go, how to go. It would be easier to walk out that door. Patrick stood. He would go.

Then Biddy McGee did something that unnerved Patrick Doyle. She reached across the space between them and embraced him. She wrapped her long strong arms around his shoulders and drew him to her breast. When he struggled to get free, she held tight and softly said, "Paddy, Paddy." He gave in to her for a moment and then began his struggle again—pushing back to get free. She held tight.

"Let me go," he asked but his voice did not demand. She held tight.

"Ye've nowhere to go." It was true and Patrick knew it. He had no place to go physically and no place to go emotionally. He gave in and let his head fall to her.

"It be fine, lad. Fine." She took his shoulders and sat him back in the chair. He leaned back, looked into her caring eyes and cried. He began to tell his story amid his tears.

"Da called me Paddy and so did Fiona. Ma always called me Patrick." Biddy listened intently, taking in every word, bringing her understanding to it. Suddenly he wanted her to know how hard it was to lose Sean, Da and Fiona. He voiced for the first time the devastation telling Da good-by, mourning for Sean, too, watching Fiona led away and his determination to find her. He told of his Ma sending him off. Finally, he spoke of Willie. He told of their plan and the attack that wounded him, but he stopped short of telling Sweeney's fate.

"We made a pact as brothers to find a way. Go to America and go for Fiona. We planned it all under the stairs at the workhouse. We thought we could. Now, it seems impossible and me not be sure it be any better with Willie." He took a deep breath. "We just didno' know."

"Go back in the workhouse to wait for Willie. Why no'?" She asked the fateful question. He avoided the truly honest answer.

"Mr. Anderson arranged passage with Jacob Brennen to take us to America. He brought me to Clarinbridge.... but me no go without Willie. The Captain sailed yesterday."

"Patrick, ye can stay in the storeroom while ye figure it out. Play music each night with ye magic flute. It be nice my patrons drop coins in ye hat...but, they no do it night after night. The coins be stoppin'. Me knows they love your music but can no' spare money."

Patrick breathed easy with Biddy. He felt better. "Me stay a while and figure what to do. Thank ye." He reached for his pouch and took out a coin. "Here, for me meals."

Biddy took the coin and set it aside and resolved to add pence to his cup each day.

"Me be movin' on soon," Patrick announced. "Each new pub means new coins in me hat. Now, the broom. Sweepin' and moppin'—me specialty.... along with the fife." His broad smile was the first in a long time. His eyes shone and his cheeks flushed with new color. Patrick looked more mature as his shoulders squared and his head went high. It was a good feeling and his first earnings paid his way at Biddy McGee's Pub.

The pub had a new burst of life. The villagers could not be dropping coins in Patrick's hat each night, but they could somehow afford to come, enjoy the music and buy a pint or a pour of whiskey. Some nights a single penny would drop in the hat. Each morning a simple but ample meal waited on the bar while Patrick tended to the floor. Each night another meal was set out for him at the musicians' break. All the while, Patrick planned to move on soon. He could not abandon the bigger plan for the food and comfort of Clarinbridge and Biddy McGee. More coins had to be in the pouch by the time Willie joined him. For that, Patrick would have to move from town to town, pub to pub.

Sunday night was another full house for the pub. All the musicians were there. Patrick was feeling at ease with them. He smiled at Biddy and went to his seat in the circle.

"Take ye solo when me says," Angus directed. "No passin' it off," he chastised.

Patrick did two solos that quieted the pub down as it did last week. Men held their drinks midair; mothers told their children to shush while Paddy Doyle stood to play. The first melody was about the hills and the cottage beyond Galway. It was melancholy and sad, as Irishmen loved—pulling at emotions and inviting listeners to bring their feelings to it. The second was lively and happy and on the third chorus of repeated melody, everyone tapped and clapped to the beat as the timpan and the bodhram joined in. They were Patrick's original melodies. The room was enchanted.

When Patrick sat down a lovely woman rose from a back table. The lightness of her appearance contrasted with the browns of the room. She was short and perfectly proportioned. a white ribbon gathered up her golden curls. Her dress of soft billowy gauze flowed like white clouds on a blue sky. Her eyes matched the blue in her dress. She walked with confidence to the center of the room. Patrick had never seen such a vision. Whispers started among the patrons.

"That be Sallie?"

"'Tis Sallie."

"Glory be, Sallie Brennen." The whispers turned to exclamations.

Biddy rushed from behind the bar to greet Clarinbridge's only famous native. She took her hand, gave a sign to a drinker at the bar to move, and invited Sallie to take the seat.

"So good to see you. 'Tis been years. We hear about ye great success."

"I still be Sallie Brennen and I love a pint," she smiled warmly.

"Of course." Biddy fell all over herself to round the bar and draw the brew.

Sallie lifted the glass as to toast the whole room, "Slainta," and took a hearty drink, erasing her foam moustache with an impeccably groomed hand. The pub resumed its friendly buzz and drinking.

"Ah, the last time ye sang for us—afore ye go to Dublin and the world. We never forget, ye sang here as a child, too. Right in that corner with Angus." Biddy took a moment to remember young Sallie singing like a bird.

"Aye."

"Will ye sing tonight?"

Sallie moved like a breeze to the music corner. Angus rushed to greet her. "Sweet Kitty Neil?" she asked.

"Ye start. We be joinin'." Angus spoke as he drew the bow.

Sallie turned to face the room. Placed her hands together and began singing.

"Sweet Kitty Neil. Rise up from your wheel.

Your neat little foot will be weary of the spinning."

By the fourth line, Patrick picked up the melody and added his notes to her pure sweet voice. Angus and the others in the circle, picked up the timpan and bodhran. The pub corner became a grand stage as the singer captivated the room. The balladeer and music makers blended in the song and Biddy McGee's Pub had another memorable night. On the last verse, Sallie paused and gave Patrick a nod to play solo. She closed her eyes and listened to him play eight bars before she finished the song.

Then, Sallie returned to Biddy and her drink. "That was somethin'. Jacob be right. I had to hear this piper, Paddy Doyle."

"Ye brother left last Monday."

"Aye. Afore he sailed he sent me a note about this lad." She pointed to Patrick. "Said I must come hear him." She lifted her glass again, drank heartily, and said. "Remarkable."

"He be special, for sure."

Sallie finished her beer and went over to Patrick. He stood as she advanced and extended her hand, pointing at the fife. Patrick surprised himself by placing it across her palm. She stroked it and gently returned it.

"I be stayin' at Jacob's tonight. Come see me tomorrow morning ere I be gone. Early. Bring the fife."

❖ ❖ ❖

The next morning, when Sallie went to the door to see if he was coming, Patrick was sitting on the step. He had been there since the sun came up. She gathered her skirt and sat beside him.

"Have you been taught music?" Away from the hometown folks, she spoke the King 's English but still with an Irish brogue, laced sometimes with a few improper pronouns and verbs.

"Taught me self."

"Can you read music? Do you know the scales?" Patrick's head went from side to side on the first question and continued on the second. His spirit fell. He was disappointing her, and he wanted more than anything to please her. He was enchanted by her beauty and voice.

"Lift ye fife, Paddy. Play this note." She sang a pure *f* sharp. He played it. She sang *c* above high *c*. He played it. She sang the scale. He played it.

"Listen carefully, Paddy." She sang several bars of a classical piece. He played it.

"Lad, there be a bag of clothes Jacob left for you. They belonged to his son a long time ago. He wants you to make use of them." Patrick returned with the bag and sat across from her and waited.

What does she want of me? He thought.

"Paddy Doyle, I want to take you to Dublin with me. Bring your fife and those clothes. You have a natural talent and I want teachers to teach you what to do with it. Is there any reason you cannot go to Dublin...with me today?"

Patrick was astounded. He did not know what to say. *Dublin? Today? How far? Who is this woman?* "Music schoolin'?" he asked.

"Music schooling with the best in Dublin." She let Patrick's thoughts fill the next few minutes.

"Is there anyone responsible for you?"

He thought of his mother, but he could not go back to the workhouse. He thought of Mr. Anderson. He thought of Willie. Patrick knew none of them were responsible now. He was the only one responsible for himself.

"Me has to talk to Biddy." He started running down the hill.

"I'm waiting for you, Paddy Doyle," she called after him.

Patrick was out of breath when he got to Biddy. "Sallie Brennen wants to take me to Dublin."

"Oh, Paddy. Go! Go, lad." She stopped her work behind the bar to talk to him.

"Who is this lady?"

"Sallie Brennen is the most famous Irish singer—called the Irish Songbird. She is Jacob's sister. She performs all over Ireland, England, and America—even in Russia. Her home is Dublin now, but she grew up in Clarinbridge. What did she say to ye, lad?"

"She wantin' to take me to Dublin for schoolin' in music. Today."

"There be nothing holdin' ye back. 'Tis a chance to learn all ye can wit' ye fife. Go."

She reached out and took his hand. "Me believe, wit' all me heart, if ye Ma be here she be sayin' same. Go, Paddy."

He was quiet as her recalled Ma's last words. *'Twas the same—go,* he thought. Biddy was right.

Then he looked at her and said, "Willie."

"Ah, Willie. I understand." She was quiet for a moment, too. "Willie would say 'go', too."

"Mr. Anderson be tellin' him, at Clarinbridge. Willie be lookin' for me here."

"And, I be tellin' him, when he come, ye in Dublin wit' Sallie Brennen. He be comin' on to Dublin soon, for sure."

"Dublin be a long way, eh?"

"Aye...but not so far as ye have come from the workhouse. Only miles, nay a lifetime. Ye be travelin' more than miles, lad. Not too far for ye. Not too far for Willie, either."

Patrick stood up and walked a circle in the pub. He pushed his hair off his forehead as if that helped him to think. "Twelve days...." he muttered, ".... workhouse to Dublin." He paced past Biddy and she heard him say, "Da.... fife.... school.... Willie.... Dublin." He returned to Biddy and she stood for his decision.

"Biddy, Paddy Doyle goin' to Dublin with Sallie Brennen. Takin' me fife to town." He smiled a big grin and wrapped his arms around her and squeezed. They jumped up and down together and laughed out loud. She stood in the road outside Biddy McGee's Pub and watched him run up the hill until he was out of sight.

"Patrick Doyle. Piper from Portumna, now. Piper to the world, soon, Come back someday. I be wantin' to see ye and hear ye again." Her words went gently into the May air.

Half-way to Captain Brennen's house he stopped running and sat down. Old fears came over him. "Me can no' go any further without Willie. Biddy wrong. Dublin too far." Patrick was deciding to stay in Clarinbridge. By the time he got to Sallie, his spirit was gone. He was prepared to tell her would not go with her.

Sallie was waiting by the carriage when he finally appeared coming up the hill. "Patrick, hurry. We must be going," she called to him.

Her voice came to him in the wind, but it sounded like his mother. He heard Ma say, "Patrick, hurry. You must be a'goin'."

Patrick climbed in the carriage.

Chapter 25

Patrick moved further and further from the workhouse, from Willie, and no closer to finding Fiona. He was in the great city, Dublin—the first in his family to ever travel there. The streets—noisy, buildings—drab, horses—abundant and smelly, and carriages—going in every direction, overwhelmed. Sights, sounds and smells accosted him. None of it was appealing and yet, it had an excitement that Patrick could not deny. His heart raced. The only color he saw was on the brightly painted pubs and window boxes trailing flowers. Patrick felt small—very small.

Sallie took him to the Ancient Concert Room on Pearse Street, home of the newly formed Royal Irish Academy of Music. Three stories rose from the road and steep steps led to the door beside which hung a bell, identical to the one at the workhouse. He hesitated as old thoughts and feelings came. Sallie, seeing him pause, took his hand, and pulled slightly. They ascended the steps to the door, passing the bell, without ringing it.

"What happens?" he asked.

"You will play the fife for four professors on the admission panel. One of your original compositions."

"If they donno' want me in their school, will ye be gettin' me back to Clarinbridge?" His mind was still set on going backwards.

"Of course." The grip on his hand tightened. "Ye will not be going back Paddy, I heard your music." Sallie assured him.

The room was large with tall windows allowing light to highlight the architecture and the Admission Panel. Patrick trembled and stepped behind Sallie as they entered. Four men formed a semicircle with an empty chair for Sallie. She walked him to the center of the room and left him there. "Take out your fife, Paddy," she whispered. Sallie turned to the panel and spoke. "This is Patrick Doyle. Thank you for giving him an audition today. He plays the fife and would like to be a student here. Today, he will play an original composition on his own instrument. Patrick?" She addressed him formally and with an open hand gesture, invited him to play.

Patrick lifted his fife, wiped it with his sleeve, as was his habit. Before he could raise it to his mouth, one of the professors rushed forward and reached for the fife. Patrick, in reaction, pulled back, holding tight.

"Lad, where did you get that instrument?" It was the sudden movement toward the fife that alarmed Patrick. He reacted quickly, putting the fife behind his back.

Sallie came forward between Patrick and the professor. "Patrick, let him see your fife." She spoke in a commanding but quiet, soothing tone. Patrick took two steps back and brought his fife tight to his chest. Suddenly he was the boy in the workhouse protecting the only treasure he owned. His face went dark and he began to tremble. He pushed the fife into his pant waist and Sallie saw him turn to bolt from the room. Shaking his head from side to side, he refused to look at her. Sallie moved fast to catch his arm and lead him through the door as his fife disappeared into his pant waist.

"Gentlemen, please, give us a moment," She shot back over her shoulder as they went out.

"He only wanted to look at your fife. It's alright, Paddy. 'Tis alright, I promise ye. Please, let me have ye fife." She spoke in the country way. "Ye can trust me,"

It was a pivotal moment. He looked in her eyes, pleading to be rescued from this foreign place. She smiled and lifted her hand to receive the fife. "Please. I will keep it safe and give it back to ye." He recalled Malcolm Anderson's words last Christmas. His separation from his fife had been a hard five months. He never wanted to give it to anyone again. Yes, to Sallie but not to these strange and foreboding men. "Please, for just a few minutes. Come, it will not leave your sight."

Patrick had to trust her. He pulled the fife from his waist and placed it in her hand. Then with her other hand, uplifted, she invited him to take it and walk back into the audition room with her. He closed his fingers around hers and held tight so he would not melt away.

"Let's begin again," she announced to the panel. If not for her prominence, the audition would have been over. Sallie Brennen had a little leeway with these professionals, but not much.

"This fife was made by Patrick and his father," she addressed the panel while Patrick took a couple of deep breaths. It is a priceless treasure that he has protected on the hard road of his life. Look....," she handed it over, ".... such workmanship brings great music. It is a true work of art and there is none other like it. Please do not take offense."

She walked over and handed it to the first professor. He passed it around. Each man handled Patrick's fife with reverence, immediately recognizing its unique qualities. "Maple?" One asked.

"Aye." Patrick responded.

"Smooth on inside?"

"Aye."

"Mid length?"

"Aye, to fit my music."

"Two blow holes?"

"Me can blow from the end or side, if me moves the wooden peg to cover d'other. Better variety of tones."

"Play!" The panel leader commanded.

The fife came back to Patrick. He wiped it again gently with his sleeve, lifted it to his lips and flexed his fingers. Music filled the room and captured the small audience. He was in his element. The gentlemen and Sallie disappeared. Nothing remained but the piper and his pipe. They let him play his song and then said, "More." He played another.

Sallie Brennen sat with a satisfied look on her face. Her smile beamed for Patrick. "Paddy, sit down, you have played well. Relax now."

She turned to the panel. "Patrick Doyle cannot read a note of music. He is totally untrained, self-taught. We need to teach him without diminishing his natural ability. He has perfect pitch. He can play any note he hears. I could be selfish and take him on tour with me. His notes complement my voice beautifully. It would not be fair to Patrick. He is young and bright. And, I'm sure you agree—his talent is special. He needs schooling here at the academy. Will you take him as a student?"

Patrick was excited to be learning and growing in music. He resisted nurturing from Sallie. She wanted to give him a room in her apartment, pointing out that she was gone most of the time. He refused. After his audition before the professors, he was offered a bed in a loft room. Sallie set up an allowance for food. Although his clothes from Jacob Brennen seemed luxurious to him, they were not by Dublin's standards. The country boy from the hills beyond Galway followed his fife into the Royal Irish Academy of Music.

A lot of things in Patrick's life had been hard, almost impossible. The one thing that he held on to would make his life good—his fife. It began opening paths for him, even before he left the workhouse. Now, Patrick lay in his bed, his first real bed since his own, built by Da, was bartered for food. He played the fife and settled his mind. *Me be in Dublin. Gettin' music schoolin'. Me fife take me away from the workhouse, to Biddy, to Sallie. Someday to America, to Fiona.* His notes took on a jaunty air, a happy tune. He lay back and played his music. It was an hour of complete happiness. Then he got out of bed, went to his desk, and took pen in hand.

> *Dear Mr. Anderson,*
>
> *Tell Willie he can write to me at the Royal Music Academy, Pearse Street, Dublin. I be waiting for him and studying music on me fife. Is he healing?*
>
> *Patrick Doyle*

The next morning, Willie was still strong on his mind. He talked to him as he walked to his first class. "Take ye time, Willie. Ye be healin'. Me be learnin'. Three, four, five months? It be fine."

He looked each day for a return letter from Mr. Anderson. Whenever he walked out the door of the academy, he looked for Willie. Patrick had dreams and visions of Willie suddenly appearing in Dublin. The thing he could not envision was Willie not leaving the workhouse or unable to recover from his injury. That was simply not in Patrick's list of possibilities and he never let his mind go there.

Chapter 26

The Royal Irish Academy of Music filled Patrick's days, but the nights were his. The first night he slept, exhausted by travel and stress. Starting the next night and each after, he took his fife and hat and quietly left his bed for the streets of Dublin where there was a pub on almost every corner. Patrick needed coins in his pouch—enough for two passages to America.

Paddy Doyle joined musicians in the nearest pub. He remembered Biddy's caution that patrons would only tip money in the hat two nights—after two nights he moved through the streets of Dublin to another. A few coins fell into his hat each night. A nearby bank changed the pence into a shilling.

The chance to make friends with fellow musician was in every pub. The men and ladies who combined their talents had a natural camaraderie. At each location they urged Paddy Doyle to stay and be a regular. That friendship was tempting, but he could not. He had to move on to gather more coins in his hat. Up and down the streets of Dublin, at each pub, Paddy was making a name for himself. His reputation as a distinguished music maker was moving though the city, but pub-goers had their favorite oasis and the boy with the fife was soon gone. The invitation, "Come again on the morrow," was acknowledged with a nod as he put his hat on and left. "Soon," he called back.

Patrick's repertoire of favored pub tunes was growing. When a new song was presented, he listened carefully and joined in by the eighth bar. Then the song was his.

Meanwhile his studies were going well. Patrick studied hard, devoured every lesson and savored the music he was exposed to. He studied music history and the classic composers and took delight in learning to read music. The simple act of looking at a sheet of music, reading the notes and bringing them out of his fife, delighted him. Patrick took blank music sheets and committed his original compositions to the pages. There was great satisfaction in having his music in written form. He was even introduced to the classic orchestral flute and liked it.... but his own fife was favored. Soon his professors saw the uniqueness and significance of the sound he could produce with it. Every request from accomplished musicians to play his fife was politely denied. Soon it was accepted at the Academy—no one else played Patrick's fife. Requests stopped. The other students and the professors respected his stance as his musicality grew.

Four months went by quickly. Patrick did not make friends. He really did not know how to act and react in group situations, especially with his isolation experience at the workhouse. Patrick could only interact with the fife at his mouth—with pub musicians or Academy classes. He was waiting for Willie. Each afternoon he looked for a letter from Malcolm Anderson. Every day he expected Willie; looked for him in the faces of boys he passed on the street. Night after night Patrick prayed that Biddy was sending Willie to Dublin, but it would be difficult—Willie had no money. It would be a hundred-mile walk with no food. Here at the Academy, each over-filled plate gave Patrick guilt. *Me have too much,* he often thought. He often skipped meals to get that old hungry feeling back and relieve his guilt.

The Royal Irish Academy of Music's fall orchestra performance would include a short solo by Patrick Doyle on his wooden fife. It was only sixteen bars in the middle of Mozart's Sinfonia 41, Jupiter, the flute solo. He stood, wiped the fife with his sleeve, and put it to his lips. The sweet, full notes repeated the joyful melody of the piece and took the audience by surprise. Applause erupted as Patrick sat down and the orchestra resumed. Sallie Brennen was in the audience that evening.

"Paddy, you did so well. I'm proud of you." They embraced behind the stage.

"Me be learnin' much."

"Now, we will have dinner and talk." She led him out and down to Dublin's most famous pub, The Crown. As they entered, patrons rushed Sallie and asked if she would sing. "Not tonight. My voice needin' rest from my last tour. Thank you."

Patrick walked over to the musicians and greeted each. Sallie watched as the once shy boy moved in the pub like an accomplished young man. "Me no' be playin' tonight. Maybe tomorrow."

"Come, let's sit here." She led him into an enclosed booth that gave privacy.

"Well, it looks like you have made a name for yourself here."

"I play the pubs at night. Last week me played at The Crown. Makin' money for me and Willie."

She ordered food and drink. "You have changed, Paddy. Grown up." She reached over to touch his burnished red hair. He pulled back slightly as she smiled.

"Aye changed...but still the same. I am lovin' the Academy

and learnin'." He drew his fingers through the hair she had touched and smiled back. "Tryin' to be patient and make money. Waitin' for Willie and go to America. Fiona somewhere in Canada waitin' for me. I'm learnin' a lot of music and learnin' to wait." He relaxed and took a piece of bread. "Even with all this at the Academy..." the bread, uneaten, went back to the plate. ".... I am keepin' my mind set."

"And improving your language, I notice."

Patrick was embarrassed by her notice. "I have to concentrate and practice with you and the professors at the Academy. But, in the pubs I go back to the old ways." He stopped to smile. "Ma wanted me to study on it. But, me be me," he joked and laughed. "And ye be ye," he continued, and they laughed together.

"Keep some of that Irish," she agreed.

"Me wants to be able to talk to Willie when he be here."

The evening was relaxed and enjoyable. Sallie waited until they finished dinner and walked back to the school before she told Patrick what was on her mind. They sat on the brick wall beside the steps.

"My next tour is performances in Ireland. To Wexford and Cork by boat, then inland by carriage and rail. I have six concerts in southeast Ireland before sailing back from Galway by Christmas. I want you to travel with me and play the fife. We will be gone during your Christmas break. You will be back to Dublin for the winter session at the Academy." Sallie stopped to get his reaction. Patrick said nothing.

"We need to start rehearsals on the program and be ready to leave December 15th."

Still, Patrick remained silent.

"Paddy, you must tell me what you're thinkin'. Tis no time to be silent in your thoughts. I'm givin' you a chance to make some real money, to do something exciting, to show your fife to the world beyond the pubs." He continued to look away. "This is no time to close down, lad. Talk," she demanded.

"Me could miss Willie, if'n me goes and he be comin' to Dublin."

"Aye, that could happen."

Patrick got down from the wall and stood before Sallie. "'Tis a lot to think about." He walked a small circle, started to talk and circled again. "Me learnin' more here than music. Even if me got a pence a day in me hat, that only be about three pounds in a year. It be years earning enough for me and more again for Willie." Sallie continued to wait, while Patrick paced. "Me think a lot about Willie and Fiona. 'Tis a big world. Gettin' from here to America.... gettin' to Canada...." He walked away in thought; turned back just before she started to go for him. "Ye brother sail without me. Me canno' pass every chance waitin for Willie in Dublin. Me be makin' me way, he be doin' the same, when he can."

"Go with me on this tour and make enough for good passage to America, not steerage with disease and rotted food. You stay here in Dublin, saving coins and probably never get to America, even if Willie came." She took his chin and delivered her last words. "You left the workhouse with a dream. This is reality. 'Tis not what ye dream that makes a difference; 'tis what ye do. That's the hard part." Sallie slipped her hand from his chin and circled his head with a hug.

"Come, ye have had a busy night. Time to rest...and think, my young musician." Sallie smiled. "We will talk about it again tomorrow."

It was a difficult night. Patrick had to move his thoughts from Willie, and it was hard. He admitted to himself that he had become disheartened by the thought that Willie might never come. Sleep evaded. Thoughts went back to Da and Ma. "Find ye way." Patrick spoke his parents' words. Before he slept, he wrote a note to Willie telling him to wait for him here. He would be back by Christmas.

After intense rehearsals and shopping for clothes, shoes and a coat, Patrick followed Sallie Brennen out the Academy door and down the steps to the waiting carriage. It was time to go. He looked up and down the street, hoping Willie would miraculously appear and he could move backward into the plan they hatched many months ago. Instead of going into the unknown with Sallie, he wanted to wander the pubs and build pipe dreams with Willie. If only he would appear today on Pearse Street. *Willie,* his mind screamed. He pulled the collar of his new coat up to his neck against the cold December wind and climbed into the carriage. His good sense told him to go with Sallie, his heart and soul said, *wait for Willie.* It was all very scary.

What me doin', he asked himself as he climbed in the carriage and looked at the door on the other side. The temptation to exit and run was overwhelming.

Sallie took his arm. "Paddy," was all she said. He fell into the seat and wondered why he felt so defeated. Only Sallie's strong persona moved Patrick into this day.

The steamship was ready to take the singer and her accompanist down the coast, south to Wexford and Cork. Patrick felt he was betraying his poverty and starvation. He skipped dinner and tried not to be too excited, but he was. His first trip in a sailing vessel, his first trip around Ireland, and his first concert were much to be excited about. He did not understand the quivering in his stomach and the conflict in his brain.

Sallie's young protégé was uncomfortable. "Paddy, what can I do or say to help you? A concert tour is a lot of work but fun, too, if you'll let it be. We will be out on the tide by sunset. Start enjoying the trip now, lad."

"The rehearsals were fun," he admitted. "Thanks again for takin' me."

"Where is your fife?"

"Here," he opened his coat and drew it out of his waist. He felt better just holding it.

Sallie opened the package she carried and handed him a stitched leather bag, with leather drawstrings, just the right size for his fife. "Slide it in here and slip the strings over your head. See? Fits perfectly. Now, Paddy Doyle, your fife is secure, and we are ready to sail."

❖ ❖ ❖

The tour started off with two great successes. Patrick began to relax after the first performance in Wexford. It was in a manor house with fifteen people gathered in the drawing room. It was not unlike the rehearsal experience back in Dublin. The boy with the fife was well received. Applause was generous and resounding.

The music was the only real part of the evening for Patrick. It was not the pub tunes he loved but it was beautiful. Being in the fancy home, and the luxury it provided, made Patrick uneasy. He was given a room and as soon as he could, he slipped away from the drawing room while Sallie enjoyed the praise and company of the manor house. He ate very little food from the tray that was brought and did not touch the bed. He slept on the rug beside it.

"You did a fine job, Paddy. Everyone appreciated your music. Now we are on to Cork. That will be much different."

Patrick was awestruck, stage struck, and overwhelmed by the concert experience at Queen's College, Cork. He lay in bed after the performance wondering who he was, where he was and why he was. The stage and lights unnerved him, but Sallie demanded his attention and gave silent demands for him to watch her and begin on the count of four. Patrick played the first note and went into the song with her. He had overcome stage fright, thanks to the music. It transformed and transposed him to a place far above the setting. He blew with joy and most importantly, with confidence.

He went to bed feeling good about it all and then in the dark, old doubts crept in. The most compelling feeling was guilt. Guilt for his good fortune, the bed, the food, the good graces of Sallie and the people around him. Most of all, he felt guilty because he did not deserve all this. His stomach ached. He was too young and inexperienced to understand his feelings but this tour, and all the advantages it was providing could not be appreciated by the boy from the stone cottage, starvation, and the workhouse. His emotions were an up and down ride. All was well when he was with Sallie making music but all else unsettled and unnerved him.

The other strange feeling he had to deal with was applause and acclaim. After the resounding demand for an encore, Patrick's head swirled. Sallie stepped aside and gave him a bow and the audience shouted, "Bravo!" She had to take his arm and lead him off stage; he did not seem to know where he was.

In bed that night, Patrick spoke to the dark ceiling. "Me love doin' this, whatever it is." He could still hear the roar of the audience when he stepped on stage the second time. It caused him to question his worth and just before drifting off to sleep he asked himself the hard question, "Me doin' right by me family and Willie?" Patrick was conflicted.

The next morning at breakfast Sallie handed him the Cork Examiner, December 19, 1850. It was folded over twice so he could read:

> *Sallie Brennen, the Irish Songbird, internationally known soprano from Clarinbridge, Galway County, sang for the audience at Queen's College last evening. She brought her beautiful, lilting voice to entrance the audience—and, entrance she did. This was Miss Brennen's second concert at Queen's and the overflow audience was evidence of her welcome back. The repertoire of traditional music was nostalgic and her addition of lively tunes of the day, a delight. Miss Brennen in concert is truly an important event. She gives the world our music, our culture and an example of Irish talent waiting here to be discovered.*
>
> *A welcome addition to the presentation was a*

new talent—a young piper, Patrick Doyle and his fife. The instrument, of polished wood, added charm to each song Miss Brennen invited him to join. His notes were mellow, rich and truly wonderful. After he played, accompanying her lovely voice, his return to the stage was highly anticipated. They did the final piece, appropriately, The Minstrel Boy, and the audience demanded two encores. Bravos for Miss Sallie Brennen and the boy with the fife!

Sallie jotted on the side.

"I will cut this piece out for you to keep. It is quite wonderful."

Chapter 27

A letter waited for Patrick back at the Academy. While he was performing with Sallie Brennen, it lay unopened on his desk.

The tour continued with great success at every venue. By the fourth performance, they were in Limerick and Sallie had Patrick on stage with her for each song. News of her adding a young boy with a fife to the performance was in the local newspapers and traveled ahead of them. New playbills were printed for their performance in Galway. His name, in a slightly smaller font, was listed under hers.

Patrick Doyle, Fife Soloist

The next morning, Sallie did not come down for breakfast with Patrick. Instead there was a playbill for his souvenir and a note on the table. "Enjoy your day in Galway. I have business to tend to. Boarding is at 6:30"

She hired a carriage and told the driver, "Portumna."

Malcolm Anderson was surprised when the clerk announced, "Miss Sallie Brennen to see you," and stepped aside to invite her in. She came dressed impressively, bright and cheerful, in sharp contrast to the surroundings. Anderson welcomed the ray of sunshine in his office and was obviously intrigued.

"Malcolm Anderson," he bowed. "Miss Brennen, what a wonderful surprise. Come in. I heard you sing in Galway two years ago. Beautiful, absolutely beautiful. I am so pleased to meet you. Did you come to sing for us?"

"Mr. Anderson, my pleasure," she acknowledged him. "I cannot sing here today. Time will not allow. But I will plan to do so the next time I am in Galway." She smiled the smile she usually saved for her audiences. He responded easily.

"That would be special." He waited for her request. "To what do we owe the pleasure of your visit?"

"I would like to speak with one of your residents." She paused and added, "Privately."

"A resident? Of course, who?"

"Annie Doyle."

His eyebrow rose as he turned for the door. "I will summon Annie Doyle. You can talk with her here in my office. Please take a seat. She will be here momentarily."

"Thank you, Mr. Anderson. You are very kind."

When Annie came in, she stood before the lovely lady, bewildered by the summons and the possible reason. Sallie invited her to sit and she went straight to the chair she was used to using. Sallie pulled her chair over by the window.

"Annie Doyle?" she asked

"Yes."

"I am Sallie Brennen. Do you know about me?"

"No."

"No matter. Are you Patrick Doyle's mother? His only family here, including a sister?"

"Yes," Annie began to squirm and became alarmed. "My son...," her voice quivered, "...Patrick. Is he hurt, in trouble?" She turned her head and looked far off out the window as she prepared, in her usual way, for the bad news she expected. Her breathing became shallow and her hands clasped tight.

"Annie, he is fine. Look." Sallie gave her the playbill from Galway and proceeded to tell her who she was and her relationship with Patrick. She started with her brother, then Biddy McGee, the academy and the concert tour. "You see, we have discovered his talent with the fife. His music is like the pied piper. To hear him once demands a repeat performance. Surely you know how beautifully he plays."

"Yes." It was the only thing Annie could attest to.

Slowly she relaxed and listened as Sallie began to tell why she had traveled here. "Patrick is in Galway today. Although he knows he is close to Portumna, he has not asked to come visit you."

"No, no. He must not come back to Portumna." She became animated and fear came over her face. "He knows it. I know it. Please Miss Brennen, do not bring him here. I love my son dearly. We said our farewells."

"As you wish, I will not. Before I go on to tell you of Patrick, tell me what you know of Willie. Do you know his friend?"

"Yes. Isn't he with Patrick?"

"No. Patrick thinks he is still here."

Annie dropped her head. "Miss Brennen, information is never shared in the workhouse. I have not heard anything about Willie. I'm saddened to know they are not together."

"They are not together but Patrick is fine. He is traveling with me back to Dublin tomorrow. He will resume his studies at the Royal Irish Academy of Music after Christmas."

Annie looked up in amazement. "My Patrick!"

Sallie continued. "For the last few weeks he has traveled with me playing his flute at my concerts."

"Glory be. Glory be," was all Annie could say.

"Listen to me, Annie," she spoke intimately and took her hand, "I need to be sure you approve of all these things for your son. He's only fifteen. Not sixteen for five months, right?"

"Yes, that is right."

"I want to assure you that I will look after him. My concerts take me out of Ireland. Next spring, I go to England and in the summer—the United States. I would not take him without your permission. And, I have not spoken to him about this. Not before I got your approval."

Annie was quiet. She withdrew her hand from Sallie's and sat like a statue. Finally, after what seemed a lifetime, tears drifted from her eyes. Sallie watched Annie's face turn from stone to soft, wet humanity. A lifetime of anguish passed through her eyes. Annie reached to take Sallie's hand back—a bold move. She reached across her poverty, her station, her destitution, her sorrow and took the lady's hand. Neither moved. Annie needed a few more minutes. And, Sallie gave her the time she needed. Annie straightened her back and wiped her tears. She stood to address Sallie Brennen with all the class and strength she could muster. It was a scene that would never be expected. The poor woman in beggar clothes, doled out by the workhouse, dark and dreary, rough, plain and straight, stood with commanding presence, clear of purpose and strong demeanor, and spoke to the high lady in billowing, glowing silks and slippers. Her voice was strong.

"Miss Sallie Brennen take Patrick where I believe the Lord wants him to go. My prayers have been answered with your visit today. All of his life I have seen his capable brain, his music, his good character. What more can a mother want for her son than to go into the world using what God has given him? You say all this is possible and I bow to you." Annie bent her knee and lowered her head. "I will trust you and the Almighty. Take my son, with my blessing."

Sallie took Annie's elbows to lift her to eye level. The two women stood as equals, each recognizing the strength in their sisterhood, each caring about Patrick in her own way.

"I will take him, if he will go. If he stays with me six weeks, six months or six years, I will nurture his abilities. Even as I present this to you, we do not know what Patrick will choose to do. He left Portumna with a plan and dedication to his friend, Willie," she paused, ".... and his independence. He has a mind of his own and walls that won't allow him to make friends at school or with me. I'll treat him as a mother but never expect him to accept me the same. Work, music, and respect. I do not expect devotion. That's yours. I'm merely doing what you cannot do for your son, a very talented piper."

The two women parted as friends and each knew the possibility of meeting again was slim. Annie did what she had to do. She let Patrick go—again. Sallie knew what she wanted to do and had no idea if she could. She came to Portumna wanting to do great things for the boy; she left wanting to do all these great things for his mother, too.

"Goodbye, Annie Doyle"

"Goodbye, Sallie Brennen."

At the door, Sallie whispered so it could not be heard, "My sister."

It was a cold, snowy day, one week before Christmas when Patrick and Sallie, exhausted from travel and performing, returned to Dublin. They climbed into a carriage at the dock. Sallie touched his shoulder. "Here are two shillings, Paddy. You earned them and there will be more as soon as the receipts come in." She dropped two shiny coins in his hand. "All the other students are home for the holiday. Come to my apartment. Stay until the next session after New Year's. No reason for you to be the only one here."

"I be fine, Sallie," he refused, and she knew it was useless to urge him.

"Good night, lad. Rest well. I will expect you for Christmas dinner. I'll send a carriage for you."

"No need. Walking good for me." He started away and turned. "Thank you, Sallie—for everything, and this warm coat and shoes." He smiled broadly, climbed out of the carriage and looked up at the Ancient Concert Room, home of the Royal Irish Academy of Music. For the first time since he left, he looked for Willie. *Could he be waiting for me somewhere in Dublin, here on Pease Street? Over by the streetlamp? Sitting on the wall, bundled from the weather?*

Patrick did a complete turnaround and called out, "Willie!" Then he went in the Academy and fell into his bed.

He found the letter from Malcolm Anderson in the morning light. His hands shook as he pulled it open.

> *Patrick,*
> *Willie has recovered from his injury well enough*

to emigrate. He sailed with Jacob Brennen on the 12th of last month for New York. However, he is permanently lame. Willie will apprentice at the Baldwin & Winston Furniture Company in Philadelphia.

Malcolm Anderson

Then folded separately inside was another letter.

Patrick,

I be leaving tomorrow for America. Walking good but not good enough to move from village to village pub to pub. I pray that God will be good to you and me and we meet again my brother.

Willie

Scribbled at the bottom was one word.

Philadelphia

Patrick panicked. His breath was short as he read it again. He turned it over. *When? What month? In Philadelphia, now?* No date. *August, September, October, November?* He backed up to the edge of the bed as if he had been hit. He lay back with the letters resting on his chest and reached for his fife. Songs from the workhouse, songs from the concert tour and plaintive notes, not part of any real song, told of truth, disappointment, and lonesomeness. They filled the empty room with reality. Willie was gone. Patrick was totally alone, and he felt it. He had lived and breathed the possibility of seeing Willie in Dublin, of working their way to America, of finding Fiona—together. Tonight, he saw the folly in that dream. Even if Willie were here—how difficult it would be to work their way anywhere, how hard it is to survive in this world, how much this world was like the workhouse. It separated; it wore you down; it denied. It made a mockery of dreams. Patrick knew he had traded the awfulness of the workhouse for the harsh reality of the world. His music told him—that dream was dead. Willie was not coming.

There would be no sleep tonight. Patrick was weary, bone weary. He was tired of playing the fife. He was tired of looking and waiting for Willie. He was tired of feeling *good* and then *bad* about this life provided by Sallie. He did not fit in here with her.

He wanted to sleep but it did not come. Depression came over him like a dark wet blanket. "Willie not comin'." Suddenly his mind was empty. All the thoughts of going to America with Willie were gone. Thoughts of adventure—gone. Thoughts of Willie, his brother—gone. Thoughts of all that Willie meant to him—gone. Patrick was mourning a great loss. Unwillingly, he thought of Sweeney. In the dark, empty dormitory, Patrick began to talk to himself. "If'n it weren' for Sweeney, I could go back to Ma." His words came back to him from the empty room. "Sweeney still has hold on me." He heard his voice saying things that his heart knew were not true. His mood became darker. He pounded the bed that would not let him sleep. "Me canno' go back. Me canno' stay here. Me canno' say 'me and Willie' no more. 'Tis just me. Just me."

He got up from the bed and wrote Sallie a note.

> *Sallie,*
>
> *Willie has gone to America. Time for me to make me own way, too.*
>
> *Thank you for everything.*
>
> *Patrick Doyle*

Patrick put on the clothes he got from Jacob Brennen and the coat and shoes that Sallie bought. He needed them—hated to take them, but he had to. All the other clothes, bought on the tour, were neatly folded and piled on the foot of the bed. He thought of the shillings, felt them jingle in the pouch. He considered leaving them. "Donno' be stupid," he said aloud dropping them in his money pouch. He slid his fife into his pant. The beautiful leather flute case was placed on top of the clothes at the foot of the bed.

The food on the dinner tray that Sallie had sent was uneaten and cold. Patrick tied it in the napkin. He patted the money pouch and the fife. "Better than when I left the workhouse. Me has shillings, one meal, clothes that fit, shoes, and a warm coat." He was trying to look on the brighter side, but his last thought brought him down again. "But, donno' have Willie." Patrick stood at the door and looked back. He assessed all that he was about to leave behind. He spoke to the room. He used the best language he could. "I cannot stay here. I am my own problem, not Sallie's." Then he said in his old cottage way, "Me be a'goin'"

He could not stop the sob that came up from his throat and lungs as he closed the front door of the Academy, pulled the coat collar up and went into the cold December dawn.

❧ ❧ ❧

Patrick headed for the docks along the Liffey River. He crossed the Butt Bridge to the north side and traveled along the river, heading east. Sallie would look for him in the pubs near the Academy. He would work through the ones along the lower river. He walked until he was at the edge of the city and exhausted. A sheltered spot in an alley, two hundred feet back from the water, became his bed. He curled up and fell into a deep sleep. His fife was tucked far into his pant and his money pouch, attached to his button, was grasped in his hand. Patrick slept past the morning hours and into the afternoon. Alarm brought him from sleep when he felt a hand touch his. He reacted quickly with arms flailing. His eyes, unaccustomed to the light, saw a figure grab his food and pouch. "Sweeney," he shouted and came up swinging. A solid blow to his head sent Patrick reeling. His head landed on a rock. He tried to catch himself with his hand. It twisted under him and he landed hard on his arm. He felt it break. His assailant pulled at his coat. Blood blinded him and everything went black.

Pain brought Patrick awake, his head pounded, but the real pain was from his right forearm and wrist. He was cold and scared. *Not Sweeney,* he thought. He pushed his right hand into his pant and felt the fife. With immeasurable relief, Patrick lay back and endured the pain. He took inventory—*money, food, coat, gone, arm, wrist—broken, head—cut open.* He looked down at his useless, agony-causing arm, and realized, *canno' play the fife.*

Patrick lay shivering on the ground without the means to go on. The early winter sunset darkened the eastern sky and a cold December wind brought a chilling mist. He had no way to stay dry, no way to stay warm, no way to support his arm, no way to clean the blood off his face. He looked down at the Liffey River with dark thoughts and passed out again.

Ma lifted his head and cleaned the blood. She gently washed his hair and kissed his cheek. She tucked the blanket in close and gave him his fife to hold. "Ma," he whispered.

Fiona touched his broken arm, and although it hurt, because it was Fiona, he allowed it. "'Twill take time, but will mend. The wrist not broken," her words were music. "Play the fife again," she sang the chorus. "And walk the glen."

"Fiona," he cried.

"Sleep, now." Ma patted his shoulder

"I donno' want to sleep. Stay with ye." He protested but they went away, and he slept.

Chapter 28

Patrick woke up to a voice urging him to drink. He opened his mouth and accepted the warm, sweet tea offered. *Warm,* his first thought. His second thought, *fife,* forced him to move—get up. He pushed against the blanket and the hands holding his shoulders. He tried to lash out but immediately had pain in his right arm and head.

"Easy, lad. It be alright." Hands held him down. "Easy."

He stopped the struggle because he could not push, he could not pull, he could not think.

A lovely, comforting voice relieved his panic. "Ye safe. We be takin' care. Safe." Patrick listened and yielded. "Ye arm broken, ye head will be fine in a couple of days. Good news, wrist not broken. Donno' fight against ye bed, 'tis where ye need to be for now. Safe, warm, n'healin'."

"Where am I? And, where is me fife?" he asked, his voice rising in alarm.

"This be J.J. Dwyer's Livery Stable. Warm and safe."

"Me fife?" he asked with more urgency. But she went on with her explanation. "J.J. me Da, fix animals—broken bones, injuries. He fix ye. A splint for ye arm and bandage on d' head."

"Me fife," again, rising up looking at the girl for the first time. "Fife?" he begged—he had no strength to demand—and, fell back exhausted from the effort.

"Drink ye tea." She held it to his mouth. "Then, I be gettin' the fife."

Patrick took the fife, place it on his chest, running his hand overall, testing each hole for damage. “Perfect,” he declared.

“Of course, ‘tis perfect,” she defended. “Tucked in where ye keep it,” she teased. “Da gave it to me for safekeeping. Now, that ye have that important thing, maybe ye will lie back and behave whilst we take care of ye.” It was a gentle chastising and with lilting tones mixed with humor. “Seems ye’d be more concerned wit’ ye head.”

“Mary Rose Dwyer,” she introduced herself. “Ye?”

“Patrick Doyle.”

“Rest now, Patrick Doyle. We bringin’ some broth soon.” She was gone.

The stable had warm animal smells and he could hear the sounds of horses back in the stalls. He was on a pallet in a small room, surrounded with saddles and tack hanging everywhere. Saddle soap and wax added to the aromatic mix. Patrick looked around the room. It was all very neat and clean—each thing in its place and well cared for. A small wood stove in the far corner gave warmth. A rough horse blanket was drawn around him. Patrick pulled the fife in, under the cover, and closed his eyes.

Mary Rose came back with a tray. “Patrick, me Da wants ye to stay awake now. Would be best for ye head injury.” She put the tray down and slid her hand under his head to bring him up and rolled another blanket to support his back. “Sit up for ye broth.” She lifted his injured arm and hand from the cover. He saw it for the first time.

“Me hand!” Frightened by what he saw at the end of the splint holding his arm, Patrick drew back in alarm. “Me hand?”

“Swollen. Be better in days. Not to worry, Patrick. Ye can eat wit’ this one.” Mary Rose pulled the blanket back over his arm and slid a spoon into his left hand. Patrick was not worried about eating. He was worried about playing the fife, earning money, and living. Right now, in this moment, he had to believe her and eat the broth. Mary Rose was bossy.

While he ate, Patrick relaxed and that reduced the pain in his arm and head. Her chatter continued. "I'm to keep you awake. Tell me about your fife. So beautiful."

As always, this topic was his favored. He could tell her about it and not talk about himself. He told about making it with his father and promised to play it for her as soon as he could.

While he was talking, he looked at the girl. She had a pleasant face and continual smile, showing laughing blue eyes and lovely white teeth. Her freckles were confined to the bridge of her nose and only a few marched over her rosy cheeks. Mary Rose was close to Patrick's age and of medium height and size. He guessed she would rise to his shoulder—not a skinny hungry girl. He wondered at his interest in such thoughts. Her dark blond hair, thick and wavy, was tied with a string of leather and looked like a horse's tail. When Patrick thought, *so appropriate,* he smiled and even chuckled.

"Somethin' funny, Patrick?" She asked.

He pushed the broth bowl back and tried to ignore her question, but Mary Rose insisted. "Somethin' funny?" Again.

"Mary Rose Dwyer, I be very lucky to be here and nursed by you. Almost ironic, me be in a livery stable and the girl takin' care of me has her hair tied up like a horse's tail."

"Well, I'll be...ye makin' fun?" She huffed toward the door, her head jerked in indignation as she passed the window and caught her reflection. She burst into laughter and pointed at herself in the glass. "Patrick Doyle! Right ye be—like a horse's tail."

Together, they laughed.

"Mary Rose!" John Joseph Dwyer came in the room. "Disturbing our patient? He should be quiet."

"Nay, Da...but, a little laughter never hurts. Does it? Ye told me to keep him awake. Maybe I overdid it." Mary Rose smiled at her father then waved to Patrick and swished her hair purposefully as she left the room. An air of levity and pleasure remained with Patrick. For an instant he forgot his plight.

J.J. pulled up a chair. "Patrick Doyle—J.J. Dwyer. How ye feelin'?" he asked.

"Good, if'n I lay still."

"Lay still, lad, and tell me how we come to find ye in such shape?"

"Me travelin' and got tired. I was awakened by a thief stealing me money and coat. Took me dinner, too."

"Why ye be sleepin' near the river?"

A cloud passed over Patrick's face and J.J. Dwyer saw it. His head began to hurt again. His brain became confused. Old reservations and protective attitudes washed over him. One thought came to him. *Leave. Go Now.* He moved under the blanket and took hold of the fife.

J.J. was a step ahead. He was a man who understood animals and at this moment, Patrick Doyle was an injured animal, possibly with more injuries than the obvious ones he had tended to. He lay his huge hand on Patrick's chest, with slight pressure and said, "Whoa." Comfort radiated where J.J.'s hand lay. His other hand came down on the injured arm and floated up to the shoulder with a gentle healing touch massaging his tense muscles. "Easy." He looked the boy in the eye. "Easy, lad," J.J. spoke and waited for Patrick to relax under his touch just as a stallion would.

"If ye have a story to tell...if ye tells it or not.... this be the place of ye healin'. Ye trusted me when ye be unknowin' and it turned out good. Mary Rose and me did good by ye. Now that ye mind be comin' back, ye can trust us even more. Think about it." J.J. stood and took his hands back.

"I be tellin' Mary Rose to come back and read to ye. Stay awake until after the evenin' meal. That's best."

Patrick missed J.J.'s touch immediately. A spark of well-being was gone. It was mystic.

Patrick could not nod, smile, or respond in any way. He knew for the first time in twenty-one months, he was in the right place—not the workhouse, not Clarinbridge, not the Academy, not touring with Sallie, not out in the road, not lost, not scared. Patrick did not think of another place he had to be, another struggle he had to make, another concession or another obligation he had to meet. He did not struggle about his past. He was not frantic about his future. He did not take out his fife to withdraw to music. Willie did not come to mind. Fiona did not haunt him. And, he did not think of Sweeney, either. Patrick relaxed, let himself be in this time and place. He began to feel rescued.

Patrick turned his head to watch the door. Mary Rose would soon come in to read to him.

Mary Rose returned and found Patrick sitting up, waiting.

She brought a Bible and turned to the book of Daniel. "Do ye know the book of Daniel?" she asked.

"Nay."

"'Tis exciting and you will like it. Sleepy?"

"My eyes are heavy. If ye stop readin' they go down."

"Listen to me, Patrick Doyle." Her eyes flashed and her horse's tail hair flipped. "If'n ye eyes close me Da'll beat me and throw me in the river. Ye want that to happen? Me in the cold, cold river in December—missin' Christmas— all because of a boy who could no' keep his eyes open?" She tried but could not keep a lilt out of her voice.

Patrick smiled, "Read."

"This be the story of a young man who had many hardships, but he used his brain and faith to overcome. The hardest when he was thrown into a den of lions."

"Read," he said again, with interest and remembering his mother reading about the lion's den. That was a lifetime ago.

She began the story of Daniel, hostage to the Babylonian court. With unusual skill and animation, she read the colorful and mysterious passages about dreams, kings, and jeopardy.

"Listenin'? Eyes open?" She asked.

"Keep readin'. Me not let ye be thrown in the river." Patrick sat up to fight off the urge to sleep and listened to Mary Rose's sweet voice read two chapters.

"Stopping right here for a while." She closed the Bible. "Patrick Doyle, do ye read?"

"Aye. Me had schoolin' but, there be nothin' t'read. Where did ye get such a book? The Bible?"

"Father Murphy let me bring it home. Ye can read to me now...or ye can talk about ye life afore." She offered the book.

"Read or talk?" Mary Rose was making a demand while offering friendship in such a way that Patrick could not refuse her.

"This book is big and heavy for one arm to hold." He made an excuse for not reading and began to talk. "Me Ma had such a Bible. It from her Ma but it was traded for food before we all went to the Portumna Workhouse. Da died there." Patrick had never said those words before, and he did not know why he was uttering them now to Mary Rose. He looked off into the distance and started his story. Briefly he told of Sean, Mavis and lastly Fiona before describing the cottage and hills he missed so. "Do ye know about starvation, Mary Rose?"

"Nay, no much. We saw it. Strangers beggin' at the stable. J.J. tended the horses from the manor houses and we niver be dependent on a crop. 'Twas worse in country. Do ye know starvation, Patrick?"

"Aye, for sure hunger stings afore ye go into the workhouse. The Doyle family knew what *nothing* was. When me left, me had nothing. Out of the workhouse, I gained two shillings, new shoes and a coat." He turned his head and looked at her. "All gone now."

"Nay, ye shoes under the bed. All not gone."

"Good, me has shoes. Stay in this bed till spring and me no need a coat and perhaps it'll rain pennies." Together, they enjoyed his sarcasm.

"True though, I have me fife. 'Tis me life. I play in pubs and get a meal and sometimes a pence." As he spoke of his treasure, he brought it out from the blanket. "Mary Rose," he paused for emphasis, "Patrick Doyle is nothin' without the fife." For this moment, he was engaged with another human being. For this time, he wanted her to understand the fife. He wanted her to understand him, and his loneliness softly melted away.

Mary Rose listened intently. When he was finished talking and put the fife away, she pulled closer and reached for it. He allowed her to take it from his hand. "Ye be just a boy, Patrick Doyle. Nothin' more; nothin' less. And, ye would never be nothin', Patrick Doyle, even wit'out ye fife. God would not allow it. We not heard ye play this but, the fife is not the boy." Mary Rose offered it back to Patrick. "Here! Donn' lay *it* down in a dark alley and wait for a thief to take it or break it. Ye has to take as good a care of Patrick Doyle as ye does this fife."

"And, what was my choice, smart colleen? There be no place for me."

"Ye could knock on a door and ask for help. People are kind. Ye need to believe it."

Shadows were filling the room and it was too dark to resume reading. "Must be mealtime." She changed the subject. "I be fetchin' ye tray now." As she moved the chair and put the Bible away, she asked, "Do ye know what date today be?"

Patrick struggled with his thoughts as he tried to count the days since his return to Dublin. Mary Rose saw he was having trouble thinking it through. "December twenty-second. Christmas soon."

"I canno' leave. Me and me fife have to stay in this place even if it be Christmas."

"Aye, me lad. Ye gettin' some sense back." And, in her usual teasing manner added, "if'n ye ever had any. Christmas in the livery stable—just like the first one. Ye be one of the animals in the Crib—cows, lambs, camels, mules and Patrick." She laughed at her own words. "But for sure, me Da will take ye to our table for dinner and leave the other animals behind eatin' hay and straw."

Patrick smiled and then turned his head away so she would not see the darkness pass over him as he recalled the days when he ate straw.

❖ ❖ ❖

J.J. brought Patrick's meal tray. "Mary Rose?" Patrick inquired.

"She has chores. When housin' and tendin' animals, 'tis every day. No excuses, not even a boy in the tack room needin' company can put off those chores. Mary Rose feedin' the chickens and horses. 'Tis her job. I be helpin' with ye dinner."

Patrick had some appetite. The potato soup tasted good and he ate part of it and most of the bread. "J.J. I canno' eat it all."

"We cover and keep it for mornin'. No waste here." He cleared the tray and brought the chair to the bedside.

"Ye look better, lad. Tell me how ye feelin'?"

"Very tired. Mary Rose did not let me sleep. Me hand throbbin' and not lookin' so good. The hand be there but feels like it not belong to me."

J.J. gently moved the blanket and lifted the injured hand and arm. "Mmm, I see. We should have had it raised up." He folded the edge of the blanket to cradle and elevate Patrick's arm. "Now, lay back. I be checkin' your hand again to be sure no broken bones. It won't hurt. Shut your eyes."

Patrick relaxed and did as J.J. ordered while the man took his swollen, distorted hand. He applied a liniment, surely meant for the horses. Without moving the arm, he gently massaged and manipulated the fingers and tendons. Patrick felt relief, warmth and comfort in J.J.'s touch. He was drifting off to sleep thinking, *He be healin' me.* And, his hand came back to being his. It was a good sleep, deep, restful and untroubled.

Before J.J. left the room, he laid his hands on Patrick's head, gently squeezed, and said a prayer of thanksgiving.

Chapter 29

Christmas Day was cold and snowy. The wind blew and the snow went sideways, never seeming to settle. It was a dry, light snow that finally built up in the corners and crevices. Patrick was feeling stronger. His hand, amazingly, began to resume its size and purpose right after J.J. worked his magic on it. For the last two days, Patrick exercised his fingers as Mary Rose instructed.

"Do this." She took his hand and moved each finger back and forth, folding and unfolding. "It be good for ye hand and the muscles in ye arm to move thus."

"Much better if'n ye do it for me.""

"Not my job. Me exercise dumb animals for Da. Ye a dumb animal? Me thinks not."

The lively banter continued between these new friends. "Besides, me has work to do in the kitchen. Da come for ye at noon to eat wit' us."

Patrick liked Mary Rose and surprised himself with anticipation to see her each morning. His outlook was elevated and yet in quiet moments he thought about his situation and decided it was all about Christmas. *Me can stay here and celebrate Christmas then be gone.* Christmas has always been a time-out from reality. The day after Christmas—the hard life resumes. *What am I to do?* He asked himself. *Why here? Why the Dwyers?* Patrick did not know the answers to those questions. He only knew that here in this tack room with Mary Rose and J.J., he was content.

"I be gone tomorrow." He stopped this purposeless thinking. It would not be easy to leave J.J. Dwyer's stable. Here, especially with Mary Rose, he remembered happy. He remembered laughing. He remembered carefree. He remembered who he was before he went to Portumna. And, he remembered hunger, yearning, begging, almost dying for food. Now he was hungry again, yearning, begging, almost dying for something else—ease, softness, what was right here—family. It was not like the luxury of Sallie's tour—that unsettled him. The tack room was simple, plain and warm. J.J. Dwyer Livery Stable was different and good. Patrick did not know the word satiated, but his inner spirit yearned to be satisfied. Mary Rose's words came back to him as he walked to the washstand to prepare for his trip to the Christmas table. "*.... just a boy, Patrick Doyle. Nothin' more; nothin' less.*" He combed his hair sat on the side of the bed, waiting for Mary Rose. "Just a boy. Not sixteen yet." It was the first time that he admitted to himself that he was too young to beat the world, too young to master continents, too young to do it all as soon as tomorrow. "Willie and me be big dreamers." He reached for his fife and tried to bring it to his mouth. He could not bend his arm enough to reach the holes. His right fingers were not agile enough. He put the fife back under the blanket and said aloud. "Soon, but not today." It was a big step for Patrick. He admitted that things would get better and he did not have to fight the world until they were. While waiting for J.J. to take him to Christmas dinner, Patrick's thinking came full circle. *Me not leavin' the day after Christmas. Not tomorrow. Stay awhile.*

The kitchen was full of delightful aromas of food and pine. A garland hung on the doorframe, a small basket with three apples decorated the space. A table to the left of the stove gave a warm inviting place for Christmas dinner. The chicken coop and root cellar provided bounty. A beautifully roasted chicken surrounded by carrots and potatoes centered the table. Mary Rose had chopped, seasoned and cooked apples to add a sweet taste to the savory meal. J.J. brought Patrick to his place as Mary Rose removed her apron and joined them. She set a plate of warm soda bread on the table beside a dish of butter. She invited her father to say grace.

"Da."

"Bless us dear Lord and the bounty ye provide. For the birth of Jesus, we celebrate this day and remember all the loved ones who are with ye, oh Lord, and missed today. Amen."

J.J. carved the bird with great flair and served everyone. He took his seat and began the feast and conversation.

"I hope ye are feelin' stronger, Patrick."

"Aye. Me head and hand much better now. Arm, not so."

"That will take a while, lad. It canno' be rushed and ye have time."

"Ye and Mary Rose be healin' me and I be so grateful."

"God doin' the healin'. We be his servants."

It was a Christmas dinner to be remembered. The food was delicious and the small company around the table, congenial. Patrick managed to eat with his left hand. The exceptionally generous menu quieted the diners. They paid attention to each mouthful. Mary Rose was unusually silent. Her Da and Patrick talked. She cleared dishes and paid close attention when they began discussing Patrick's plans.

"I canno' stay, being helpless to work for me bed and food."

"Ye must. Give yourself more time and then we be findin' work a one-arm boy can do."

"Even tomorrow. Me canno' sit around doin' nothin'."

"Ye canno' go out in the street, lad. Sometimes life takes away ye choices. Better to be helpless in a safe place. Time not ye enemy. Pride—that be ye enemy. From the stories ye tell, it be ye habit to run away when ye canno' figure things out. Nay, here. Ye stay and figure things out. The Good Lord let ye be injured so ye could learn that lesson."

Patrick was very quiet while J.J. talked. He took in his every word. Mary Rose came back to the table to lighten the conversation. "Be there gifts on this Christmas Day or only profound lessons?"

"Gifts," J.J. replied.

Patrick fidgeted. He had no gifts to give. "If I could play me fife, that would be ye gift from me. A poor piper's gift."

"We be waitin' for that gift. As soon as ye able, we will be grateful."

J.J. gave Mary Rose a small potted rose that he had saved from the cold and nurtured. She hugged him joyfully and placed it on the windowsill. Her gift to her Da was a belt that he had worn, loved, and discarded. She had restored the leather and shined the buckle. He was pleased. Then Mary Rose turned to Patrick.

"For ye." She brought out a piece of cloth that she had hemmed and sewn into a half circle. When it went over his head it formed a sling to support his arm. "There. Perfect."

"Yea, perfect." He was delighted and his arm felt immediate relief. "It be easier to do one-arm chores, J.J." He turned to Mary Rose. "Thank you. 'Tis the nicest Christmas. I never thought I would have another after me family left the cottage." Patrick did not cry but several tears escaped his eyes.

Chapter 30

J.J. Dwyer was a big man, burly with curly blond hair. He had a strong chin and patrician nose—a handsome man with a beautiful speaking voice that rolled his Irish brogue out like satin. Dwyer was comfortable wearing leather and was one with the animals he tended. His hands, which had brought healing to Patrick, were big and gentle. J.J. was known on the north side of the Liffey River, east of the Butt Bridge, as a man of God with unusual powers. He could talk to the animals and calm horses with his touch. Some believed J.J. had clairvoyance and saw things no one else could see, even the future. He never claimed that but did not deny it, either.

Mary Rose was twelve years old when her mother died. J.J.'s sister wanted to take her. She had two babies and two older children. She wanted Mary Rose and the help she could give. J.J. refused.

"We be a family, me and Mary Rose."

"A stable is no place for a girl," his sister insisted.

"Nay. No. Not. Niver!" He threw every negative into the air. "*This* be Mary Rose's home." It was final. Mary Rose flew across the room and threw her arms around her Da's waist. She would not lose her father, too.

❖ ❖ ❖

J.J. had a vision of Patrick Doyle months ago. On a beautiful day in November, when warm temperatures belied the date, he walked into the tack room and saw a vision of an injured boy on the bed. As was his usual habit when visions came to him, J.J. sat down and waited for understanding. The vision evaporated, but the knowledge he waited for, came. The boy would be hurt and lost. He would come and stay long enough to serve. *Serve?* J.J. thought. *Serve who? Serve what?*

And then, the air cleared. The vision and understanding were put away. J.J. was patient, he would wait for meaning. It would come.

Weeks later, driving his wagon home from the wheelwright's shop, he saw a foot extended from a narrow alley. On investigation he found the boy in his vision. When he put the unconscious boy on the bed, in the tack room, he knew it was meant to be and immediately called Mary Rose to attend to him.

"Mary Rose, bring clean warm water. I will get a splint from the cabinet and build a fire in this stove. This young man to be with us for a while."

J.J. never told of his special *sight.* When he saw Patrick wrapped in a blanket sleeping on the bed in the tack room it was a fulfilled vision. He accepted this and waited for the full meaning and purpose to unfold. He was sure of one thing, Patrick Doyle was not going to leave the day after Christmas nor any time soon, but J.J. was the only one who knew that with absolute certainty.

❖ ❖ ❖

J.J. went to the tack room early the day after Christmas. Patrick was sleeping soundly. His shoes were under the bed. J.J. took a chair and watched the sleeping boy. Soon, in that quiet pre-dawn room, he felt Patrick Doyle's story, he felt Patrick Doyle's trials, he felt Patrick Doyle's future. J.J. took time to sort all the information coming fast at him. Then he heard Patrick Doyle's fife. It was peaceful and beautiful. A young girl walked across his vision. *That be Mary Rose?* He thought. He looked closely. It did not seem to be Mary Rose. *Who?* The girl bent to tend a child and he could not identify the faces of the two figures. Intuitively he knew the girl was not anxious, scared, or troubled. He took consolation, if in fact, it was Mary Rose. As always, he waited for the unfolding of time and events to define what it was all about.

The bright sun falling across his face brought J.J. back from his trance. Patrick was stirring.

"Good mornin'"

"Good mornin'," Patrick sleepily replied.

"Me wanted to be sure ye did not intend to leave today. I be glad ye shoes are under the bed."

"I be stayin'"

"Ye knows ye are free to go, Patrick. But, promise me this. Ye'll not leave without tellin' us. It be important that ye stay until the time is right for ye to go."

"Promise. I'll not steal away. Promise." After that serious moment, Patrick smiled. "Ye promised me some one-arm chores."

"Aye. A saddle and some soap and wax await ye in the stable. Rest often, lad. Ye are not ready for a full day's work. Do enough to make ye self feel better about it. First, breakfast wit' me in the kitchen. Now let me check ye head."

They went to the kitchen where a simple meal was prepared. Obviously, Mary Rose had fixed it but was nowhere to be seen. Patrick wanted to ask but held back. He kept an eye out for her all morning but she did not appear. He was busy with the saddle most of the day; taking breaks often. He refused the mid-day meal and slept though the time it would take to eat. In the afternoon, Patrick was exhausted and went to bed. *Stupid,* he thought. *Stupid to even think me could leave here today.* That small amount of work wore him out and brought his headache back. Mary Rose brought his evening meal on a tray and left it. When hunger brought him awake, he saw the food and the Bible marked where she had stopped before. He could only eat and hope she would come back soon. Mary Rose did not come back to the tack room that night. Patrick slept peacefully.

Chapter 31

Patrick was up early the next day. The morning was without conflict, uncertainty, or even doubt. He leaned back on the pillow and enjoyed the first thoughts that crossed his brain. *All is well here.* All the requirements were manageable. For the first time since the potato vine blackened, Patrick did not have to *go* someplace else; he could *stay.*

He caught sight of Mary Rose crossing the paddock. "Mary Rose, so early? On ye way?"

"Aye," she answered and continued her path.

"I be walkin' with ye?"

"If ye like. And tote this," she handed him a large cloth bag while she held to some items under her arm. They rounded the stable to the east and proceeded to the crest of a hill. The sky began to color in anticipation of a beautiful winter sunrise. "Here," she directed as she put her bundle down. She talked as she set up an easel and took out paints, brushes, and a folded tri-legged stool. Mary Rose pointed to the empty cloth bag. "Guess ye will sit on the ground, if ye want to stay." It was an off-handed invitation and he accepted readily. Patrick watched as she prepared to work. She put an unfinished canvas on the easel. It was full of a colorful sky without definition. As soon as she started her strokes, he was alone; she was immersed in her work. The sun was changing the sky and Mary Rose had minutes to capture today's blaze of glory before the sun melted the brilliant hues to gold and brightness. She added this dawn to the previous one she had started on the canvas.

Patrick understood and left her uninterrupted until she spoke to him.

"Hungry?" The sun came into their eyes. "Leave everything. We go to eat now." Mary Rose covered her easel, put each brush away carefully, ready for later. "After breakfast, I be comin' back to work on the background landscape wit'out the sun in me eyes."

"Ye be an artist," Patrick stated as they moved away from the scene and walked in silence. He noticed how comfortable it was—just being with her.

❖ ❖ ❖

After breakfast Patrick returned to his task in the stable. He wanted to follow Mary Rose back to the hills but reluctantly stayed behind. It had been a long time since he had given himself to the hills. With Dublin out of his sight line, being off to the south and west, he could imagine the hills near Galway and the Shannon curving like the Liffey. He became entranced with his memories as he rubbed the leather. He did not notice J.J. observing until he faced Patrick from the other side of the saddle and began working with him.

"Ye seemed to be day dreamin', lad." J.J. spoke and began rubbing the saddle.

"Aye, 'bout me home near Galway. Our stone cottage, the hills and rock walls dividin'. 'Twas paradise until the blight."

"Does it make ye sad to think thus?"

"Sad for that time.... miss me family and playin' me fife."

"No point in agonizin' over things ye canno' change. But, tis good to remember the good."

"The hard part is, me thought we had a plan, me friend, Willie and me. Big plan to work our way to America together. Now nothing. Willie be gone wit'out me." His voice dropped, "No plan a t'all."

"The question for ye is this. Did ye really have a good plan?"

Working together on the leather seemed to open Patrick to talk. Without hesitation he answered J.J.

"Nay, that be the hardest part. I have learned after almost a year leavin' the workhouse, we did not have a plan. Even if Willie come to Dublin—no hope. What happened to me would happen to both of us. Surely. We never get to America. Me had the chance to go and didno'."

"Ye had the chance and didno'? Tell me."

It was so easy, sitting in the chair, rubbing oil into the saddle leather, and watching it regenerate in his hands. Patrick did not even raise his eyes as he began his story of friendship with Willie, Malcolm Anderson's interest and offer, of Sweeney's abuse, of his refusal to sail with Jacob Brennen and finally of Willie's departure for Philadelphia.

"You escaped Sweeney when you left the workhouse. Why he be a part of this story since ye left? And why didno' Willie leave when ye did?"

For the first time since that fateful night, he talked of Sweeney—the attack and Willie's injury. It became therapeutic to tell J.J. "I pushed his own knife into him." Tears came unbidden. "Me be a different boy when I left the workhouse. Times Sweeney comes to me dreams. Times guilt comes. And times me canno' think what is best." He stopped to take a breath. "Me no' worthy of Mr. Anderson, of Biddy, or Sallie...even of ye kindness." He stopped working on the saddle and looked J.J. in the eye for the first time as he told his story. "I killed a man." No more tears, just admission. "When Jacob Brennen said go, me needed Willie to help me face the fact that I killed a man. Now me knows, even with Willie, that donno' change. I killed a man." He thought about Willie and admitted to himself for the first time that Willie had the street skills for a tough life, and he did not. When he left the workhouse, Patrick went into a world that was foreboding, scary and foreign.

J.J. put his cloth down and came around to stand beside Patrick. He took hold of the chair that Patrick sat in and turned it around so he could look the boy in the eye. "Do no' think those words again," he put his hand on Patrick's head. "Ye saved Willie's life and ye own. That be what happened that night." At first Patrick reacted to J.J.'s hands and tensed his neck. J.J. stayed like a stem of truth with an unbelievable, gentle pressure. Patrick's head bent in submission and then rose up and looked into eyes that he could believe.

J.J. moved his hands to Patrick's shoulders until he felt the trembling stop. "Ye hand was in it, but Sweeney was dead by his own hand. Willie hurt but ye both would be dead today if he had accomplished his purpose. To yield to Sweeney's murderous sin would have been suicide. Ye could no' do that."

"I canno' go back to the workhouse and it happened that Willie had to go without me. I was not smart. Me Da told me not to be foolish. Foolish, I was. I be in America now if I leave with Jacob Brennen."

"Aye, ye could be there now but ye would be just as injured wit'out the broken arm. Patrick, there be healing here and when ye go, ye will be renewed, whole, and strong. More than that ye will fulfill ye purpose."

"Purpose is to save Fiona, me told ye, Fiona lost somewhere in Canada."

"No, Patrick. Fiona no' ye purpose. Ye purpose to be all ye can be, wit' all the talent ye have, for all the good ye can do. Fiona awaits ye but she no' be ye purpose. God gave each life to be, to use, and to do. Be a boy, Patrick, and when ye are a man ye will know how to find Fiona and if ye have to make a difference, ye can."

Patrick seemed to understand, not with logic, but with feelings. He felt an easement in his heart and brain. J.J. worked things out, such that a boy could never do. Most importantly, Patrick believed, and he did not want to move from this circle of trust, revelation and truth. He did not want to cry or run. He wanted to take a big breath and be himself for the first time in over two years. Only one thing would improve this moment—his fife.

J.J. heard that thought. "Patrick, I think we can put a shorter splint on your arm tomorrow and maybe you can play the fife again." J.J. received Patrick's smile.

"Oh, I meant to ask before. Who is Sallie? You talked to her in your delirium and mentioned her in your story today but, ye never told us—who is Sallie?"

Chapter 32

It was hard to find the words to talk to J.J. about Sallie. How could he explain why he walked away from her and all she offered, when he did not know himself? "Sallie Brennen." He announced her full name.

J.J. looked up in surprise. "Sallie Brennen? The Irish Songbird?" he asked in disbelief. J.J. knew of her international fame and of her residence in Dublin but he had never heard her sing. "You know Sallie Brennen?" he asked.

"She be sister to Jacob Brennen the sea captain. Was to take me to America on the money Malcolm Anderson paid. He told her—come hear me fife. Sallie be the one what brought me to Dublin and the Irish Royal Academy for learnin'. Me be ashamed to say....me ran away from that, too." Patrick lowered his head. Just saying it caused him pain. He recalled Sallie's interest and the fun learning at the Academy. He was humiliated to admit his actions with no excuse for them.

While Patrick talked, J.J. brought his chair around to sit with the boy. This story was such a surprise and revelation.

"J.J., I canno' go back but needs to let Sallie know...." He paused to think. "She was so kind and generous. I was thoughtless and unkind." His voice told of his regrets.

J.J. slipped his arm around Patrick's shoulders. "Aye, ye canno' go back *yet*. If ye like, I be lettin' Miss Sallie Brennen know ye are safe here. And that you be stayin' for a while."

Again, Patrick felt rescued. "Thanks."

"That splint changed first thing tomorrow. We wantin' to

hear ye fife. Get ye arm mended; all else can be, in time." As he walked out the door he whispered, "Sallie Brennen. Our Patrick knows Sallie Brennen."

True to his promise, a letter was dispatched to Miss Sallie Brennen, in care of the Royal Irish Academy of Music. The next morning, J.J. came to the tack room with a shorter splint. "Now, lad. Let's have a look at that arm. Stay in bed and lay it beside ye." He carefully removed the old splint and set the arm securely in the new shorter one that did not extend over the wrist. "Bend," he directed. "Pain?"

"Nay." Patrick lay very still.

"Bendin' the wrist be good for ye arm, but only for short periods of time. Understand?" He gave him the fife from the table and waited to see if the new splint allowed the movement Patrick needed.

Patrick stayed on the bed. He pulled the injured arm across his chest and took the fife, brushed it with his sleeve and flexed his fingers. He felt the tendons in his right arm pull and looked at J.J.

"'Tis alright lad, if there be no pain," J.J. assured.

Up and down the scale, then his own favored composition. Music filled the room.

After the first tune, Patrick played some pub songs. It was pure joy. The scene was so unusual—a beautiful boy, lying on a bed in a stable tack room, expanding the stable world with delightful music.

Mary Rose, as if summoned by the Pied Piper, came to the door and sat on the floor, entranced.

"Enough for now, Patrick. Come for breakfast. Ye must not overdo it. And, continue ye work on the saddle wit' ye other hand." He walked over, took the fife and replaced it on the table.

"'Twas no pain, J.J. I be doin' as ye say so my arm and hand get better and better."

Mary Rose and J.J. left Patrick alone with his music and went into the kitchen to finish putting breakfast on the table.

"Mary Rose, this young lad makes life with his fife."

"Aye, Da. Life." was her short reply to her father's musing.

J.J. understood the boy and his history so much better as he listened to the notes from the fife. He knew why Patrick was mentored by Sallie Brennen and why he would do the same.

❧ ❧ ❧

"After ye finish ye work, come join me on the hill. The light perfect then," Mary Rose invited as Patrick finished breakfast.

Patrick took his fife and went to find Mary Rose as soon as he could. The sun lit the back of the stable and the huge tree that shaded it. She had turned her easel and was working to bring to her canvas the weathered boards and filtered sun. He was captivated by the light, life, and illumination in her work. She was fully engrossed, so he sat on the cloth bag, which she had obviously spread for him. The day was cool, but the sun was warm. Patrick and Mary Rose were happy sharing the day, warmth, and time.

Almost as an afterthought, Patrick remembered the fife tucked in his waist. She painted and he played in complete tranquility, compatibility, unity. It was a special time and both were aware. Mary Rose put her brush down and came to sit with Patrick. He dropped the fife to his lap.

"Donno' stop."

"J.J. said not too much at a time."

She nodded agreement and took his injured hand. "Feel better?" She asked as she massaged it.

Strange sensations traveled from her touch to his core—as if he had never felt anything before, his senses magnified. Patrick took a deep breath and smiled.

"Ye me nurse?"

"Nay, me be but a girl. Ye be but a boy." She laughed her wondrous way and he laughed with her, but she did not release his hand. "It be two weeks, since ye came here. Da say ye half healed of ye injuries. At least two more weeks in the cast. He say ye needs more healin' than the arm. Do ye know what he means?"

"Aye. He teachin' me how to pass by all the hard things in life."

"Da be good at that."

They took some time to be quiet and together. Talk did not seem important. Neither wanted to find a reason to end the pastoral perfection of this time and place. Patrick and Mary Rose were one with the earth, the sun, the river, the trees, and the light. Neither of them knew what it was all about. They were just there—together. Mary Rose did not realize she was still holding Patrick's hand. Patrick was not going to move a muscle or tendon so she would.

Finally, she broke the spell. "We be the best of friends." She took her hand back without embarrassment, got up to put her paints and brushes away.

"Did I tell, I used to draw pictures on the wall at the workhouse?"

"Pictures?"

"Aye, me job was paintin' walls but before coverin' the grey walls with new whitewash, me painted pictures. Even used wood ash for shadin'."

"What kind of pictures?"

"Likeness of me family. 'Twas like visiting them but all erased," Patrick drew his hand through the air, "a'fore the workboss could see 'em."

"If'n I was to give ye some of paint would ye paint again?"

"Maybe," he laughed as he put his fife away, gathered her easel and stool into the cloth bag. They started the walk back.

"Now that I know ye draw and hear ye play—Patrick, ye be an artist, too." There was pure joy and delight in her voice.

Patrick had never in his whole life felt so good. So wonderfully good. Not even back in the cottage, on the hills. Mary Rose could not see his face as she walked beside him but there was a glow to his smile and a light in his eyes.

Chapter 33

Healing continued for Patrick and bonding continued for the unusual family unit at J.J. Dwyer's Livery Stable. Each day J.J., Mary Rose, and Patrick had a routine of work and meals. Mary Rose and Patrick found time for their music and painting—sometimes together—sometimes not. Patrick became stronger and required less rest. The fully restored saddle that Patrick had worked on emerged as a thing of beauty. J.J. posted a bulletin on his door inviting his customers to bring saddles in disrepair. J.J. would do the mending; Patrick would work the leather to renewed life and beauty. Restoring saddles made him feel better about accepting food and bed from J.J. He planned to go to the local pubs again to earn money, as soon as the splint came off. He truly missed the camaraderie of other musicians.

Changes were made in the tack room to make it a more human place. The horse blanket was exchanged for bed linens; a washbowl, a razor, and a stand with a mirror were provided to tend to the emerging beard. A couple of hooks that once held harnesses gave him a place for clothes and a towel. Patrick was comfortable and pleased with the meager accommodations. No more meal trays; he was expected at the table.

On the wall beside his bed, Patrick hung a recently completed, small portrait of Fiona and made room for one he was painting of Annie.

At quiet times he remembered and mourned each of his family members. With J.J.'s help he turned these thoughts to positives. "Ye canno' change what God has wrought for each, only what the possibilities are for ye self, Patrick," was said to him, over and over. And he accepted that for Ma, Da, Sean, Mavis.... but never fully for Fiona. The responsibility he accepted for her well-being could not be put aside. It could be forestalled for a while but not forever.

The splint came off on a long-anticipated day. Patrick was surprised at how emaciated his forearm was. The bone was healed but the arm was weak and almost useless. His shoulder was stiff—with limited motion. J.J. noticed the shocked look on Patrick's face as he gazed at the unrecognizable limb.

"Worry not, lad. Ye muscles have rested a long time. Exercise and they soon be strong again. Mary Rose! Come, help Patrick with his exercises." She gladly responded and aided in Patrick's recovery again. They spent an hour each morning and evening working with the arm and shoulder that had been immobilized so long. It was the best part of his day.

"Patrick," she announced during a morning exercise session, "workin' on the washboard is perfect exercise for ye. Let's go there—get the laundry done and ye exercise, too." She laughed at her cleverness.

"As long as it be for me shoulder and arm but no longer."

She was right. The pushing and pulling of the wet weighted items and the wringing to get the water out did exercise the exact muscles Patrick needed. He pretended to mind the woman's work but saw it was good. He enjoyed every excuse to do *anything* with Mary Rose.

Most of the day—March tenth—marking his birth, Patrick thought about his mother. In the evening, Mary Rose prepared mutton and potatoes and the newly formed family sat for dinner and celebrated the occasion. When the plates were clean, Patrick played a familiar tune, J.J. and Mary Rose sang. It was very festive. J.J. brought his bottle of apple cider to the table. Mary Rose filled the glasses; J.J. raised his in a toast.

"To Patrick on his sixteenth birthday, to the blessings in this family, to the future which we canno' know but is full o' promise." They drank hearty and sang one more song with Patrick's music.

Mary Rose began the clean-up. J.J. invited Patrick to sit outside the kitchen door while he enjoyed smoking his pipe. The early evening was warm, and the smell of spring was in the air.

"Sixteen, lad. On the brink of manhood."

"Do no' feel like a man."

"No happen on one day, but day by day. I be wantin' to talk to ye about goin to America. Still ye plan?"

"Aye. To America and then seek Fiona in Canada."

J.J. put his pipe down and took a moment to find his opening words. He had planned this discussion with Patrick for many days.

"Ye canno' do that *now.* No money, no prospects, no direction."

Patrick interrupted. "Aye," in the most dejected voice, "I canno' stay here and canno' go either."

"Give me a chance to tell me thoughts. Time to listen, Patrick. Ye can stay here as a place of preparation. Finish ye journey into manhood. Make a plan that will work. Ye have found how difficult it is to make ye way on the roads and byways. Imagine how it would be in America in the same situation." He resumed smoking and gave Patrick time to think about what he said. "Stay in the tack room, take ye meals here. Know each day ye has a safe place—no alleyways, no beatin's, no thievin'. No more runnin' away. No more punishin' ye self. Be the piper, take the fife to pubs, save money, work in the stable for ye keep. A little more recovery, a little more growin' up, and a little more plannin'. Right here at J.J. Dwyer's Livery. Ye will know when ye are ready to go. And, Fiona still be there, makin' her way, too. We pray to God for her way. That is all to be done for her until ye are ready." He blew several smoke rings and waited for effect. "Take an honest look at Patrick Doyle. Would he be any help to Fiona as he be today?"

It was a profound question—one that Patrick had to consider. He stood up and walked in a circle before J.J. Then he took his fife out and began playing a soulful tune. He acknowledged J.J. with a nod and walked toward the hills behind the stable. Mary Rose came from the kitchen when she heard his music and saw Patrick disappear behind the stable. J.J. pointed, indicating she should follow.

"Follow the music, Mary Rose." She dried her hands on her apron, pulled it off and dropped it before she ran like lightning.

When she rounded the corner, she heard a lively tune drifting over the meadow at the crest of the hill. Patrick turned, played several more bars of happy music, dropped his fife, gave Mary Rose a broad smile and ran to her.

"Mary Rose," he declared, his eyes wide, obviously happy to see her there. His happiness swept to her before him. She was not sure what the transformation was or why his music went from melancholy to joyous. She just opened her arms. The embrace was spontaneous and warm. He lifted her and spun her around.

"Patrick!" She found her footing and laughed the laugh that he had come to expect and love. They were both a bit dizzy. "Are we still celebratin' ye birthday?"

"We are celebratin'.... nay me birthday, ...me life." He took her hand and drew her to sit on the grass where they usually painted. Mary Rose gave him her devoted attention. She became quiet and waited for his words.

"J.J. wants me to stay here and work on a plan for the future. I'm gonna do it." He squeezed her hand. This was the most profound decision of his young life. He made it without Ma or Da or Willie. Patrick reached deep inside and knew time for running, fearing, or dreaming was over. The ever-elusive plan was spreading out before him. "'Tis hard to believe. I'm gonna do it—just as J.J. says. No runnin' away. No strikin' out." He took a breath, realizing he was talking too fast. "Me acceptin' J.J.'s help. I thought I could no' but I can." *Accept help!* An idea he had always rejected. "I do need help and I do not need to be alone. No runnin'," he repeated. "No runnin' to nowhere. Stay here." He was so excited he could not sit on the grass with her. He started walking around while talking. In his excitement he spoke the language he learned in school. His head went high and shoulders squared...

Mary Rose could see the change in, not only Patrick's music, but in him. *He not just a boy,* she mused as he went on.

"When I decided to stay, when I told myself 'twas what I should do, I became excited and happy. That changed my music." He came back to her and knelt before her. "I can look in the mirror now and be me. Mary Rose, I can be me. You can be you. 'Tis wonderful." He took a deep breath and spread full body out on the cool spring sod.

"Well, Patrick Doyle, Mary Rose be what me was all along, in case ye never noticed. 'Twas ye who saw nothing in ye mirror!" She laughed and lay down beside him. They laughed and laughed and laughed—giggles of youth and laughter of joy—sounds of happiness.

Finally, when their laughter waned and they began to wonder what seemed so funny a moment ago, she sat up and said, "Patrick Doyle, the discovered one, time to feed the chickens. Me hopes they can see ye." Mary Rose ran off to the kitchen.

Patrick scattered the chicken feed feeling good about everything—good about himself—good about his decision—good about J.J. and Mary Rose. Especially about Mary Rose. He recalled her flying into his arms and, forgetting he was holding a bucket, dropped it. The cracked corn spread over the ground. The chickens joined Patrick in glee. Shooing the birds and gathering up the corn, Patrick laughed out loud.

That night he lay awake in bed. Many thoughts kept him awake. He thought back to the full year since leaving the workhouse and wished he could talk to Willie. For the first time in twelve months, he believed he had a plan and a safe place to work on it. He had true regret for leaving Sallie as he did. He did not know what he could say to explain, He only knew he could not stay in that abundant life.

Patrick's thoughts went to his Mother. He got out of bed and found paper and pen in J.J.'s desk and wrote to his mother. Patrick hoped she would get it. He knew she could not buy postage to write back so there was no return address. He wrote in the language she would appreciate.

Annie Doyle
Portumna Workhouse
Portumna, County Galway

Dear Ma, I am in a good safe place. Today is my birthday. I know you are thinking of me. I work and play my fife. I miss you and my family but try to go on. Make sure Mavis remembers me.

Love, Patrick Doyle

At the bottom he drew a picture of himself playing the fife. For the rest of Annie's life this little note and picture was tucked in the bosom pocket she sewed in her frock. Other than Mavis, it was all she had of her cottage life and family.

The next day, when Mary Rose and Patrick were gone, J.J. walked into the tack room to hang up a harness and saw Fiona's picture on the wall. It was the face of the girl in his visions—the faraway girl. He sat on the bed and studied the face he had seen before. He knew the lines of chin, the look in her eyes and her persona. Fiona came into focus for J.J. He had seen so her many times. Today she had a name—Fiona Doyle. She was the young girl tending children. He had seen her walking across the workhouse yard, looking back. He saw her sailing away from Ireland with the same sad eyes. He saw her in her new home with a child and swollen with another in womb. He saw her with a husband. Her eyes had changed—no longer sad. Almost on demand, he stayed with the vision, trying to learn all he could about Patrick's sister.

When he finally walked out of the tack room, several hours had passed. J.J. was exhausted and hungry. He went for a piece of bread and to bed. Mary Rose found her father in bed in the late afternoon. "Ye ill, Da?" She asked. "Needin' tea?"

"No' ill but tea would be nice. Worn out."

"Oh, dear. Visions again?" She put the kettle on. His special gift was often taxing.

"Aye. It be a while since such."

"Me hopin' it no' be hard on ye, Da."

"Me has to think about it but...." He stopped to gather his first impression, which she understood, ".... Aye, 'twas a *good* vision. Me not distressed, just tired."

"Good." His visions could be very stressful and often foretold tragedy. He smiled to reassure his daughter. "Wait until tomorrow to figure it out, Da. Dinner soon and we'll have Patrick give us music before the piper goes to town with that fife o'his."

❧ ❧ ❧

J.J. was quiet during dinner. Mary Rose had seen her father like this many times. She picked up the conversation with animation, which Patrick fully enjoyed. "We need a bit of music before ye go out tonight, Patrick. Something lively."

He went for the fife to accommodate her. With Mary Rose's attention, he was most inspired and finished with his new latest composition.

"A new tune?" she asked, "Are there words?"

"No words, yet. I just wrote it last week." He was too

embarrassed to tell her it was titled, *Mary Rose*. He changed the subject. "Will ye be comin' to the pub tonight? I be goin' to the Jolly Tinker. Love t' have ye."

"Maybe aye, maybe nay. Ye never know," she teased.

J.J. walked to the door with Patrick. "A'fore ye go, lad. Me needs to talk to ye." They walked together down the lane. "Me needs to tell ye. Ye sister, Fiona was in me eyes."

"Fiona?" Patrick interrupted.

"Listen t'me," J.J. took his arm to stop the walking. "She be contented. There in the vision. Not distressed. Me can only assure ye. Me never understand it all but 'tis me feelin'. She waitin' but nay cryin'."

"Thank ye, J.J.," was all Patrick could manage to say.

Chapter 34

All through the next week, Patrick tested himself for old feelings. The familiar urge to flee came unbidden at night and in the early morning. It became a fear that he had to struggle with. Da's words came to him again and again, cautioning him to resist *foolishness*. The *unknown*, which had always looked better than the *known*, did not entice him from J.J. Dwyer Livery Stable. That simple fact finally settled into his being. Patrick did not run.

Day by day he became more assured of the path mapped out ahead. He now had the means to be safe and work for the money to go to America. It was a blessing he would not even have thought to ask for, not even of God. The words that stayed in his mind were, *soon, when I'm ready.* The constant in his days was Mary Rose.

Patrick could not be fully content—there was Fiona, always Fiona. Thoughts of her caused a restlessness but he was learning to be happy again.

Sunday was a day of rest at the livery stable. This one was warm and sunny. After mass, the small family had a cold meal. J.J. dozed in his chair. Mary Rose gathered her easel and painting materials and headed out. She knew Patrick would find her later. He went to the tack room for his fife. Before heading out to find Mary Rose, he polished his fife, played one tune, put it away, and stopped in to check on J.J.

Patrick was shocked to see J.J. with a guest in the kitchen. "Sallie," he exclaimed. "Sallie," he repeated as she rose to come to him. *Here, Sallie here?* He thought, as he froze in the doorway.

Sallie was a lovely vision—her hair loose on her shoulders and her full-skirted, cotton dress floating around her. He had a quick flashback to the luxury which surrounded her...and yet, she fit in this humble place.

J.J. spoke. "I told ye I wrote to Miss Sallie Brennen to say ye are safe. Ye wanted her to know."

Sallie looked twice at Patrick. Her smile was steady and did not reveal her surprise at his appearance. He had changed so much. Not the skinny boy of last year. His hair was darker, the red subdued. His shoulders broader and he stood taller.

"I came straight away after my last tour." She took him by the shoulder and looked into his eyes. "Hello, Patrick. So good to see you and know you are well. I heard your music drift in from the stable." She smiled a happy and generous smile that told him she was not angry. "Beautiful, lad, as always."

"Sallie." He could only say her name.

"Sit down. I be lettin' ye have some time wit' Miss Brennen." J.J. picked up his pipe and headed for the door. "I'll tell Mary Rose of our guest."

Patrick was ill at ease; Sallie was relaxed and radiant. She straightened the full skirt, sat, and invited him to relax with her casual air. "Patrick, go get your fife," she directed. "Play for me." While he was gone, she looked around the simple, well-kept kitchen. This household was not wealthy but enough for the Dwyers, plus one. "Ah, yes, the beautiful fife." Patrick had returned. She laid her hand on the fife and started with the words she came to say before he could blow a note.

"I want to tell you I am sorry. It was not wise of me to cast you into school and touring so suddenly. It was not right for you. Too soon out of the workhouse. So...." She looked him square in the eye with a soft gaze. "Patrick, I understand why you left, and I....am.... sorry."

"I am sorry to leave without talking to you." Patrick used his best schooling language for her.

Sallie gave Patrick the first hug ever and pulled back with a quiet laugh. "Well," she said, bringing the mood up, "let's have some music now." It was the only way he could relax and make it through this awkward reunion.

Patrick happily obliged with a bright, fast pub tune that had her tapping her foot. On the next familiar tune, she sang. "That was fun. I don't get to sing for fun very often. I think the last time was at Biddy McGee's when I came to hear you. Remember?"

They reminisced about those days and their tour around the coast. He recalled the hard parts and she recalled the excellence of the performances. Together they honestly pieced together how good, and bad, it was.

"I was never comfortable."

"I was too selfish to see." She reached across and embraced him again, finishing the apologies. "Another tune, Patrick." He played and she sang again.

Sallie went to the bag she had deposited at the door. "I brought your things—the clothes, and this." She took out the leather bag for the fife. Then she handed him a pouch which jingled with coins. "One pound, twelve shillings. I told you there would be a payment to you when the receipts came in."

Then with laughter she chastised him with an exaggerated brogue. "Never leave wit'out ye pay, lad."

Conversation turned from the past to now. "I had a long talk with J.J. He is a fine man and has your interest at heart. This is a good place."

"Aye. And you haven't met Mary Rose, yet."

"Are you still planning to go to America?" He could see that she was interested in what he wanted to do. Unlike last fall, when her interest was only what she wanted him to do. He settled back in the chair and told her of his determination to prepare for success in America and finding Fiona. "J.J. has made me see that I need to prepare before going. He and Mary Rose are giving me a safe place. I am happy here, but I will go.... when I am ready."

"What of Willie, did he come to Dublin?"

"Nay, Willie is in Philadelphia. Sailed with your brother some time last year. He is a fine carpenter working in a furniture shop. Willie finding his own way."

"That is good. You will be finding your own way...actually, I think you have found your way. The next term at the Academy starts May first. What do you think about going back for the summer session?" You must see the value in it, especially in America. If you go back to school, you will not only be able to work with an orchestra, you can write, perform, and even teach music. Your fife and music will be the key to your future, no matter where you are. I will advance tuition—a loan, if that will make you feel better."

"A loan. Yes, Sallie, a loan. Let me begin." He reached in the pouch and took out two of his shilling coins. "This is the best start on my future. Here." It was an important part of his preparation for the future—paying his own way and accepting an obligation for it. Sallie took the coins.

"Let me know if you want to join me on stage again. I leave that up to you. No traveling. The Academy always posts my local concerts."

Patrick felt better. He had some clothes, some money, and more support than he thought possible. *Back to the Academy,* he was excited by the thought. He always liked school and did well with his studies. It was a long walk from the stable to the Academy, but he could do it. He began to think of rising early, doing work for J.J., going to school and returning in time to help Mary Rose with the evening chores. And starting all over the next day. *A real plan!* Screamed in his brain.

Sallie called him back from his reveries. "Patrick, we never know if we can accomplish all our goals but nothing assures it more than diligence. If a poor girl from Clarinbridge can travel from country to country and across the sea singing, a piper from Portumna can play his fife for the world. It matters not if that world is in a livery stable, a pub or on a concert stage. It matters only that you know you can do it all. Believe it."

As Sallie was finishing her speech, Mary Rose came into the kitchen. She advanced to Sallie and curtsied. "Miss Brennen, my pleasure. Mary Rose Dwyer." She extended her hand.

"Mary Rose, my pleasure."

"If n' ye have finished talkin', I be makin' tea. Da's comin'. Tea and biscuit for all on this special visitor's day."

"Lovely." Sallie accepted the invitation. "Paddy, a little music to help the colleen with her tea making." It turned into a party.

After tea and easy conversation, Sallie bid J.J. and Mary

Rose, good-bye. "'Twas a lovely afternoon. I hope I can come again to see Patrick and his new family." She took his hand. "Walk me to my carriage, Paddy."

At the carriage she asked him to sit beside her. "I have more to tell you." She waited for him to settle on the carriage seat. "My brother Jacob has half of your fare to America from Malcolm Anderson. He is keeping that for you. In truth, with what is in the pouch, and the two shillings you gave me, there is enough for steerage passage." She took the two coins out and offered them back. "You are sixteen now. You can be on his next crossing..." she paused, knowing how profound this was, "...to America. Now." She leaned back and let silence and the magnitude of the facts sweep over Patrick.

He looked off to the distance blankly. *Now,* he thought. "Fiona," he whispered. This did not relate to the impossible dream he once had. This had nothing to do with the unknown place he would go. This had nothing to do with the awkward unprepared boy he was. It was about reality. *Get on board. Sail. Now.*

Patrick climbed down from the carriage, walked away from Sallie and all that she said. His hand caressed the fife in the leather pouch, but he did not take it out to play. The air stirred and a bird chirped as Patrick walked a wide circle in the afternoon sun. Sallie's gaze was steady upon him but he did not look at her. She and the fife were distractions to the thinking he had to do. They were a refuge he had to ignore.

Sail. Now? Patrick had been to this place before and he let Jacob Brennen sail without him. He thought again as he walked another circle and thought of Willie. Sallie did not hear him speak aloud, "Willie." Willie had been his confidence, his ability, his courage, his crutch. Now, as he walked the maze of his thinking, Patrick knew. He would sail when he did not need all he thought Willie provided.

And now, standing beside the carriage with all the possibilities Sallie presented, he knew why. It was a revelation and epiphany. "I was not ready to sail with Jacob Brennen last year..." he paused for clarity, and looked up at Sallie, "...and I am not ready now." Patrick climbed back in the carriage and gently pushed her hand with the shillings back. "The time is not right for Patrick or Fiona Doyle. I will return to the Academy and continue getting ready. I will go but not now."

"Paddy, I am so happy to hear you say that. You are growing up and you will, someday soon, be ready."

Patrick smiled for Sallie. He was not anguished by his decision.

"One more thing before I leave." Sallie demanded his attention with a serious tone. "Remember when we were in Galway and I went off for business?" Patrick nodded. "I went to Portumna to see your Ma." He sat up. "She is fine....and a lovely mother. I told her of the tour and the Academy. She gave her blessings to all your efforts with your music and schooling. She truly wants you to go ahead with your life and appreciates any and all who help you."

Patrick was quiet for a moment. "Ma believes in schooling." And with that broke into tears. "Ma," was all he could say.

"'Tis alright, lad. Ye Ma would not cry. She be so brave. Ye be brave, too." Sallie went to her native speech for this boy from Portumna. "What we do for ye future, we do for Annie Doyle."

"Thank ye, Sallie Brennen. Ye give me the best present of

all."

As he climbed out of the carriage, she said, "Mary Rose be named right—like a lovely rose. Me likes the lass."

"Me, too," he shouted back as he ran for the hill behind the stable.

Chapter 35

Warm spring days made everything easier around J.J. Dwyer's Livery Stable. The grass grew and horses grazed. The earth was soft and receptive, so Mary Rose planted the kitchen garden. Patrick greeted each new day with anticipation of his chores, his fife, and time with Mary Rose. His arm and shoulder were fully recovered. He could lift saddles onto the wooden horse. Watching aged and neglected leather come back to beauty, softness, and flexibility gave Patrick a sense of accomplishment. The stream of work seemed endless as word passed though the horse community. J.J. offered Patrick a share of every shilling earned but Patrick refused. "Nay, J.J. 'Twill pay for me keep here." He was adamant.

Patrick developed a discipline about his work and went straight to it from breakfast. He resisted seeking Mary Rose until late afternoon so they both could meet their obligations before the pleasure of time together.

As soon as his arm was strong enough to play the fife for hours, Patrick took it and went to the closest pubs where his reception into the circle of musicians was assured. His hat was set on the floor. Each night a few pence accumulated. Although small sums, his pouch grew. Pence or not, his pleasure was being in the pubs making music. After a few weeks he became known and welcomed. His arrival at the various pubs was anticipated and received with applause. "The piper be here!" was the call when he and his fife arrived for an evening. "The piper be here!" became his greeting all over southeast Dublin down by the Liffey.

He sat in the tack room one afternoon and composed a music piece he called *The Piper Be Here.* It was lively and distinctive, and it featured all the special sounds Patrick could produce. The piece always commanded attention and certainly dancing. Patrick became a showman. He entered the pub with his fife to his lips and played his newly composed tune. Soon patrons in the pub could hear him approaching. They began to greet him chanting, "The piper be here. The piper be here." Shortly thereafter the musicians in each pub played along with Patrick on his entrance. In this pub, on this evening, with this entry, all would know it was a special night of music—Paddy Doyle, the piper, was here. Occasionally J.J and Mary Rose came to the pub to be with their minor celebrity. J.J. stayed for hours to enjoy the music, drink and atmosphere. Mary Rose always went home early but never left without a special smile for Patrick.

❧ ❧ ❧

Mary Rose became more and more dedicated to her painting. She ventured further down the river to get away from the city and closer to the pastoral scenes that she loved. Her work came easier when Patrick played his fife while she worked. His fingers danced over the fife; his eyes followed her form. The fife music told of her beauty, her charm, her unaware enchantment. He noted the sun on her golden hair and the blowing of her full skirt. Time became unimportant, as did the setting of the sun. They stayed as long as they could.

Patrick was falling in love. His mind was full of Mary Rose. His dreams included her. He was not sure what to do with these feelings, he just spent great blocks of time looking at her—while she painted, fixed meals, fed chickens or did chores around the stable.

"The light is leaving us," Mary Rose announced as he helped her to pack up.

"Mary Rose, I have watched ye paint wonderful pictures but except for two in the kitchen, I never see 'em again. Where?"

"They be sold. The English want them for their manor house. One bought to go to America. Me paintin' gets to America afore ye, Patrick." Mary Rose continued to answer his question. "A man walkin' up the Liffey saw me paintin' of the river and went to the stable to ask Da if he could buy it. It be painted wit' me first paints and brushes. After it be sold, Da gave me money for easel, many brushes and paints. See all this?" She pointed to her easel, palette and brushes. "Did ye wonder where me gets such? Three pictures painted and sold." They began the walk back to the stable.

"Ye paint to sell?"

"Nay, me paints because that be what I love. Like ye fife, money not the reason. But, can be the result. Da put the money away for me. We be alike, Patrick. Be it paintin' or playin' the fife. It be for makin' a dream."

"What's your dream?" he asked as they reached the stable.

The conversation had become too serious for her. "Me dreamin' of a knight in shiny armor, ride on a white horse and takin' me off to his castle." She turned her laughing eyes to him. "Fool!" With that she dropped everything she was carrying, except her canvas, and ran for the kitchen. "Meanwhile, best get dinner on the table. Ye do the dreamin'," she called back.

As he gathered up the easel, brushes and paints, Patrick looked at the empty space she had, moments ago, filled. He wanted to chase her, to catch her. Instead, he took his lovesick self into the stable and cleaned her brushes.

❧ ❧ ❧

J.J. was in the kitchen when Mary Rose came in carrying her latest picture. "Ah, me love. Another masterpiece?" He asked.

"Another picture, for sure, Da." She turned it so he could see the perfectly executed scene he knew so well. "Not for sale, this one. Me loves that spot down the river and me never wants to forget it."

"Aye, 'tis a beauty and to be kept," he agreed. And, in that moment he saw her hanging this picture in her own home. The vision was clear, but the home was foreign. He studied the edges of the vision but could not see where it was. He knew by his feelings; it was her own home—not the livery stable in Dublin.

Mary Rose walked over to her father and hugged his neck, bringing him back from his vision to the kitchen.

Chapter 36

From May first, when the session started at the Academy, through the whole year, Patrick was busy. He rose early, worked in the stable and then walked across Dublin to Pearse Street by nine o'clock. He left with a slice of bread and cheese in his pocket for lunch, refusing Sallie's offer to pay for his meals. His fife was stored in its bag, strapped over his shoulder, and firmly carried under his arm. Classes during the morning included music theory and history, plus language arts. Patrick was expected to speak with proper pronouns and verbs at school. In the afternoon he had *practicals*, with the other students—it was the time to be a piper, so he pulled the fife from its pouch. Once a month the Academy held student concerts. Sallie came to listen when she could. On those days Patrick was late returning to the livery stable.

It became a way of life and Patrick thrived in it. He loved the classes and the opportunity to broaden his musical experience. He played with musicians on every level—professional, experienced, and novice. He studied, he piped, he learned, and he thrived.

In this busy life the boy matured, not only in attitude but in appearance. Patrick's confident air made him stand taller, hold his head higher. His written assignments began to reflect what he believed in, what he was gaining, and what he was learning to give. The Academy and his work at the stable filled his days, but he had two other things he needed time for—Mary Rose and the pubs. They were easy because he loved both. On Tuesday and Thursday evenings he went back to the pubs in the center of Dublin near the Academy. They were his old haunts and Patrick was remembered. The patrons and musicians in The Crown, O'Grady's, The Leprechaun, and Full Pint greeted him warmly. "The piper be back! Play Paddy, play!" His hat was laid out and he brought the fife to his lips. It was as if he had not been away eighteen months. A few pence were gained and often an evening meal provided before he began the walk home.

On Monday, Wednesday, and Friday Patrick moved quickly after his last class to be in the kitchen with Mary Rose to set the table. "I am going to feed the chickens while you finish dinner, Mary Rose."

"And, who be ye, me lad? Speakin' such?" She chastised when he forgot to adjust his grammar for home life. "If'n ye see Patrick Doyle yonder, tell 'im, me be lookin' for 'im."

"Ye niver be lookin' far for Patrick. He be next to ye, a pest and bother. Always in ye way." He shot back to her.

After dinner, Patrick held out his hand. Mary Rose took it and they walked out together to enjoy the long summer day and each other. It was as natural as the sun and the rain, and needed as well to nurture life around the livery stable.

Late in July, the Academy held its Annual Mid-Summer Music concert. Patrick spotted Sallie in the audience and fully expected her to wait for him afterwards—she always did. He put his fife away, threw the loop over his shoulder and hurried to the side entrance. She greeted him with a hug. Sallie and

Patrick's relationship had become easy and comfortable. "It was wonderful, Paddy."

"I love playing with the orchestra. You see the conductor has made a place for the piper. My fife notes are soft, but pure, and he knows how to use them."

"That's what music education gives you—understanding and possibilities."

"And appreciation of all music. I can love this and pub music, too. I remember the days when I thought I had to choose."

She hooked her arm into his elbow. "Walk me to my flat, Paddy." They walked, just enjoying being together in the warm, still light, summer night. When they arrived at her door, she insisted he come in for a minute. "I have something for you." In the drawing room a light spread of biscuits, cheese and room-temperature tea waited. She poured. "Here....," she reached in her purse, ".... this is from your mother." Sallie handed him a folded letter and started for the foyer. "You can read it here, alone.... or take it with you. Which do you prefer?"

"I do not think I could walk all the way home with this in my pocket." The food before him was forgotten. He unfolded the letter as she disappeared. "Ma," he whispered as he began to read. Annie's beautiful face was before him. He saw her smile and her sad eyes of the more recent past.

Patrick my son. The Doyle family is no more. Only me, you and Fiona. We are survivors and the workhouse could not make us less. Mavis died in May. I leave the workhouse now. I have a job and room as nanny to three young children in Derry. Mr. Anderson spoke for me. I am gone when you read this. I trust Sallie Brennen can give you this letter. I do not worry for you are strong and able to make your way. Find your life and only look back to find happy memories of our family at our cottage at the foot of the hill. If love can keep us together, you are never far from me. My heart beats for you and Fiona. My mind is full of Da, Sean and Mavis.

Your mother,

Annie Doyle

Fiona—Glace Bay Cape Breton Island Nova Scotia Canada

He called Sallie back in the room.

"Are ye alright, lad?" she asked.

"Aye, it's a lot. Ma has left the workhouse and is in Derry as a nanny. Mavis died....," he stopped to count the weeks. ".... gone about twelve weeks. No mourning for my little sister." His voice told of his deep despair. He handed the letter to Sallie and gave her time to read.

"I am so sorry, Paddy. So sorry." She read down to the last line and looked up at Patrick. "Now you know where Fiona is."

"Aye. And, I must go." He took the letter back, pressed it to his chest, grabbed his fife and moved toward the door.

"Patrick, you must still consider wisely what you will do and when you will do it. Your mother did not mean to give you urgency."

He heard her words and clutched the precious letter as he left with a backward shout. "Thank you, Sallie." And, ran all the way to the livery stable.

Chapter 37

As he bounded across the Butt Bridge, Mary Rose nearly ran into him coming the other way. She was out of breath. He took her into his arms and held tight. Together they breathed—in and out, clinging together.

"What's happened, Patrick? Da told me to run to the bridge to meet ye. He said ye needed me. Why?"

"Sallie had a letter from Ma. Full of sadness." He handed her the letter and found a place beside the river where they could sit. She read it once, then twice and gave it back. Mary Rose gave Patrick time. She did not speak; she waited.

"Mary Rose, my family gone like the setting sun. It went piece-by-piece, chopped and ended by the workhouse. The Doyles went in to live, not starve to death, and we be just as lost as if we starved, one by one. We starved not for food but for one another. 'Tis another kind of hunger." He turned and demanded her eyes. "I thought I could bring them back to the cottage and be happy again. All I had to do was want it bad eenough and strive to do it." His chin went to his chest. "Nay, nay, niver." The negatives were low guttural mutterings. His eyes closed; his body went limp. His hands could not hold the letter. The breeze picked it up and carried it. Mary Rose jumped to catch it. "Let it go," he commanded.

Mary Rose would not let this last bit of Patrick's mother blow away. She ran along the edge of the river, following the wind. She grabbed at it to keep it out of the water and fell in. Her arm raised high, except for a few splashes, she kept the water from the ink, but she was wet up to her waist. When she looked back, Patrick had disappeared.

"Be at the stable, Patrick," she prayed as she climbed up the bank. "Do no' run from us," she implored. "Dear God," she turned it over to Him and started her walk home sloshing in wet shoes and heavy in her wet skirt, carrying Annie Doyle's letter.

Patrick was not in the kitchen. He was not in the tack room. J.J. had not seen him. Mary Rose carefully laid out the letter to dry and went to bed with a heavy heart but refusing to cry—weeping would mean she had given up on him.

❧ ❧ ❧

Breakfast was somber for J.J and Mary Rose. No Patrick. They worried in silence, neither voicing their fears for Patrick. After the mid-day meal, Mary Rose's spirits lifted. "He'll be on the hill," she told her father. After she ate, she gathered her paint supplies, and hurried out.

Patrick was not on the hill.

At dinner, she was totally distraught. "Da, look to a vision. Where be Patrick?"

"Ye know it do no' work like that. Me only know, in me heart, Patrick be well."

"He comin' back?" She asked, nearly begging.

❧ ❧ ❧

The days are long in Ireland in mid-July. The setting sun waits until past ten at night before it yields to the horizon. For two nights, Mary Rose, against her father's advice, sat by the kitchen door to watch for Patrick. It had been forty-eight hours since he left her by the bridge. She had suffered through every one of them. The sun sank low, the ten o'clock hour struck. As she gathered herself to go into the kitchen, she heard soft fife notes drifting in the twilight air. Mary Rose took a deep breath of relief, let her skirt down and resumed her seat to wait a bit longer. She sat, silent and unmoving. It seemed an eternity before the piper came out of the evening mist.

She looked at him with new eyes. He was taller, more manly than she had noticed before. Patrick was not a boy. He was a man, and as such, required her to contain herself, not run like a schoolgirl to him. She had to allow him to have control and she had to show control, too. By the time he crossed the meadow and drew close, it was dark.

"Patrick." Her voice told him she was there, beside the kitchen door. He lowered the fife and saw her.

"Mary Rose." He said nothing more as he took the chair next to her, ceremonially put his fife away, drew the strings around the pouch, and reached for her hand—as if he were getting things in order.

He spoke to her in his new improved language—still with some soft inflections of old Ireland. Between the old ways and the new, Patrick was unsure. He was confused but he took her hand, he tried to tell her how he felt.

"I been down by the Liffey watching the endless river flow by. 'Tis like life, going on, no matter what. When I put my hand in it and pulled it out again—'twas as if me be nothing in this life. But when I launched a leaf, it floated on and on, a part of life. Be making sense?" He turned and looked at Mary Rose. Even in the dark he could see her soft countenance and approving smile. "Me trying to stay on top, not get over washed and overwhelmed with life itself. That where I be all night and all day. How long, Mary Rose? I lost track of time."

"Have ye eaten?" She wanted to tend to him.

"Nay, I wanted to be hungry. It makes me stronger. Even in the workhouse, I missed meals so the memory of our starvation would not be lost. That gnawing in my stomach and the quest to relieve the wanting, are strength to me. With so much on my mind, I needed hunger again. Hunger is not just for food; hunger for Ma, Da, Fiona, Sean and Mavis, for the cottage and the hills, for a good place to be. Now, I am learning to accept being fed. Ye and J.J. have taken some of that hunger from me. I be with ye to be fed, not by food, Mary Rose." He folded over his cramped stomach and rocked back and forth wrapping his body with his arms—his agony causing physical pain. "Things are clear with this pain."

Mary Rose gently placed her arm across his shoulder and with her other hand lifted his chin, looking into his distorted face. It took a lot of courage and determination to hold back her tears to give him the support he needed. She had to lean in close in the dark. He raised his eyes and saw love in the smile she had for him.

"Can ye eat now?"

"Aye, now."

At the table, he ate—slowly and deliberately small portions of soup and bread that Mary Rose set before him. There was no conversation; he was lost in thought as he released his hunger. She went to get the letter and laid it beside his plate. Patrick took it up and stopped eating. "You have fed me body and soul, Mary Rose." He touched his mother's signature. "Ye did no' let it blow away."

"To bed, Patrick. Tomorrow is another day. Ye and me, we be in it. Tunes to be piped, lessons to be studied, pictures to be painted, saddles to be cleaned, meals to be fixed and chickens to be fed."

He walked to the tack room and repeated the phase that stayed with him from Mary Rose's night song: "Ye and me, we be in it." *Ye and me, we be in it.*

Chapter 38

The next morning dawned bright and beautiful. Patrick slept past time to go to school and Mary Rose did not waken him. When he came alive the sun was high. J.J. and Mary Rose had gone to their chores. Breakfast was set for him. He ate and felt contentment. No need to judge his food, his place, his future. Time to just *be.* Not sure what contentment was, he went out to find her knowing that she was part of this new-morning feeling. He started around the stable and turned back, he needed his fife.

Mary Rose was hanging wash on the line. The breeze picked up the linens and put her in a cloud of white. Her hair was pulled loose and blew around her face as she tried to hold the tablecloth and push her hair back. Her laugh floated out to greet him. Amazing happiness engulfed Patrick as he heard her—even before he saw her.

The wind tipped over her basket and she went to the ground to save her wash from getting soiled. When Patrick arrived, she was awash with her laundry on the green grass. Her hair was helter-skelter. The cloth on the line was beating her head. Her cheeks were flushed from exertion and her eyes were flashing with frustration.

Patrick had never seen such a beautiful sight and rushed to join her. Mary Rose saw him running to her and suddenly began to laugh at the ridiculous scene. Her lilting laugh completed the joy for Patrick. He plopped down beside her.

"Would be wonderful to stay here with you, Mary Rose."

"Here? On the ground wit' d'laundry?"

"Here." He pushed the basket away and pulled her close. They knew in an instant, the laughing was over. This was serious.

"But....," he returned her steady gaze, "after this Academy session and the winter one, I be goin' to America and Canada. I promised Da, promised Fiona. America and Canada." He took a deep breath as Mary Rose waited. "In the next spring." He pushed here flying hair from her face with a touch that lingered on her cheek.

She squeezed his hand and leaned forward. Her face came to his face—closer than he had ever been. All that he knew of Mary Rose from a distance was within a breath. He saw a curl falling close to her eye, the few freckles across her nose, the peachy color of her cheeks, the outline of her chin, and the approach of her lips. Patrick waited on heaven and it came with the slight pressure of her mouth.

Mary Rose moved slowly back, and then, came to him again to receive his kiss.

Patrick knew he would never be the same. They were not ready to leave this place of discovery and revelation. So, they stayed on the ground—wrapped in love, desire and laundry. She took his hand and pressed his fingers to her cheek. He leaned in close to smell the joy of her. There was an ease in the air. A comfort in their being. Patrick placed his hand on the small of her back to pull her to him. Mary rose yielded. With their kisses, Patrick made all assumptions possible for their future.

The piper put his fife to his lips and played the wonderful music of their love. It *was lyrical, melodic and romantic.*

It swayed, it echoed, it had a smooth soft beat matching his heart. He moved the fife in circles as he blew the notes. Round and round at the end of the fife, he saw all that he had suffered and all that was his world today. The notes went higher; the fife moved in an orbit of discovery—he was the piper he had always been, and now, Mary Rose was part of his music. Patrick played full, complete, glutted, gorged, sated—no longer hungry.

Chapter 39

J.J. watched his only daughter grow into a woman. In the spring and summer of her seventeenth year. He saw Mary Rose laugh and light up when Patrick was around. She looked so much like her mother did on the day in June when they married. These were happy and sad thoughts. He did not want to see his daughter reach beyond the homestead for her future. But, J.J. was a wise man and knew it had to be.

During this profound time in the life of his daughter, J.J. was plagued with visions of the future. Sudden glimpses of Mary Rose or Patrick flashed when he was working, driving the horses or relaxing with his pipe. J.J. knew change was coming and he knew it would be big.

Mary Rose was like her mother in so many ways and one of the striking characteristics was her absolute confidence and certainty. She and her mother always seemed to know they were making the right choices. Now, at this time in her life, Mary Rose's obvious choice was the piper who had entered life in the livery stable. She began to prepare herself for a life with Patrick, starting with a frank discussion with J.J.

"Me life be wit' Patrick," were her opening words when they were alone after breakfast.

J.J. showed no surprise on his face or in his voice. "Ye and Patrick have discussed this?"

Mary Rose ignored his question and went on. "Da, me be thinkin'. We be so good together. Canno' have enough time together. Me canno' imagine me wit'out Patrick. That be what marriage is. Two, so good together?"

"Oh, Mary Rose....," he put out his hand to hold hers across the table, "if only ye mother be here to talk to ye. 'Tis a big part of it but, not everything. Takes love to get past the hard times life gives. Takes more than likin' to be wit' each other."

"Da, me lovin' Patrick."

"Does he love ye back? Goin' to America and then to Canada for his sister be his only thought. Ye could be left behind."

"Da, no left behind. Where Patrick goes, so goes Mary Rose," she spoke in a quiet tone laced with sadness. Mary Rose went to him, believing her words were hurting. J.J. drew her to his knee as he did when she was a child.

"Me love, do not put sadness in your words of joy and rich anticipation. If ye love Patrick and he be lovin' ye, sing it." He turned her to look in her face. "Make sure he loves ye, Mary Rose. His dream and plan are part of his being and ye must know if it includes ye. If so, your Da will sing wit' ye."

Mary Rose went quiet with her father's questions. She cleared the table; he lit his pipe. Each in their own thoughts. Finally, she put the plates down and announced. "Me be findin' answers to those questions, not only for ye, but for meself, too." Her smile was lit with confidence and happiness. She kissed her Da and danced and whirled toward the door. "Next March, Patrick be eighteen. Finished at the Academy in the fall. Almost eighteen by Christmas. "Maybe at Christmas next, it be announced. We be makin' our life together." Her words and thoughts were rolling out. "How old be Ma when ye two went to the Priest? Eh, Da?" As always, Mary Rose left a void when she disappeared.

J.J. headed out to the stable to think about what had been

said. "We be not eighteen," he muttered.

None of this surprised him. Since the day he found Patrick and brought him home, he looked on him as a son and he watched his daughter give her heart away. He knew someone would have a broken heart. If Mary Rose went to America, his would break. If Patrick left without Mary Rose, the pain would be hers. J.J. put his pipe aside and went into the stable to go on his knees to tell God how important his daughter's happiness was. He had to have faith in Patrick, too.

Mary Rose found Patrick in the chicken yard spreading feed. "Come, gather eggs with me," he invited. They went in the warm coop where the chicken smells were blended by the heat of the nests. Each egg, like a treasure, went into the basket while Mary Rose waited for the right words to come. Patrick took the egg basket from Mary Rose and took her hand.

"Will ye marry me? As soon as the Academy graduates me next spring?" She looked at him with astonishment, her big eyes stretched to their fullest. "Or at Christmas?" She was speechless. "I love you, Mary Rose." Patrick was rich with words and feelings. "We be so good together. Me canno' imagine days wit'out ye next to me."

"I love ye, like Fiona, but different. I love ye like nothing else I know. And thinkin' about ever being apart, tears me heart. Can I say these things to ye?"

"Aye, ye can, Patrick Doyle. Me knows what love is."

Then Mary Rose spoke and validated all of Patrick's choices, trials, and tribulations. She opened her lovely mouth, smiled, and said the words that gave his life meaning and made every step of his journey worthwhile

"We be goin' to America, Patrick—together."

Chapter 40

Six Years Later - 1859

Patrick and Mary Rose stepped off the ferry at Cape Breton Island, Nova Scotia, Canada. He took her hand, not only because she needed his, but because he needed hers. "The parish church, there," he pointed to the steeple above the trees and moved toward it. Patrick wanted to run to get the information he needed from the priest, but Mary Rose could not. She was six months pregnant.

"Easy, Love. We be there soon enough," She cautioned, knowing his anxiety.

Father Murphy welcomed the couple into his office. After offering tea and a chair for Mary Rose, he began. "Ye letter came last month, Patrick Doyle. I have been through our records for a marriage nine years ago. 'Twas February 15, 1850. Fiona Doyle to Walter Collins. Interesting notation—only the bride, Fiona Doyle, was Catholic. Most marriages of miners take place in the Anglican Church. But, the note says, 'by the request of the bride', they came here. That did not happen often."

"Do you know my sister, Fiona?"

"No. I have only been here a short time and cannot place Fiona Collins."

"How can we find her?" Patrick began to fear he would not.

The priest summoned Patrick to the window. "Look there," he pointed down the road toward rows of identical small, drab houses. "That row of connected homes. They are owned by the mine. Ask about. Someone will be able to tell where the

Collins' live. If not there, in homes beyond. All miners."

"Are ye ready, Mary Rose?" he took her elbow. He was impatient. "Fiona," he whispered as if he had to explain. Then he turned to thank the priest one more time before leaving.

She saw him coming. She knew it was him. Fiona dropped her hoe and ran. "Patrick," she screamed. "Patrick," she cried. "Paddy," she exhaled a prayer to God. Her words soared into the breeze. "Me knew, me knew! Ye'd come." She called as she flew to him.

Patrick was there. His arms went around, and she melted into them. He lifted her, light as a feather. All left-over burdens of his life in the workhouse evaporated. All promises kept, all faith assured, all hope realized. Fiona was everything he ever loved, everything he lost, everything he treasured from his past life. And, right now, in this moment, he had it all again.

She dropped her head to his chest and took in all that her brother was, ever had been, and ever would be. Time stood still as years melted away in their embrace. "Paddy. Paddy."

"Fiona, my Fiona." Both cried tears of joy. As their tears poured forth, happiness broke through—they wept and laughed.

"Ye changed, Paddy. Not a boy—a man, tall and handsome—like Da—but, lookin' like Ma. A wondrous sight." She reached up to his hair. "Darker. Me still a carrot." She pulled one of her curls forward.

By the time Mary Rose, walking slowly, completed her walk across the yard, they were sitting in the grass. "Mary Rose, here is Fiona." He rose to take her hand and present her proudly to his sister. "Fiona, my wife, Mary Rose."

She saw the tears on Fiona and Patrick's faces and began to shed her own. "We be a fine family of weepers," she declared, smiling through her tears.

Fiona got up to embrace Mary Rose, saying her name. "Mary Rose Doyle, me sister."

At that moment, a young child came to the door to call. "Ma, Mavis be awake."

"Comin', Annie." Fiona answered. "Patrick and Mary Rose, Time to meet ye family. First, me girls." Unable to let go of Patrick, she drew him to her side to walk into the house. Mary Rose took his other hand.

They entered the drab house into a plain, but well-kept room, narrow and deep. It was the only room on this floor. To the right, one window lit the kitchen. The hearth centered the opposite wall where a cradle and small bed filled the closest corner. An open stair rose to a bed/loft area.

"Annie, bring Mavis." The beautiful little girl, with hair identical to Fiona's, carefully lifted the infant and came to her mother and visitors. "Annie, this be ye Uncle Patrick and ye Aunt Mary Rose." She smiled at her sister-in-law. "Give Mavis to ye Aunt," Fiona directed.

Mary Rose put out her arms to receive the baby. It was a welcoming gesture from Fiona that Mary Rose would never forget. Until this moment, the only baby that she had held was in her womb. The warm baby smell and deep blue eyes enchanted Mary Rose. She fell in love with Baby Mavis and bonded to this newfound family.

Patrick looked on and beamed. He thought his heart

would burst with happiness. All around him he saw signs of Fiona's life and her contentment. Over by the window on a small table, an open Bible waited. Spread on the dining table was a cloth of beauty and handiwork. Not quite the tablecloth that his mother had treasured, but surely there to keep that memory alive. While Fiona and Mary Rose talked of the children, Patrick walked around the room. It felt so good here. Fiona had made a home as close as possible to the cottage by the hill in Galway—and yet, different. This home had a floor and glass in the window. No potatoes were growing outside the door and no walls of Ireland's beautiful stone circled the land. Fiona had an *Annie* and *Mavis* inside her walls and today, *Patrick* was with her in this place. It was more than a dream come true. It was a miracle.

Patrick turned back to look at the four girls and tears again burst from his eyes. Neither Fiona nor Mary Rose commented on his tears. They were expected.

Patrick was anxious to learn of Fiona's life since leaving the workhouse, but he knew by what he saw, that she had found a good, new world. He saw the light in her eye as she said, "Soon, ye be meetin' Walter, after work. He be fifteen sailin' from Lancaster and lost his family on board. That's why he came here to the mines, sixteen years ago. Walter be a work boss now," she spoke with pride. "He no longer goes down in the mine. For that, we are grateful."

As soon as the tall slender man entered the house, Patrick did an assessment of him. Walter was considerably older than Fiona, dark-haired and fair-complexioned with intelligent, kind eyes. His arms were muscular and strong. His walk lanky, but commanding.

"We have visitors, Fiona?" He voiced surprise. Walter Collins was soft-spoken, and obviously dedicated to his wife and children. He looked on them with love. Walter continued his greeting to the children while Fiona made introductions.

"This be me husband, Walter Collins." Fiona went to him and slipped her arm into his. "Walter, me brother Patrick and his wife, Mary Rose."

Walter went straight away to the children, showing his priorities above the strangers in his home. He lifted Annie in greeting before he took Mavis. Walter kissed the babe's forehead and returned her to Mary Rose's arms. Then he took Patrick's outstretched hand. "You are most welcome here, Patrick." Finally, he addressed Mary Rose. "And, you too, Mary Rose." Fiona stood by and watched her husband move easily with children and visitors. "Your visit here has been long awaited," He smiled for his wife and turned back to Patrick. "It is time you came to meet your nieces and bring my Fiona the family she has longed for. Our home welcomes you and your wife, heartily."

"We be having a family dinner together," Fiona announced as she got busy in the kitchen.

Meeting Fiona's husband was one more, good thing Patrick celebrated since stepping off the ferry today. His deep sigh was one of total relief. He stepped away and addressed Da. *All is well with Fiona, Da. All is well.*

After a good meal and conversation, Walter returned to the mine to supervise the changing shifts. Fiona turned to Mary Rose. "Me havin' a great need to talk to Patrick. Would ye be walkin' out wit' us now?"

"Nay, Fiona. I be staying in. Annie and Mavis needin' to

know their aunt. Go." She already knew his stories. Brother and sister would have some time alone.

"Come, Patrick," Fiona led him to a small stone wall behind the house. "Walter built this for me." The stone was different from the grey/white rugged boulders of Galway, but the sentiment was truly apparent.

"Walter is a good man, Fiona. How blessed are you....and me, in your union."

She did not answer, just took a seat and waited a moment for Patrick to settle on the wall to begin the history she had to hear. Before he started, he opened the pouch he carried under his arm. He drew out two small pictures and laid them in her hand. To her amazement, likenesses of Ma and Da looked back at her. Fiona was at a loss for words as she drew them to her chest and looked at Patrick with thanksgiving in her countenance. She would not have to struggle to keep her parents' faces from fading from her memory through the years. Her brother had just given her a priceless gift.

Fiona got down from the wall and walked in circles, first looking at the drawings, then hugging them—looking and hugging—until she was ready to sit again. Meanwhile Patrick reached back into his pouch.

"Ye fife!' She exclaimed. "Ye fife," she reached out to touch it claiming its importance and connection to Da. "Are ye the Patrick Doyle we hear about? Me wondered but could not believe it be me own brother—Patrick Doyle—the famed piper in pubs and concerts?"

"Aye." He put it to his lips and played for his sister—songs of their youth and family, songs of Ireland, songs of sorrow and songs of joy. The notes drifted back to the house. Mary

Rose sang the words softly for Fiona's babies.

"Thank God, ye managed to keep the fife in the workhouse and now play it for the world."

"'Tis an amazing story. Have you heard of Sallie Brennen?"

"The Irish Songbird? Aye, as does every Irish lad and colleen. Ye know her, too?"

Patrick took time to tell of Sallie and the Academy before he started the stories about their family.

Fiona wanted to know every tragic detail. She mourned Sean, Da and Mavis, each in turn as he told. Then he told the circumstances of their mother's life.

"I went to see Ma in Derry."

Fiona was overwhelmed. She could only say, "Ma, Ma..." Her eyes begged for each and every fragment of her long-lost and ever-missed mother.

"Fiona," he took her hand, "Ma is incredibly strong. She endured and when given the chance to leave the workhouse after Mavis died, she took it. She is living in Derry as nanny to three English children in a manor house. She has a room of her own and has made the children and manor grounds her world. I wanted to bring her back to Dublin when Mary Rose and I married, but she refused, and continues to refuse. I celebrate her survival. Can ye celebrate with me?" He reached up and wiped a tear from his sister's cheek. "Fiona, Ma is strong and has made her world as good as possible—just like you. As you are happy, we must accept that Ma is happy in the world she has found."

"Just as ye are happy in the world ye have found, Paddy."

"My home is Dublin. My plan to leave Ireland is gone. I thought I would have to emigrate but my fife and the music it makes, changed that plan. As long as Ma is there, I am too. I will see her at Christmas. Mary Rose's father is there. We have a Ma in Derry, a Da in Dublin and a sister and nieces in Canada." He took the fife lovingly in hand. "This fife has made it possible to travel to all the places where my family is. The workhouse put us asunder, the fife put together again. Actually, Da put us together again when he taught me to carve the fife." They sat quiet for a while. Then Patrick changed the subject.

"Remember Willie? The boy who helped us the day we went into the workhouse?"

"Aye, me remember. He be your age. Willie came to me the day me left the workhouse. He whispered to me. 'Patrick—me friend.' It was almost like ye was there."

"Ye saw me in the window."

"Aye. Me saw ye promise to come find me...and ye did." They embraced in the memory.

"Willie was a great friend to me in my workhouse days. He is in Philadelphia now and I be seein' him when me and Sallie go there next month for a concert."

"He left the workhouse, too?"

"Aye. That be another story, for another day. I be tellin' ye... he worked with Da in the carpenter shop. He learned much from Da and now makin' furniture in Philadelphia."

"Da lives on." Fiona paused in that memory, too.

The long summer days gave Patrick and Fiona a lot of time. And yet, as they returned to the house, so much was still to be shared. "Time to tend to my babies, Paddy. Will ye and Mary Rose stay?"

"Stayin' the night but must go on the morning ferry." She

took his hand and thought of all the times as children she reached for it. "We be comin' back when Mary Rose be delivered. Our babe'll be Andrew Sean or Mary Fiona."

"That be perfect because I have little Walter Patrick comin' along in November."

"You know your babe be a boy?"

"Of course, me ask God."

Chapter 41

Patrick took a deep breath and opened the door to Baldwin & Winston, Furniture Makers. He stepped into the shop where sweet aromas of pine, mahogany, and polish, accosted him. He closed his eyes to enjoy the remembered smells of wood shavings and pine tar. He opened his eyes, knowing Da was not among the smells and dust but Willie was here—somewhere.

Willie dropped his makeshift crutch and ran a few jagged, jerking, off balance steps to Patrick. "Paddy." He collapsed into his arms and regained his balance. Except for lameness, he looked good—well groomed—quite handsome. His dark unruly hair was combed straight and his eyes bright with happiness at seeing Patrick. He was bent over, still skinny as Patrick remembered. "My brother!" Patrick exclaimed as he assisted Willie back to his workbench.

"Me knows of Patrick Doyle, Piper to the Erin Isle and now America. Me own Paddy, the piper from Portumna, in concert here in Philadelphia. 'Twas in the paper. Now, ye be here!"

"You expected to see me, right?"

"Aye, me did. Me knew it was ye and ye magic fife. I be waitin'..." he took hold of Patrick's upper arms, "...waitin' a long time." He looked into Patrick's eyes and squeezed his arms again to be sure he was alive and here. "Twas ye arm me took to make ye talk on those hard nights under the stair." He squeezed again. "Me listening." He invited the stories to begin.

"I waited and looked for you in Clarinbridge and Dublin

until I got your letter. Then I started my life." Patrick went quiet in thought. "'Tweren't easy starting a new life and I made mistakes along the way."

"Wit'out ye sayin', me knows. The ole life was no' good but, ye and me, we did what needin' bein' done."

Willie was always more at ease at talking, so he took the lead. "Malcolm Anderson did good by us. Where would we be today if not? Me be afeared to think."

"Is he still at Portumna?"

"Nay, he left shortly after me...but where?" he shrugged his shoulders. "Me hopes he be well, wherever. He protected me and got good care." He patted his bad leg. "Then kept his promise—took me to Jacob Brennen." Willie paused in thoughts before continuing. "Will there be time to tell and hear the stories we have? Are ye here long?"

"I have a concert date Sunday. Leave Monday. We have tonight and all day tomorrow. Then I'm gone."

"Ye can stay wit' me and we can talk in the dark." Willie's laugh was old music to Patrick's ears. "Let me show ye me shop. Then we can go to the pub where ye can tell me of ye self, Ma, Mavis, Fiona. They be me only family, too, Paddy."

"We lost Mavis in the first year after I left Portumna. But our family has grown. There's Mary Rose, my wife, and a baby comin' in another month. Ye be Uncle Willie, then." The air and spirit were light. Willie's surprised laugh was infectious.

"A wife and baby!" Willie slapped Patrick's back.

"Now show me what you do here at Baldwin & Winston."

Willie took his crutch and set out to walk with Patrick around his shop as other workers were leaving for the day. "No like the shop in Portumna. Here at Baldwin & Winston, me has the very best wood and tools. Look," he pointed out the oak, cherry, maple, walnut and mahogany wood in luscious piles, carefully stacked to prevent warping. "Can ye imagine what Andrew Doyle could do here?" He picked up the bright, clean, and sharp tools that were initialed, WC. "Mine," he explained. "Ye Da has made me life possible and good. Me canno' thank him enough." He uncovered a completed chair of dark mahogany, perfectly crafted and finished. With his hand motion, he invited Patrick to sit.

"Willie, this is wonderful. You did it all?" Patrick exclaimed as he ran his hand over the wood.

"Me design. Fellow workers help me, but I do the fine carving, the turning, the inlay, and the finish. Finishing be me specialty." He took a deep breath to say something very important, "It be for the White House. Federalist style ordered by James Buchanan. Makin' twenty of em." As Willie talked, he ran his fingers over the fine inlay design on the chair back.

Patrick was impressed. He reached across the chair and shook Willie's hand.

"Each chair be Baldwin & Winston with a WC under their mark. Willie be in the White House! Patrick Doyle will have to wait to be invited to the White House, if ever a lowly Irish country lad gets there—to keep up with Willie Carney." They enjoyed the teasing comradery of the moment before Willie became serious again.

"It be as if ye Da wit' me. We could not do this kind of work at Portumna, but he talked about it and of what the wood would do if be treated right. When I got the tools and the opportunity, I understood what he taught. Ye Da gave me love—love of wood and its craft. So sad that he could not live his life doing it."

"He be doin' it... everyday, here with you, Willie."

As they walked around the shop, Willie stopped often, pretending to extend his explanations, when in reality, he needed to rest. Patrick quickly saw that Willie struggled with exhaustion. And, although the crutch helped, it did not give Willie the strength he needed on his right side.

"Da gave much to me, too. If not for his love of wood, no fife would be carved by this bumbling boy turned piper."

Patrick helped Willie put his tools away. Then he hooked his arm around Willie's waist and grabbed the crutch to help his brother out the door and down the street. As they walked, Willie barely put his bad leg to the pavement. Patrick bore his weight effortlessly.

Dinner and cups of brew accompanied Patrick and Willie's reminiscences about shared experiences at Portumna. They managed to laugh about some of the horrors and torments. They managed to accept the cold, the discomfort, the lice, and routines while carefully avoiding bringing Sweeney into the conversation. There was a mutual effort to keep the discussions light while they were in the pub.

"Is it far to your flat?" Patrick asked as they left.

"Nay, across and down." Willie pointed to brick townhouse on the street. Patrick assumed the task of assisting Willie and they slowly made the trek across and down. Willie had a ground floor unit, consisting of a large room. A meager kitchen in one corner, a bed in the other and an outside toilet, shared with another tenant. The room was clean and well kept.

"Ain't much but all together for fewer steps. Close to me shop and the pub. Very important for me. Me has few requirements." Willie invited Patrick to sit, as he began removing a bulky wooden brace and fell into a large overstuffed chair. "Some nights this be me bed. Tonight, for sure. Ye gets the guest suite, Paddy." He pointed to his bed across the room and pulled a blanket up from beside the chair. Willie was exhausted.

Patrick surprised Willie by pushing the chair and him across the room. He stopped beside the bed. "If we talk all night, ye canno' be across the room." Then he fell on the bed and the two boys, who had become men, laughed together. "We have almost nine years to cover."

"Ye first, Paddy," Willie invited.

Patrick started and the flood gates opened. Willie sat enraptured while Patrick told of his life in Dublin. "When I learned that Ma was in Derry and Fiona was in Canada, I didn't know what to do. How could I go across the sea and never come back? So I stayed in Dublin. It was the fife that gave the answer. I travel to America and Canada and home again on tours—playing the fife. I saw Fiona in Canada last month." He told of Sallie Brennen and the Music Academy, and finally of J.J. Dwyer Livery. "There I found Mary Rose Dwyer," he said. "My wife... and soon, we will have a child."

Willie cried when need be and laughed with joy at better news. "Was a long story. Glad I did not have to lie on the cold dark floor to tell it," Patrick remarked.

"And, me did no' have to lie on the cold dark floor to hear it," Willie retorted.

Their stories came in zigzag fashion in the dark. It was well into the wee hours, when after a pause in their chatter, Willie said, "Sweeney."

"Sweeney," Patrick repeated.

"Sweeney the goat. Sweeney the swine. Funny thing, me stopped hating him a long time ago." Willie surprised Patrick with his words.

"I don't think about hate..., just wish I could forget what happened. He gets in my dreams, sometimes in my mind. Me... Patrick Doyle...killed a man—be he goat or swine—a man. Me be the one who killed him." Patrick reverted to his manor of speech of long ago. "The knife that took ye leg was meant for me. Ye cripple be me guilt, too."

"Ye be feelin' guilt?" Willie raised his voice. "Guilt? That canno' be. Ye saved me life. Ye saved ye own life. Paddy, no guilt." He lowered his voice, "No guilt," he repeated.

"In dreams, me feel the knife goin' in Sweeney's chest. Now, I see the crutch, the brace, Willie. Now, I see your leg." Patrick began crying. He released thoughts that had been held within for so long. "You bear the scar of that night. 'Tis me guilt."

"Nay, brother, ye bearing the deeper scar. Me hears it tonight and it hurts more than my leg ever did."

With all his strength and crushing pain, Willie stepped on his unsupported leg, came to Patrick's bed and threw himself over his friend. With all his weight and intention, he pounded his words in as if they were dovetail joints holding a table together. "No guilt, Paddy. None. What happen was caused by Sweeney, himself. When ye thinks about the killing, think of Sweeney with his knife in the air. Me canno' move. Sweeney's next slice be at me heart. When ye fought with him, it could have been ye with the knife in the chest and then me be next." He took Patrick's head in his hands. "Put this in ye brain, Paddy. Not another tear over that night. Not another agony about that life lost or me leg. Remember me. Think of ye self. We be the lives ye saved. Me be cripple but me be alive! Ye be alive and playing the fife. Me be alive makin' chairs." Willie rolled off Patrick. "Ask Mary Rose, and ye unborn child. Should ye have guilt? Should we be dead at the gate to Portumna?" He lay still on the bed beside Patrick for a long time. Finally, Willie heard slight snoring. He took his tired body and suffering leg back to the chair and slept.

The next morning Willie and Patrick slept late. A rap on the door brought them awake.

"Gilly! Come in," Willie shouted. Patrick turned to see a young boy come into the room. "Paddy, ye are about to meet me helper." He turned to the boy. "Gilly, this is Patrick Doyle, me old friend." The boy nodded a greeting and went right to Willie's brace and crutch.

Patrick stayed out of the way as Gilly, assisted Willie with his morning bath, shave, clothing and brace. By the time Patrick had washed his face, a breakfast of bread, cheese, and tea was on the table. Gilly disappeared after Willie gave him a coin.

"Gilly be on the street beggin'. Me usually helps wit' a coin for young boys. That be what me does wit' me earnings. Gilly be different from the other boys me helps. So, me took an interest in him."

"Different? How?"

"He put his hand in his hat and returned to me—the only coin he had—thinkin' me be cripple and needin' it."

"Gilly be me right hand man now. He has the job and the pay, as long as he stays in school. Life much easier with Gilly."

"You be Malcolm Anderson to him, eh?" Patrick asked.

Willie shrugged with a grin on his face. "Maybe." Willie thought a moment, "'Tis more like—he be Sean to me. We donno' know where Sean be. Beggin' maybe. Me hope someone drops a coin to him."

They continued their breakfast, both thinking about Sean, the lost one.

"Paddy, me knows ye are thinkin' bout takin' care of me. Helpin' me...or some such. Part of ye guilt. But since there be no guilt, and ye met Gilly...see me getting' along. Get it outa ye head."

"I can help."

"Nay." Willie sat up straight and delivered the words he had rehearsed in his head. "Me be doin' well. Ye life good. Me life good," he repeated. "So much more than we ever expected."

"Your injury is more than I expected. You get exhausted. Is there more than I can see."

"They tell me the infection that nearly took me life came from the dirty knife. It weakened me heart and took me manhood. Willie survived but never be the man ye be, Paddy."

"Oh, no," Patrick was beaten down with this news. His head hung low and his eyes filled with compassion.

"Can ye see how important ye Da's lessons are? Twas the only good thing I had when me finally walked past that gate and didno' look back. Ye left the workhouse whole, strong and full of dreams and possibilities. Nay, me. Me be broken, without dreams...so much less than perfect. Malcolm Anderson insisted me get on that boat to Philadelphia. Each day since then has been a success—just getting up and goin' to me workshop. Now after so many days, so many years, me has a life worth living. Me canno' make dreams outa me own body.... but with wood and all that Andrew Doyle taught me, ole Willie can pick up a piece of rough cherry, shape it, plane it, carve it, inlay it, polish it and make it an important part of a whole." Willie was giving Patrick the truth he had waited years to tell. He was compassionate, factual, and compelled to share it all. "Tell me Patrick, what can ye do for me to improve that? Make me dependent on ye? Nay, nay. Me thinks not." He drew a breath. "No sympathy, Paddy." He lifted his friend's arm, picked up his crutch and started for the door. "No sympathy, life's good. Come, let's sit in the sun. Ye and me no longer part of the darkness. Me pulled up the sun today after all the rain and clouds of yesterday." With his usual good humor and openness, Willie told Patrick what he needed to know...and what he had to do with the facts.

Patrick recalled Willie's attitude the first day he took him to his dormitory. It was the same today. It was good to recall after all these years what is so good, so strong and sensible about Willie. Patrick walked behind him to the bench in the yard. Now, he knew. Willie did not want or need help—with walking—or living.

❖ ❖ ❖

The concert on Sunday night was for Willie. Nearly two hundred people fill the concert hall to hear the Irish Songbird and the Piper from Portumna. But, Patrick played his fife for Willie. He and Gilly sat on the front row. Sallie took center stage and sang songs of Ireland. Then she invited Patrick to join her. Willie straightened in his seat. The Piper raised his arms and brought the beautiful fife to his lips. The first pure note went out to Willie, the next notes floated into the concert hall and carried Willie to Portumna and back. Patrick played of hours under the stairs, of times painting wall, cleaning latrines, of the importance of his friend. He gave the lilting music to his dear friend. He gave their sad memories a burst of spirit. Then Patrick lowered the fife, smiled at Willie and played This Is Our Christmas Day, his song of Christmas in the workhouse. The only music Willie had previously heard from the piper. The audience may have been surprised to hear a song of Christmas in mid-summer, but Willie understood.

Sallie came back to center stage and joined Patrick in lively pub tunes to end the concert on a happy, toe-tapping note. As an encore they played Johnny Get Up and invited the audience to dance in the isles.

After the last bow, Patrick walked to the stage directly in front of Willie and jumped down. In a warm embrace, he bid his friend goodbye.

"I'm comin' back with Mary Rose and the baby, soon. I want them to know ye, Willie."

Willie stood up and, with all his strength, pulled himself tall and straight. Patrick had to see—Willie standing tall and straight, with the same smile that the ragtag boy had when he greeted the Doyle family on their first day at Portumna Workhouse.

The End

Discussion Topics

Workhouse:

What did you learn about the Irish workhouse system? Discuss the workhouse as an English welfare system developed for the Irish. Would you have taken your family into a workhouse in 1848? Why or why not?

Sweeney:

Did Sweeney, or his death, have any positive effects on Patrick? How important was he as the antagonist in this book?

Hunger:

What did the author mean, speaking of Patrick – "Hunger became his ally—food his enemy"? Discuss the times when Patrick used hunger while in the stone cottage, the workhouse, after he left the workhouse and in J.J. Delivery Stable. Can we as a culture understand hunger? What did you learn about starvation from reading this book?

Guilt:

Patrick assumed responsibility for his family, he subsequently piled guilt on himself. Find other guilts Patrick took on himself. Explore the reasons for his guilt and how he reacted and dealt with it.

Family:

How did Andrew's, Annie's, Patrick's, Fiona's, and Sean's adjustment (or lack of) to the workhouse affect their final outcome? Explore Annie's strength, both physical and emotional. Compare Patrick's and Sean's life in the workhouse. Could Sean's tragedy have been averted? Explore Patrick's relationship with his father, his mother and Fiona.

Music and Talent:

Discuss the fife as a character. Define Patrick's artistic talents and their value. For almost a year, Patrick had to use his imagination to hear his fife. Discuss hearing his music as a reader?

Willie:

What was Willie's role in Patrick's life in and out of the workhouse. Discuss Willie's strengths? What was the most important thing Willie did for Patrick? How did Patrick and Willie interact with the Master of the Workhouse at different times in the story?

Characters:

Malcolm Anderson, Sallie Brennen, Jacob Brennen, J.J. Dwyer, Mary Rose, and Walter Collins all played minor but important parts in the lives of the Doyle family and Willie. Discuss each influence on Patrick or Willie or both.

The End:

The author did not tell what happened to Sean or Malcolm Anderson. How would you write their endings? Most Irish famine stories are about emigration. Were you surprised at who did and who did not emigrate? Discuss how their final choices effected Patrick and Willie.